"Oh," Mack said as if he were dumbfounded that he still stood there. Featherlike laugh lines crinkled around his eyes. "I guess…I think…I'll go fix us a snack."

Laughter echoed in the small room as Penny lifted her fingertips and accepted the towel. She stared at him. "Mack?"

"Hmmmm?" He stared back.

"Just what kind of snack were you thinking?" Penny flushed at the brazen innuendo.

"Hot chocolate?" He answered with a question, looking her over seductively.

She didn't miss the double meaning of his question. Penny tried to throttle the dizzying current running through her as she saw the smoldering flame in his gaze. Her heart danced with excitement as the very air around them became electrified.

Indigo Sensuous Love Stories

Genesis Press, Inc.
315 Third Avenue North
Columbus, MS 39701

Shadows In The Moonlight

ISBN: 1-58571-064-4
Manufactured in the United States of America

First Edition

Shadows In The Moonlight

by

Jeanne Sumerix

Genesis Press, Inc.

ACKNOWLEDGEMENTS

Thanks to Mary Doak, forest firefighter, who graciously gave of her valuable time and information to make this story factual.

SPECIAL THANKS

Mary Poupard and Penny Brooks

Chapter 1

"Mom?" Penny Hart called out as she entered the front door of her mother's house. Dropping her gear in the hallway, she half hoped Diane Hart wouldn't be home. When no answer came, she breathed a sigh of relief. She wouldn't have to tell her mother she was moving, not just yet anyway.

The clean odors of oil soap and pine wafted through the fresh early April air. Her mother had been spring-cleaning. Penny smiled as she glanced around the home she had known all her life. What her mother found to clean was beyond her. She ran her fingers over the freshly polished piano as she passed by on her way to the kitchen. The music sheets she'd left on the piano last evening were gone, and Penny knew they would be neatly stored in the bench.

Penny glanced at her image as she paused at the mirror. After four years, it was still difficult to believe she was the woman in the reflection. She wasn't thin but she sure wasn't fat anymore. She gazed at herself for a moment. She couldn't help but wonder if her mindset would ever let her know she wasn't fat, or whether she would always have to look in a mirror for affirmation. Kind of like pinching yourself, she thought.

Grabbing a can of Diet Coke, she popped it open and

jumped as the noise seemed to echo in the quiet house. Penny laughed at herself for being so unnerved. Freshly baked chocolate chip cookies cooled on the counter.

Grabbing a cookie she munched on it and looked from the Diet Coke in one hand to the cookie in the other hand and reproached herself. "Now there is an oxymoron if I ever saw one." She laughed aloud. After all of this time she felt guilty for eating a cookie. Her weight was under control and she knew it, but she also knew it wouldn't take much to throw her back into her bad eating habits.

"I won't let that happen," she told herself as she leaned over the kitchen sink and glanced out the window into the backyard. There in the bright spring sunshine, she could see her mother kneeling on all fours in the middle of her rock garden. The small-framed woman pulled weeds with a vengeance and neatly placed them in the basket that Penny knew would be emptied into the compost pile. She had grown up on proverbs and waste not, want not was one of her mother's favorites.

I might as well get it over with, she thought. Taking a deep breath, Penny pushed open the door and called out, "Mom." She let the back door slam and then grimaced as metal cracked against wood.

Diane Hart turned and smiled at her daughter. Placing her gardening tools in their container, she removed her gloves and stood to greet her. "How was your day?"
"Great!" Penny said with more enthusiasm than she'd wanted to show. She was excited about the transfer but knew her mother wouldn't be. "How was yours?" she quickly asked to

cover her excitement.

Penny's mother surveyed the garden and then her daughter's face. "I love working in the garden," she announced as if Penny were a stranger and had no idea, and then asked. "Why don't you tell me what made today so great?"

She knows something is different, Penny thought. She had no idea how, but her mother could read the slightest nuance in her demeanor. "Well," she began, and then took a bite of her cookie. Even at twenty-five her mother wouldn't want her to talk with her mouth full, she thought, buying herself some time.

"Oh," her mother said knowingly as she watched her daughter munch on the cookie. "It was great for you, but I won't think so?" She smiled at her daughter and then continued. "I didn't hear of any raging forest fires in the country so that can't be your delight." She paused momentarily and quipped, "No more cookies until you've told me." "Well," Penny began again and then stopped.

"Yes," the older woman eyed her daughter closely. "That is where we left off before the cookie."
Their mutual laughter rang in the spring air as the warm sun poured over them. "Mom, I took a transfer to the Upper Peninsula." That was easy to say, Penny thought, but then held her breath waiting for her mother's response.

"Well," her mother said thoughtfully. "Now, that is a bit of news." She shifted her gloves to one hand and swiped at the stray damp hairs on her forehead. "I don't understand why you would want to transfer. You get plenty of action here. And heaven knows when there are fires in other states you are gone at the sound of the horn, so a change of scene wouldn't be the reason." Her mother's gaze penetrated deep within her.

Penny shook her head. "Mom, don't." She shuffled her feet as she contemplated what to say. "I want to advance in my career and in order to do that I need experience in all areas of the forest service. And frankly, Mom, it's just that I want to be on my own." Penny watched as her mother's face grew more strained. "It's not to get away from you, so stop thinking that. I'll be home often." Her gaze swept over the backyard to the house and back to her mother. She loved her home and all that went with it, but it was time to move on. "The only time I've been away from here is when I went to training for my job."

"Nonsense, you were gone most of last summer fighting fires out west." Her mother took a deep breath and then added as her voice filled with resignation, "It's time for the bird to leave the nest. I knew the time was coming. I do know what it's like to want to advance in your career, and I know you will do it." Mrs. Hart smiled in resignation. "I can only thank the good Lord I had you for this long." She gazed at her daughter through misted eyes.

Penny hugged her. "I'll never be far away, Mom. If you need me for anything, I'll come home as soon as I can. It's only a four or five-hour drive from here."

"Four or five hours, is that all?" Mrs. Hart exclaimed as Penny led her back to the house and into the kitchen. She knew her mother was summoning the courage to let her only child go.

"Where will you be living?" her mother asked as if the news hadn't knocked her for a loop.

Inwardly Penny breathed a sigh of relief. "I'll stay at our cabin. It's right between the Sault Saint Marie and Saint Ignace's ranger stations." She paused, hoping her mother would be more comfortable knowing she'd still kind of be at home, but that was not the look she was getting. "What?" she asked as her mother's face grew more strained.

"Oh, honey, we never go there anymore s"
Penny cut her mother off. "You sold it? Without even telling me?"

"No. I could never sell the place your father loved so dearly. That's where he spent the last days of his life." Diane's eyes grew overcast as she went deep within for strength. When she returned from the depths of her soul, she half smiled at her daughter. "I've rented it out for the year."

"Mom!" Penny couldn't believe what she was hearing. At least once a year they went to the cabin. The serenity of the forest, the peace of the area, and the tranquility of the creek running through the land provided their yearly retreat from reality. What had her mother been thinking?

"Penny," her mother said in an admonishing tone and then continued, "I've rented it to Mack Holsey. He needed a vacation and wanted to spend it there."

"Mack Holsey? Daddy's old partner? What could he need a vacation from?" Penny couldn't believe her luck. Just when she thought she'd be out on her own and in such a serene place, she discovered she couldn't.

"He isn't old. Mack was a rookie when he was partnered with your father. He needed to get away from the bureau for a while. Mack took a year's leave of absence…to well…work on a few things and to rest."

Penny gazed into her mother's soft-brown face and could see lines of grief forming around her mouth. "Oh, Mom," Penny breathed as she realized what was happening. "You haven't given up on the idea that Dad's death was an accident, have you?" Penny said it but she hoped she was wrong. If her mother couldn't accept the FBI reports, then she couldn't move on and put her pain to rest.

"Your father's death was no accident, and he certainly did not commit suicide," Diane Hart said adamantly. "And Mack is going to prove it. Mack is a fine FBI agent. And if he didn't have his doubts too, he wouldn't spend his valuable time chasing ghosts."

Penny dropped to a chair at the table and thoughtfully rolled her Diet Coke can in her hand. With a long sigh she agreed. "Okay, Mack Holsey can stay there, but I'll be there too. I'm not going to look for another place to live when we have a perfectly good cabin with four bedrooms."

"Penny Ann Hart, you will do no such thing!" Her mother's dark-brown eyes grew black with disbelief. "No daughter of mine will live with a man out of wedlock."

Penny laughed. "Okay, I'll marry him but I won't sleep with him." She watched her mother's face as the smile slid into place and then added, "I haven't seen Mack since Daddy's funeral, but if I remember he wasn't all that bad."

Her mother's eyebrows arched as she stared at her

daughter. Thoughtfully her smile grew wider. "You know he is only five years older than you. It might not be such a bad thing."

Penny laughed as she could see the wheels turning in her mother's head. She formed a cross with her index fingers and held them up against her mother. "Back off, you eternal matchmaker!"

Where a short time ago the kitchen had been filled with silent separation, the two women who loved each other so dearly had come together in laughter. They fell into each other's arms. The passage of time had occured and the young one was able to fly from the nest.

After a long, thoughtful silence, her mother firmly stated, "All I ask is that you stay in contact with me and let me know how you are. And young lady," Mrs. Hart continued emphatically, "I'm agreeing to you staying under the same roof with Mack because I trust you both to behave."

"If you trust him, then that's good enough for me." Penny smiled at her mother but a plan was forming to move Mack Holsey from the cabin. All she wanted was some time to herself. Time to get to know what she was all about.

When she'd lost more than a hundred pounds, the one man who'd professed his love for her, left her. The weight loss was to advance in her job, not to look for other men as Cooper Jones had insinuated. Twinges of pain gripped her heart as she thought of her lost love. She and Cooper had spent two years of high school and three years after graduation making plans for their future. Penny shook her head and heaved a deep sigh. Her only crime had been to lose weight.

Willing herself to leave the painful past, she returned her thoughts to her mother and said, "Mom, please inform him of my arrival and assure him I'll stay out of his way if he stays out of mine."

Diane Hart squeezed her daughter tightly. "Don't worry about it. Mother will take care of everything."

"That's just what I was afraid you would say." Penny laughed but she knew her mother was plotting something, and she hated to see her mother be disappointed.

A week later Penny dropped her belongings at the cabin and decided not to stay until Mack Holsey returned from wherever he was. Standing in the door of the cabin, she looked to her right at the spotless kitchen and then to her left at the open and immaculate living room. The cabin looked as if no one had been there since her family's visit last summer. He was either not living there or was very neat. She shook her head as she looked around. I moved from one neat freak to another. "Well, if I have my way, it won't be a long stay for him," she muttered to herself as she turned and trudged through the snow back to her truck.

As she drove along US-2 toward Naubinway, the spitting snow covered her windshield. Penny could see the last of winter hung on to northern Michigan with a death grip. Bare but budded trees bent stiffly and then snapped against the onslaught of the spring snowstorm that was blasting the eastern Upper Peninsula with a late but powerful Alberta Clipper. Early spring flowers had bravely popped their heads through the ground and now were being weighted with snow.

Penny peered through the windshield at the blinding flurry. Just this morning she'd been in Baldwin where spring had broken with the renewal of life and the promise of more to come. She was excited at having the whole outdoors as her playground. In the spring and summer she would fish, swim, boat, and hike to the higher altitudes and camp. In the fall she could hunt and tramp through the beautiful brightly colored foliage. The longer winter would be great to ride her snowmobile, use her snowshoes, cross-country skis and be thankful she had traded her small sports car for a four-wheeldrive truck. So far, all of her decisions had been good ones, and she hoped her luck would hold.

"God's country," she spoke aloud as she drove past the forest along Lake Michigan's most northern point. She had no idea why she was driving in this direction but it didn't matter. She was there and free to do as she wanted, even when she didn't know what she was doing.

Penny laughed at her silliness and then began studying the terrain. She had three weeks until she began work. She wanted to learn as much as she could about the area where she would be living, not just as a visitor; she was a resident now.

As she drove along Lake Michigan's shoreline, she was amazed at the differences between this almost barren shore and the very inhabited shore of the same lake downstate. The buildings along Southern Lake Michigan were interrupted by an occasional stand of trees, but here on the northern shore, it was quite the opposite. She began humming. Yes, she would be very happy here in the woods by herself. Well, by herself as soon as she got rid of Mack Holsey.

She glanced up to see the Cut River Bridge in front of her. Chills ran over her as she thought of her father falling to his death from that bridge. She looked at the date on her watch. "Oh," she breathed aloud. "It was five years ago this week." Penny had struggled with her father's death but had grown to accept the official reports. The alternatives would be unthinkable. She shook her head. "No," she told herself, "he did not commit suicide, and he was too kind a person for someone to murder. It had to be an accident."

Pulling the truck to the side of the road, she tugged her hat around her face to ward off the cold wind that stung her cheeks and the snow that stuck to her lashes. Penny had no idea why she was edging along the walkway of the bridge. Unless it was just to be where her dad had been on his last day.

Before Cliff Hart's fatal accident, he'd been spending the first days of trout season fishing the rivers near the cabin. As she stared down into the Cut River, she was sure he hadn't been fishing in this one. Peering through the snow, the cavernous hollow seemed to go on forever until she could see a narrow trickle of water at the bottom. She remembered her dad telling her it was a million-dollar bridge over a ten-cent river. Now that is definitely a ten-cent river.

Penny walked, slowly measuring and comparing in her mind, her size to her dad's. She moved around testing the probability of someone falling. No, not just someone, she thought, but a man who had great physical agility and a brain to match. Maybe…, she pondered, and then shook her head.

Mack Holsey had come to this bridge for the hundredth time since his arrival in Michigan's Upper Peninsula. As he crawled up the steep hill and regained his footing on the bridge, he noticed a young woman on the other side. He stood watching her until recognition hit. This was his late partner's daughter! Her mother had phoned and told him she would be arriving soon but he hadn't expected to see her here. But then again, he thought, of course she would come here, after all it was close to the anniversary of her father's death, and she probably wanted to be close to the memory of him.

Mrs. Hart had told him Penny had accepted the results of the investigation and wasn't happy with him or her mother for reopening the wounds. Yet, he knew his partner's abilities and he just couldn't accept the official report. A man with Cliff's physical and mental skills falling from this bridge was highly improbable. Besides he owed it to his mentor. If Mack had come on that fateful fishing trip, the ending might have been different. He shuddered. Until he laid this to rest, the guilt wouldn't let him rest.

He observed the young woman as she seemed to measure herself against the bridge and then lean forward. He could see her mentally weighing the probability of someone falling from there. She seemed to be considering the facts surrounding her father's death, as he'd been doing prior to her arrival at the bridge. She was on the right track; he'd done the same thing. Mack could see her shake her head and begin to turn away. Suddenly she turned back, stuck the toe of her boot in an opening on the bottom of the bridge, and hoisted herself up. Now she was waist high with the bridge and again leaned forward.

He quickly walked across the highway to maintain a closer vigil in case her investigation went awry. She shoved both boot toes in and thrust herself forward. He reached out to grab her but she eased back and shook her head again.

"If you are going to jump, it would help if your toes weren't locked in the bridge," Mack said quietly.

Penny screamed and twirled around. "What...?" Startled and gasping for air, she said in a choked voice, "What the hell? Are you trying to scare me into falling?"

She immediately recognized Mack Holsey. He was older but age had done nothing but improve the mental image she had of him. Deep golden-black eyes glimmered in his dark-brown almost black face. His black-laced-with-gold eyes reminded her of the tiger-eye stone her father had brought her from one of his assignments. His flawless complexion had struck her as perfect at her father's funeral and did again today. But today she was open to what she was seeing. Penny held her hand on her chest, feeling her heart as it pounded heavily against her ribs and she wasn't sure it was from being scared.

Mack sucked in a deep breath. Her beauty was overwhelming. Five years ago, she'd been his partner's grieving daughter and he wasn't sure he'd seen her, not really. He thought she'd been larger. If she had been, she sure wasn't now. At this moment, he saw the woman and not the sad young girl he'd seen five years earlier. And what a woman, he thought as he surveyed her. Soft, shoulder-length, deep-dark copper curls fell around her tender, lighter copper-brown, heart-shaped face. As she cursed at him for scaring her, one curl strayed errantly and bounced among the few freckles that were sweetly sprinkled over her cheekbones. He couldn't help laughing as he answered, "I don't think it would be that easy to fall from this bridge. Do you?"

"Oh, don't you start that with me, Mack Holsey." Penny's hands automatically fixed on her hips as if to dare him to push the issue of her dad's death. Her full lips puckered as she delivered his name. "I know you and my mother are on some kind of witch hunt, but leave me out of it."

He couldn't help noticing how she squared her shoulders and lifted her chin as she tried to sound confident. Damn she was cute, smart, and a forest ranger all rolled into one. She could put out my fire anytime. But she is Mrs. Hart's daughter, and I promised to take care of her. For a moment he struggled between honor and desire and then with a deep inward sigh, he offered, "Okay. You have a deal. Now, want to have dinner with me?"

Penny looked at him cautiously. "Why would I want to do that?" she asked as if he'd lost his mind. His long face grew a smile showing white even teeth. He was even more handsome than she'd remembered. She let her gaze drift over him, scrutinizing his long, muscular body and then with the heat of embarrassment she brought her roving gaze back to his face.

"Because we both have to eat?" Mack asked and answered as if he hadn't noticed Penny's survey.

"Look," Penny said as she drew in the cold air, "we are not here to be together. You have your agenda and I have mine." And part of mine is to have you move soon. She subconsciously slid her foot over a pile of snow and then added, "I don't want to be mean or stubborn but I came here to be on my own."

"Being on your own means you won't be eating?" Mack persisted.

She could hear a slight chuckle in the back of his throat. Maybe she was being unreasonable. Maybe if she were nice to him she could talk him into moving out sooner. Then she would have the cabin to herself. She glimpsed his handsome, smiling face while tapping the pile of snow with the toe of her boot and answered, "Of course I'll be eating, and sure, let's eat dinner together."

Mack beamed. "Let's take my truck."

"And leave mine here?"

"No, we take yours back and then leave from the cabin."

"Oh." It seemed everything she said amused him. The smile had not left his face since she turned to him on the bridge. Maybe he isn't as harmless as Mom thinks. Well, he hadn't better mess with me because I'm tougher than I look, she thought smugly. She walked to her truck, tossing back over her shoulder, "See you at the cabin."

"See you at home," Mack hollered back with a laugh as he loped across the highway and got into his truck.

"Ohhhhh, darn him," she muttered under her breath as she watched him in her rearview mirror. His broad shoulders smoothly tapered to his well-developed back and over one of the nicest butts she had ever seen...and those long muscular legs. Her mind drifted to his face with the continuous smile and she shook her head. "No," she firmly told herself and turned her truck in the direction of the cabin.

Penny was preoccupied with her unwanted thoughts as she entered the bungalow. She could smell the freshly brewed coffee and heard the shower shut off. In a couple of minutes, Mack was standing in front of her clad in a towel. She openly stared at him. Water glistened on his dark chest, drawing her eyes to sinewy muscles that flexed as he moved to pour coffee.

"Want some?" He held up the coffeepot.

Penny shook her head. Want some? she thought. Then banished that thought from her head. "Which bedroom did you take?" she asked as if there wasn't a half-naked man in front of her. She wanted to tell him to get dressed but then he would think she wasn't sophisticated and mature enough to live with a man who wasn't a member of her family or her husband.

Mack waved his hand. "When your mom called I moved to the bedroom at the back of the cabin so you'd feel more comfortable in the other one off the living room."

Penny glanced at the bedroom near the living room. That was still too close for her comfort. Her gaze moved up the stairs to the loft. "I think it would be best if I sleep up there."

Mack smiled knowingly. "Okay, but Penny, you are safe with me. I loved and admired your father. He was my mentor. We actually had many of the same dreams." As if he just realized how he was dressed, he glanced down and then said, "Just a minute, I'll be right back."

The sincerity in his voice when he said she was safe with him pulled at her heartstrings. She might be safe with him but that was not what she had planned for this summer. She just wanted time and space so she could see clearly what she wanted to do with her life. It was probably selfish of her but all she wanted was a little time. Pulling herself from her thoughts, she watched as his long strides made the towel tighten around his muscled rear. Penny shivered inwardly. *I really need a fire to put out right now.* Then she laughed at herself. She had one, but it wasn't in the forest.

Mack re-entered as quickly as he'd left. The jeans and T-shirt covered what she already knew was there, which did little to slow her breathing.

"Is this better?" he asked earnestly.

She nodded. "Yes, thank you."

"I'm sorry, Penny. I get so used to working with agents that I don't really think of the male-female thing."

"Oh." She wasn't sure if that was a compliment and she really didn't want to get into what he and the other agents did. Then as she thought about what he'd said, she wondered if he was telling her she was just one of the guys to him.

"If you are ready, we could go to dinner," Mack said,

obviously trying to ease the awkward situation.

"I have to shower and change." Her face grew hot as she thought of being naked in a room near him. And I told Mom I could do this with no problem at all.

She had to change the subject. Penny picked up the picture of her parents from the nook by the door. "So what dreams did you and Dad have that were alike?" She breathed deeply. Thankfully, she'd remembered what Mack had said earlier even though she'd been mesmerized.

"There were many. We both wanted to arrest the top ten list all at once and be the heroes." His smile left as his gaze momentarily clouded in remembrance.

She released the breath she'd been holding, grateful for the change and the memory. This was something her father had joked about with her mother. It felt good to hear it again. "I would think that would be most agents' dream."

Mack thought for a moment and then said, "Yeah, but I bet they don't all have this one, and it was a dream of your dad's and mine." His face lit with memory.

"And what would that be?" She smiled.

"It might seem silly to you," he teased.

"Try me," she poked back. Then heat filled her face as she realized how that could've been taken. She looked into his eyes and knew he considered offering an inappropriate response but then thought better of it.

"Cliff and I thought how great it would be if we could be locked in a huge room..." He hesitated.

"Well," she said insistently. "What for?"

"A huge room filled to the ceiling with m&ms and then

we could eat our way out." His boisterous laughter filled the cabin.

Penny had to laugh with him. She knew how her dad had loved m&ms and could believe that he'd think a thing like that. She reached in her purse and pulled out a bag. "Do you mean these?" she asked, holding the bag teasingly in front of him.

"Oh, little lady." His voice grew laughingly serious. "To hold those in front of me when I'm hungry is a bad thing to do."

Penny held the bag close to her and ran to the loft steps. Mack was in pursuit of the candy when she held her hand up to stop him. "Rule number one is you are not allowed in the loft."

Mack stopped on the third step, turned around, and slumped back down. He turned at the bottom and pointed a warning finger at her. "Okay, but you have to come down sometime and when you do, those are mine." He disappeared around the corner into the kitchen but hollered one more thing. "Someday you will pay for that. Now if we are going to dinner, get yourself ready."

Penny smiled. Mack Holsey was making it very hard for her to keep her mind on her goal. This could be nice, having a roommate. And then she thought, but that changes everything I wanted to do. He will only be here for a short time and not for the year Mom rented to him, she assured herself. And then I can get on with my life.

Chapter 2

Penny knew she'd taken a long time primping and dressing for a dinner date that she would insist be Dutch. There was nothing wrong with looking your best, she told herself. But she knew she wouldn't have taken the time to do her hair or her makeup if she'd been alone. She smoothed her pink cashmere sweater over her full bosom and adjusted her less-than-roomy jeans before she left her loft. All the time she was adjusting her clothing, she rationalized that all of this had been for her own self-image and had nothing to do with the man downstairs. "Oh, girl," she whispered to herself in admonishing tones, "you are so full of it."

At the top of the staircase, she pulled herself together, resolving to keep her goals and stop letting hormones dictate her feelings. After all, she told herself, you are much more mature than that. She felt better having scolded herself and righted her thinking.

She glanced out the window as she ran down the loft stairs. It was snowing even harder. She could hear a truck running but Mack was in the kitchen. "Someone here?" she asked, almost hoping she wouldn't be alone with him for the night.

"Nope, just thought I'd start the truck so you wouldn't

freeze when you got in." He smiled as he slid his arms into his winter jacket.

"Thank you," she said and pulled open the outside door. She was met with a gust of night air. The cold took her breath away but it felt good to have her cheeks feel normal for a few minutes. This wasn't going to be easy. He was way too kind, considerate, and sexy. How was she supposed to get rid of him if he was going to act like this?

She stuck her head out and then leaned back in. "Are you sure we should be going out on a night like this?" Maybe, she thought, I will just go to my room and read.

Mack came beside her. "Where's your sense of adventure? We both have four-wheel drives, and if you would feel more comfortable, we both have snowmobiles."

Oh, he thinks I wouldn't dare. She glanced at the way she was dressed and then looked him straight in the eyes. "I'm not dressed for the snowmobiles but you're right, this storm shouldn't keep us in."

"Atta girl!" Mack smiled broadly as he lightly slapped her on the back of her shoulder.

Her warm feelings changed instantly. Concealing her annoyance with Mack's condescending manner, Penny smiled broadly. She resisted the urge to rub the stinging spot on her shoulder. In the months to come, she would show him a thing or two. And there was no time like the present to begin.

"I'll drive," she shouted over her shoulder as she ran to the truck.

She saw Mack hesitate only momentarily and then

recover. "Okay, let's see if this thing has enough guts to get us to dinner and back without too much damage." His warm laughter filled the truck cab as she shifted into reverse.

"Where would you like to eat?" she asked.

Mack looked at his watch. "It's early yet. Let's drive over to Eckerman and eat at the Bear Butt Bar."

It was just five o'clock. Penny knew the place; it was about an hour from where they were on good roads. But she wasn't going to let him see her sweat. "Okay, north it is then...well northwest." Now why did I qualify that? she asked herself. What do I care what he thinks about me?

"You know," Mack began and waited for her to glance in his direction. When she looked, he continued, "I've seen storms like this come and then before the evening is done they're gone. Kind of like the rains in Florida."

"I sure hope you're right about this one." She thought for a minute and then added, "You're from Florida?"

"No, but I spent a year there one month. At least the month seemed a year long." Mack laughed.

She wanted to ask him where he was from, but then she thought he might think she was too interested in him. Instead, she asked, "Were you on assignment there?"

"Yep," he answered.

So much for small talk, Penny thought. For a few minutes, she watched the road but all she could see were the wipers throwing snow from one side of the windshield to the other. The silence in the truck grew louder as she searched for something to say. Here she was with a stranger. The only thing they had in common was her father, and they disagreed about that. She thought about how clean the cabin had been when she arrived and asked, "Are you always so neat?"

Mack glanced at his clothes and then at her. "I guess so."

"No, I mean the cabin. It's spotless." All of a sudden talking to him was like pulling teeth. She didn't know what to say next.

"Oh," Mack said and smiled sheepishly. "I hired a cleaning woman. I knew there was no way I could keep the cabin as nice as your mother does."

"Whew." Penny let out a long breath. "I thought you were going to be like Mom. I'm not like her, so I'll share in the expense of the cleaning woman." She wanted to add, until we can make other living arrangements, but didn't want to push too hard too soon.

Mack looked at her as if to object and then thought better of it. "Okay, whatever works. I guess we should decide on how we will split the groceries and utilities too."

"The utilities, right down the middle," she offered.

"And the groceries?" Mack asked with a big smile.

"I guess we'll have to wait and see who eats the most." And if I have my way, you won't be here long enough to worry about how we split anything.

"Sounds like a plan to me," Mack agreed.

She watched him out of the corner of her eye. He seemed to be searching for something as they drove. She looked too; there was nothing but highway, forest, and a few houses along the way. Whatever he was looking for she didn't want to know. It probably had something to do with her dad's death, and she didn't want to hear it.

She spotted the bar and swung the truck into the parking lot. Thrusting her door open, she jumped out and looked back at Mack. "Hey, are you coming?" Mack started when she spoke. He seemed to be in a world of his own.

Bringing his focus to her, he smiled and jumped from the truck. Quickly making his way to her and taking her arm, he answered. "Are you kidding? I'm starving. Of course I'm coming."

Penny stared at him for a moment. His silence was over and he had returned to the good-humored man who'd been at the cabin with her. He'd either been in deep concentration or was scared to death of her driving. She tried to suppress a giggle but it escaped. She glanced up to see Mack smiling down at her. She couldn't help returning the smile. There was something warm and enchanting about him that she had to admit she liked.

"Now what's so funny?" Mack gazed at her as he held the door of the bar open. Penny shrugged.

"Oh, I see," Mack spoke in jesting quips, "here we are on our first date, the first day of our new relationship, and you're keeping secrets from me." Amusement flickered in the deep golden-black eyes that met hers.

"We aren't on a date. We don't have a relationship, and we aren't starting one." Penny laughed lightly as she glanced around the bar. From the door she could see into the tiny kitchen and marveled at how clean the whole cooking area looked.

Mack was looking, too, and his mouth quirked with

humor. He nudged her and asked, "Do you think your mom got here before we did? And what do you mean we aren't on a date?"

He sounded so incensed that they weren't on a date; she brought her hand up to stifle her laughter. "You are nuts!"

"Oh, my God." Mack's expressive face grew almost somber. "I don't know how you found out but please don't tell anyone. This is a secret you and I'll have to share and keep private."

Penny stared up at him. What was he saying? Then she watched as his face evolved from dejection to his bright infectious smile. She almost yelled at him. "Stop that!" She couldn't help laughing aloud. In her heart, she could sense more of why her parents cared for and trusted this man. He was everything parents could want in a son. And she didn't want to admit it, but he was everything a woman could want in a man.

Mack had her by the elbow and was leading her to a table in the corner. As they passed the bar, she heard the men she assumed were regulars discussing the hockey game that was on the television. The small area with tables was filled with people eating what looked like half a cow to her. Mack held her elbow until they were at a little table in the far corner.

When they were seated, Penny whispered, "If you order what they're having then I know the groceries will have to be divided seventy-five and twenty-five."

"Well," Mack gave a long drawn-out low whistle. "I didn't picture you eating that much but I thoroughly understand. I don't want the twenty-five percent portion, it just wouldn't feel right."

Penny stared at his serious face. "I hope you are kidding. How on earth do you think I could eat all that?"

"Ohhhh," Mack expelled a long breath. "I thought you meant that was not enough for you." His eyes danced with each word.

Penny smiled inside at his humor but kept a straight face. "As I said, if you eat what they are eating then we have the seventy-five and twenty-five split decided." Her tone was definitely trying to keep him from being the comedian at her expense.

"Well good, that part of our arrangement is settled now too." He took her hand in his. "Do you see how well we work together? In a matter of hours, we have negotiated some very touchy subjects. Our sleeping arrangements are settled. Our housing and food are settled." He turned up his smile a notch. "And our first date is going well. Don't you think?"

Penny openly stared at him. She loved his gentle companionship and his not-so-subtle wit. Her hand burned in his. She felt as if she were swimming through a haze of feelings and desires. Her gaze dropped to their joined hands. His large hand wrapped around her smaller hand. It all looked so natural to her. Stop it, she told herself. She drew her hand from his and let it fall to her lap.

Then after gaining some semblance of control, she asked, "Should we order dinner? I still have to unpack."

"Exactly," Mack said with a chuckle.

"Exactly?" Penny asked, more baffled then ever.

"Those were my thoughts exactly. We should eat and get home so we can unpack your things." He hesitated for only a moment and then added. "You know, I would love to help you unpack but I know your number one rule will prohibit that." Mack grimaced in good humor. "So, I'll make us a snack."

Penny's sense of humor took over. She laughed as she asked, "We haven't even eaten yet and you are thinking of a snack?"

"Snacks are very important to people who are trying to develop a relationship." He answered matter-of-factly.

Penny threw her arms in the air. "I give up!"

"I knew it!" Mack said jubilantly. "Now we are getting someplace."

After dinner, Penny handed the keys to Mack. "Could you drive? I'm really whipped. It was a long drive from home to the cabin. I'm not sure I can stay awake to get us back safely." She held her breath waiting for a wisecrack or innuendo but none came. Mack nodded and took the keys. She sighed within. Penny did love his humor, but she was very tired and was just not in the mood for more. He seemed to read her mood and backed off.

How could she help but like this man? she thought as he held her jacket for her and then led her out to the truck. She shivered as she slid onto the cold leather seats. "I think I'll need warmer clothes for living here," she said as she hugged her arms tightly around her waist.

Mack smiled as he turned the key. "You can borrow mine. Since I've been here, I've spent half my time at the farm store buying warmer clothes." He peered out the windshield. "And what did I tell you? The snow has stopped and the sky is clearing. In fact, I believe I see a hint of Northern Lights."

Penny pushed the button to roll down her window and stuck her head out. "Oh, they are beautiful," she uttered in a breathless whisper. She gazed at the luminous streamers of vibrantly colored lights in the northern night sky. "And to think this is all caused by the ejection of charged particles into the magnetic field of the earth. Mother Nature never ceases to amaze me." She drew her head back in and exclaimed, "But darn, it's cold out there!" She quickly hit the button to close the window.

Mack glanced at her. "Charged particles? That is the least romantic way I've ever heard the Aurora Borealis described." He laughed. "You spend entirely too much time studying the atmosphere. And don't tell me what causes a full moon. I don't want to lose all of the romance of nature." He smiled at her with a glint of humor in his eyes and then continued. "This is the second time I've seen the lights since I've been here. One day it's like spring with the sugar-moon lighting the sky, and the next it's like the dead of winter with the Northern Lights spreading across the skies."

"That's Michigan weather for you." Penny began to relax as the fan kicked out hot air. Her faced flushed with the heat. At least that's what she told herself. It couldn't be that she was sitting next to one hell of a hot man.

Her gaze slid over him. He had a body that looked as if Michael Angelo had sculpted it. His skin was such a rich deep brown and those eyes... She took a deep calming breath, those tiger eyes. Bottomless pools of black laced with gold met her scrutiny. More heat rushed to her cheeks. "Uh," she mumbled aloud while she tried to think of something to cover her close inspection. "Just making sure you're not getting as sleepy as I am."

"Oh." Mack grinned. "Of course you wouldn't want your driver to fall asleep."

"Of course," Penny said as she sank down in her seat. I have to think of something to say that will make our conversation easier, she thought.

"Tell me about working with my dad." There, that should keep him busy and keep the subject off us.

"Cliff was the finest man I've ever met." Mack paused and his face became sad. "My parents were both gone by the time I was a teen. My grandmother raised me. Cliff was my surrogate father. He took me under his wing after I finished training and taught me to be a good agent." He glanced at Penny and then added, "But don't you think because he was my surrogate father, that I'm thinking of you as my sister." He smiled broadly

"I don't know. It might be nice to have an older brother. Being an only child is sometimes lonely," Penny offered with some half-truth. Being an only child could be lonely but she certainly wasn't looking at Mack as her brother.

"So why did you decide to become a forest ranger?"

Penny released the breath she'd been holding. Finally a

change of subject she would love to talk about. "My grand-father, Mom's dad, was in the Army Air Corps during World War II." She glanced at Mack and saw he was listening attentively. "His platoon had trained and were fine jumpers but no White commander wanted them in their outfits. So, the government made them smoke jumpers. They were dropped into some hellish fires, fought them, and proved their worth." She sighed. "Their unit was called the Triple Nickel and from the first time I saw Grandpa's picture and heard the stories I wanted to be a part of that."

Mack shook his head. "I'd never heard of the smoke jumpers in World War II. I guess there's a lot of our history we never hear." He thought for a minute and then asked, "How did you get started? Did you go to school or what? I guess I don't know anything about being a firefighter or a forest ranger."

Penny was more than pleased to tell the story. It kept the subject generic and she did love her job. She smiled at Mack and continued. "Well, I began in the office. I loved working in accounting and administration. That's what I'd studied and at least I was near firefighting. But as a couple of years went by and I watched the firefighters and saw the excite-ment in their faces, I knew that was for me." Penny thought about how she'd longed to fight the fires and how she'd done anything to be near the exciting activity. She smiled to her-self remembering how she'd delivered meals to the crews and assisted the forest dispatcher. Penny glanced at Mack. He was listening intently and waiting for her to continue. "I felt like I'd been on the outside looking in. I knew what I had to do to become one of them, so, I dealt with my problem directly. I began a physical fitness program, lost weight, and took the training. Now I'm on the inside looking out. I can't imagine my life without the feeling of the adrenaline rush when the fire horn blows."

"That's how I feel when the phone rings and I have a new case," Mack shared with her. "There's nothing like it. You know somewhere out there, people need you and you want and need to help them."

"Yes!" Penny exclaimed. "That's exactly how I feel. I can't imagine my life without the smell of smoke in my hair and on my clothes. I love sleeping on the ground, sometimes without a tent or..." She laughed self-consciously. "As crazy as it sounds, I can't imagine my life without foot blisters from a hard day's work or without sore shoulders from carrying a bladder bag or hose. I guess what I mean is, I know I've made a difference in life because I've chosen to risk mine." Penny glanced at Mack. For once, he wasn't laughing; instead, he was nodding in agreement. "And you?" she asked.

Mack looked in her direction. "You've said it all. I remember the feeling of being on the outside looking in when I was in training and had to do office duty. I was putting in my time waiting to get into the game, and when I did, your dad was there to lead the way."

Penny opened her mouth to speak again but then saw Mack's eyes grow wide and felt her body jolt as she heard screeching brakes and realized it was their vehicle. Her hands flew to the dash in anticipation of hitting it, but her seat belt thrust her tightly back against the seat. Her racing heart throbbed in her ears as she pulled herself together and peered out the window. Half a dozen or more cars were stopped in a line on the road. "What…" She didn't finish her question because she was sure he wouldn't hear.

"Damn it!" Mack's knuckles grew pale on the steering wheel as he brought the truck to a stop within inches of another pickup that had stopped in the middle of the road. "Oh," he said as he looked to the northern sky.

"Uh-huh." Penny released a breath that they were okay and at the wonderment of the night sky. What a spectacle. As many times as she'd seen the Aurora Borealis, each time was like the first. The colors were even brighter and more radiant than when they had left the restaurant. She wondered why she hadn't noticed the change. She glanced at Mack; his handsome face had turned in awe of the lights and was cast in a warm glow. He's the reason you didn't notice the brilliance of the lights. They were so bright they should've blinded her. She chided herself, Get back into the real world.

"Yeah, they are something." He brought his survey to the road filled with vehicles. "I wish people would park alongside the road instead of all over the damned place." His hand swept through the air and stopped. "They're even in the middle of the road."

"If they all parked on the side of the road there wouldn't be anyway for a vehicle to get around," she said trying to make him see the beauty instead of the impediment. "You know how it is, Mack." Penny considered the traffic jam in the middle of nowhere and smiled. "People are captivated by the Northern Lights." Of course they were; she was too.

She heard Mack grumble agreement as she turned her gaze to the spectacle in the sky. The lights played across the heavens in colorful profusion. It was as if an artist had spent the night creating a masterpiece on the black velvet expanse.

At the base of the colors were dense trees, mostly tall pines silhouetted against the brilliant reddish orange that seemed to set the forest on fire. Penny marveled at how this fire in the sky brought her peace but the real fires she fought brought her exhilaration. Hot reds scorched the treetops and as the colors stretched up toward the heavens, the shades grew to a warm glowing orange and then shining yellows as the painter's pallet stretched upwards. Feathering over the crown of the sky the colors grew into the most gorgeous teal blues and greens she'd ever seen. Breathtaking couldn't describe the wonder before them.

Penny looked to the southeast. A full moon was creeping over the sky. Long tree shadows cast on the snow seemed to point at the Northern Lights. It was beautiful but eerie. She shook her head. She had to quit reading so many mystery novels.

Returning her attention to Mack, she asked, "Can you honestly look at the lights and not be awed by them?" She playfully jabbed him in the shoulder.

He stared at the sky filled with the array of colors. "It's a beautiful sight alright. But in the past few weeks I've seen it so much that I can't see the forest for the trees."

Penny smiled at his analogy, it sounded like something

she would've said. "You know, when I was here last year, I heard that the Native Americans in this area have a theory for the lights, some spiritual meaning." She paused trying to remember and looked at Mack as if he would have the answer.

Mack was quietly studying the people around the scene. Some were standing outside their vehicles and some stood on the roofs of their trucks with video cameras. "I'm sorry, what did you say?" He suddenly turned to her as if he had just realized she had spoken.

She shook her head. "Nothing much, I was just trying to remember what the local Native Americans had said about the meaning of the lights."

"Oh yeah, I heard that. Now how does that go? It seems the spirits, just as the wind and water are spirits, warn us of good or bad. I also heard that the brighter the lights shine and the particular colors that are shown mean it's a warning of impending trouble." He glanced at her. "Now you aren't going to give me all that much trouble, are you?" An easy smile played on his inviting lips.

The double meaning of his long gaze was obvious and his voice, deep and sensual, sent a ripple of awareness through her. Penny shivered. But her in her mind, she tried to decide if he was flirting just to be nice to the girl whom he thought needed an ego boost or whether he was honestly attracted to her. Maybe he was just trying to be nice to her. He cared about her parents and maybe she was his charity case. Penny scowled at herself inwardly. Why must she always think someone had an ulterior motive for showing her attention?

"Are you cold?" Mack's voice filled with earnest concern.

Penny shook her head. "No." She wasn't cold but if she stayed with him much longer, she would need a cold shower. She just wasn't ready to work on a relationship even if he was seriously flirting with her. She'd gotten rid of the weight but the excess emotional baggage was still there. She didn't know how she would ever think of herself as anything but fat. And besides, her career just wouldn't allow for any extracurricular activities right now.

"Oh," Mack said knowingly.

"Oh, what?" Penny asked with as much dignity as she could muster. She was almost sure there was a thin thread of sexual tension growing between them and if not that, then he was feeling sorry for her. Whatever it was, she didn't want either, not right now.

Mack pulled a very serious face. "The *oh* was, I didn't know what to say."

"Oh," Penny answered and then laughed. "Guess I don't either."

The laughter lessened the tension. The couple turned their attention to the road. More vehicles had joined the midnight parking lot and more were coming.

Mack looked all around. "I'm going to try to maneuver around this metal jungle and get us home."

"Good, I'm beat. I think I hear my bed calling me." Penny rested her head against the seat.

Mack turned the steering wheel toward the only area left open for maneuvering vehicles around the late-night traffic jam, the right shoulder of the road. He glanced in the rearview mirror and saw emerging headlights that cast an eerie shadow over a silhouetted figure on the side of the road. The figure was running from the forest and onto the road. Mack rapidly sucked in a deep breath as he glanced in the rearview mirror.

Penny looked up when she heard his quick intake of air and in seconds, she saw what had drawn his attention. From behind them, a driver was rapidly weaving in and out on the narrow shoulder, narrowly passing on the right, and showed no signs of stopping. "Oh, my God," she cried as the sound of metal hitting flesh pierced the night air. A quick muffled scream from the victim grabbed at Penny's heart as she realized what had happened. "That car just hit someone." Her words came in breathless gasp.

"It threw 'em all the way across the road," Mack said as he thrust the truck door open and jumped out.

Penny's hand was on the door handle, and she flipped it open at the same time Mack did. Together they raced to the near lifeless body on the side of the road. They joined the crowd of people who'd gathered around the victim. The young woman's fading gaze looked at all of the faces surrounding her as the crowd grew. She fixed her stare on Mack and Penny, who immediately moved closer and dropped to their knees beside the young woman. Penny wiped the girl's face and whispered "Everything is going to be okay. We'll help you."

Tears escaped the young woman's eyes and her hand moved over her stomach as she spoke in a labored whisper. "Please, don't let them have my baby."

"We won't," Penny agreed as if she knew exactly what the young mother was talking about. She could see the hit-and-run victim was obviously pregnant and she knew implicitly the girl wanted someone to make sure her baby was taken care of.

The girl's face grimaced as her hand moved slowly over her stomach. "Thank you," she whispered and began shivering uncontrollably.

"Save your strength," Penny whispered as she checked the girl's pulse and noted her labored breathing. Penny released a deep breath and held the woman's hand. "Everything is going to be fine."

Penny yelled into the night. "Has anyone called for help?" And then turning to Mack she said, "I'm going to get something to cover her from the truck."

Mack nodded and firmly placed his hand on her shoulder. "Good idea, the ambulance is en route. Be calm. When you get back, I'm going to try to get these vehicles off the road so the ambulance can get in."

✄

Mack moved protectively closer to the girl. "Is there anyone we can call for you?" he asked.

The girl shook her head but then whispered, "I saw them. I don't know what is going on but I saw them deliver a healthy baby and then tell the mother it was dead. I knew then that I had to get out of there."

Mack felt a chill run through him as the young woman closed her eyes. What was she talking about? Saw who? Get out of where and who told what mother a healthy baby had died?

Mack bent very close to her, "Tell me your name."

Her eyes fluttered with great effort. "Nikki Mmm..." Her voice trailed away as she slid into unconsciousness. Mack barely had time to assimilate this information before Penny returned with a stadium blanket.

She held it to him. "This is all I could find."

"That'll work," Mack said as he took his favorite football blanket and wrapped it around the shivering girl.

❧❧❧

As Penny returned she could still feel Mack's touch on her shoulder. She had to admit the warmth of his hand was reassuring. She was good in emergencies but for a moment she felt very alone. She surveyed the crowd; they all stood watching and not moving until Mack took action. Penny heard his commanding voice as he ordered drivers to move their vehicles. She couldn't help noticing he sounded like a veteran traffic cop.

A quick glance at her patient proved she was still breathing, but barely. Anxiously, Penny glanced up to see the road almost clear and heard the siren before she saw the lights. By the time the lights were visible the road had been cleared. Penny heaved a sigh of relief. She knew instinctively the girl in her arms was hanging on to a thread of life. She offered a prayer for her and her baby.

The paramedics moved in as the young woman's head fell to one side. They quickly picked her up and loaded her in the ambulance. Within seconds the ambulance sirens were blaring again as it sped off to the hospital.

Penny moved closer to Mack. "What do you suppose she was doing out here?"

Mack was in deep concentration as he picked up small fibers and bits of spilled items at the scene. He shook his head. "I'd sure like to find out. It's not just that the girl is way out of her element here; it's that she is pregnant and seemingly alone."

Penny crouched down beside him so no one could hear their conversation. "Is it okay if you take this stuff from the scene of the accident?"

"There's plenty for the local police too. I don't think they would need what I'm taking, and I don't think it would be for the same reason." He glanced around. "None of them seem to be interested anyway."

"What reason?" Penny asked as she followed his gaze.

"I'm nosy." He shot her a crooked grin.

He was right; the police were so busy clearing away people and asking questions, the crime scene was the last thing on their minds. "I can't imagine where she came from." Penny thought for a moment and then asked. "What did you mean, you want to find out?"

"Like I said, I'm nosy," Mack said in a hushed voice.

Someone in the crowd asked. "Do you folks need a ride to the hospital?" Mack looked up at the crowd, which was becoming increasingly interested in him and Penny. He scowled. Penny opened her mouth to ask why they would go to the hospital and then she realized other than the victim they were the only Blacks at the scene. Mack shot her a look and she closed her mouth.

They stood as a policeman approached. Mack positioned himself beside Penny and put his arm around her shoulder. She glimpsed his strong face as he squeezed her shoulder. She knew she was to follow his lead. No words needed to be spoken. She just felt it.

"Good evening, officer," Mack said as the county policeman approached them.

The policeman touched the brim of his hat. "Evening. What can you tell me about the young woman?"

"We saw her run from the woods and saw the dark sedan hit her. That's it."

"Sedan?" the officer asked thoughtfully. "Did you get the year, make, or license number?"

Mack shook his head. "To tell the truth we were looking at the Northern Lights and only briefly caught that it was a dark, older sedan."

"Yep, eh? That describes half of the vehicles in the Upper Peninsula; the other half are pickups. And they are all covered with mud or dirt. I don't remember the last time I could read a whole license plate." The officer shook his head and grunted as he looked in the direction the vehicle had sped.

"I guess I've noticed that too," Mack agreed.

"You don't know her then, eh?" The officer turned and briefly studied the couple.

"I've never seen her before in my life," Mack stated and turned to Penny. "How about you, hon, have you ever seen her?"

Penny shook her head but she had no idea what kind of game Mack was playing. She stood helplessly next to him. She wanted to ask the policeman about the girl, and she wanted desperately to do as the girl had asked, even if she wasn't sure what that entailed. She glanced at his nametag. "Officer Finney?"

"Yep?" The balding, round-bellied man turned to her.

"It's just that the young woman did speak to us and somehow I feel responsible for the baby." Penny glanced at Mack who nodded and seemed to be okay with what she was saying. It wasn't that she was responsible but when the girl had asked her not to let them take the baby she had agreed.

The officer's eyebrows shot up. "What did she say?"

Penny shrugged. "Something about seeing that the baby was okay." She couldn't tell the officer the girl had said, not to let them take her baby because it didn't make sense to her. What made sense to Penny was that the young mother knew she might die and wanted someone to see to the welfare of the child. Penny looked at Officer Finney. "Do you have any idea how either of them is?"

Officer Finney smiled at them. "Just a minute, I'll check." He lumbered off to his patrol car and began talking to someone on his radio.

Mack turned to Penny. "What are you going to do? Try to get the baby?"

"I don't know." Penny couldn't think beyond the moment. "But I would like to at least know the baby will get a good, loving foster home." Penny hesitated for a moment.

"I'd like to see it placed with people of its own race.

Mack ran his fingers over his cropped hair. "The baby is kind of young to worry about that," Mack offered. He shook his head. "This does complicate matters but I suppose we can see that the baby gets to either its real family or at least a loving African-American home." He glanced in the direction of the police vehicle and knew from the expression on the officer's face the news wasn't good. "If the mother doesn't make it, we'll work to see that the baby gets to either its real family or at least a family with people of its own race."

Penny nodded as she watched Officer Finney walking toward them. The officer shook his head. "The mom died but the baby lived." He paused thoughtfully and then continued. "It's the damnedest thing. What would a girl be doing out here on her own, eh? Dispatch said there wasn't a drop of identification on her. Headquarters checked with Sugar Moon and they said all of their girls were accounted for. Probably a runaway."

Mack had considered she might be a runaway too, but somehow the pieces just didn't fit. Even the most educated Blacks were too streetwise and conscious of their race to run away and hide in a world where they would be so obvious. "Sugar Moon?" he asked the officer as if he'd just heard it.

"Yeah, the place over there for unwed mothers, eh?" His arm dangled in a southerly direction.

"Oh, I see," Mack answered thoughtfully. Then he took Penny by the elbow. "I think we should go to the hospital."

Penny smiled at him. She was relieved that he was going to help her keep her commitment because she had no idea how she would do it otherwise.

The officer shook hands with them and said, "Good to meet you, eh?"

When they were on their way to the hospital, Mack was deep in concentration. Finally he turned to Penny and asked, "Was that cop deaf or was that a speech impediment, eh?"

She laughed as she answered. "No, it's a colloquialism to add *eh*. I don't know why they do it but I like it. It adds a homey flavor to the area." She thought for a moment. "Have you heard what they call themselves and the people of the Lower Peninsula?"

Mack shook his head. "I'm not sure. I've been to a couple of the local watering holes and have heard the locals call each other a lot of things but most can't be mentioned in mixed company."

Penny punched his shoulder. "If you're going to live here you should know. The residents of Michigan's Upper Peninsula are called Yoopers."

"Why?" Mack snorted.

"I was told that Yooper was derived from U-P-er, as in Upper Peninsula."

Mack glanced in her direction and smiled. "So does that mean the people of the Lower Peninsula are called Lopers?"

Penny shook her head and laughed. "No...people in the Lower Peninsula are called Trolls."

"Now why in the hell would they be called that?" Mack laughed heartily.

Penny shrugged. "Because they live below the Mackinac Bridge." She thought for a moment. "I'm sure most states and regions have a dialect of their own."

Mack nodded. "I've lived in many areas and while it's true most inhabitants seem to have their own language, this area seems to be overflowing with it."

"Only because it's all new. We'll get used to it."

"We? Does that mean you and I have begun our relationship?"

Penny let out a long sigh. "Just drive, will you?"

"Yes, ma'am!" Mack saluted.

Penny ignored his salute. She wasn't sure what they had started but right now she wanted to get to the hospital to see what she could do to follow through on her self-imposed obligation to the now deceased young mother.

Chapter 3

Penny took a deep breath as they entered the hospital. She had no idea how they'd get to see the baby, but she knew she had to try.

As Mack and Penny waited in the emergency waiting area, a nurse came rushing up to them. "Oh thank God you're here. I'm so sorry for your loss."

Penny opened her mouth but Mack took her hand and squeezed it tightly. "Thank you." He smiled politely at the nurse and asked, "Can we see the baby?"

"Of course. Follow me." The well-meaning nurse led them to the nursery. She wrapped the infant in a blanket and handed it to them.

The nurse quietly left and closed the door behind her, leaving them alone with the baby whose mother they had seen only for minutes.

Mack looked at the closed door, then at Penny. "This is the first time I've ever had stereotyping work to my advantage." He shook his head.

Penny nodded in agreement. "Yes, but now that it has, how do we explain that we don't know the young woman?"

"We'll tell the truth." Mack smiled down at the baby in Penny's arms. "The look fits you."

"Oh yes, a baby would look great packed on my back while I fight forest fires." A baby? she thought. "I wonder if it's a girl or boy."

"We could look," Mack offered.

Carefully Penny unwrapped the baby until they could see. "Aw," Penny cooed. "It's a little girl." She ran her fingers over the baby's dark curls and then stared at her for a moment. "I think she's beautiful."

Mack looked closer. "I don't know. I think all newborn babies look alike." He studied the baby.

Penny nodded. "Still, I want to make sure she goes to a home where she can be taught our culture." She hugged the baby tighter. "I agreed to not let *them* take the baby. I'm not sure what that meant but I just feel we should at least see she is going to be well cared for. Somehow..."

The door opened. The nurse who'd brought them in ushered in another woman and then left. The woman looked at Mack and Penny and then at the baby. "She's fine-looking." She set her briefcase on the floor and held out her arms. "Would you mind if I held her?"

Penny shook her head, held out the baby, and then protectively pulled the small bundle back against her chest. "Who are you?" She cringed a little inside. Sometimes her directness surprised even her.

The middle-aged, heavyset woman answered, "Oh, of course, let me show you my ID." She reached in her pocket and held up a card. It read Carol Young, Michigan Department of Social Services Caseworker.

"Nice to meet you, Carol," Mack jumped in. "I'm Mack

Holsey and this is Penny Hart."

Carol Young smiled at the couple and accepted the baby Penny relinquished to her. The caseworker smiled down at the sweet package and then looked at the couple. "Does she have a name?"

"Aurora," Penny said. "Well...I mean...that's what I'd name her because of the Northern Lights and all." She gave Mack a pleading look.

Mack smiled at her and then turned his attention to Carol Young and the baby. "The truth is, Carol, we came on the accident and the young mother was dying." He took a deep breath and continued. "She looked at all of the faces and ours being the most like her own, she asked if we would see to her baby."

The caseworker's graying eyebrows lifted in question but she waited for Mack to finish.

"What we are saying is, we'd never seen the young woman before tonight. It's just that we did agree to help. And we fully intend to oversee the placement of the child."

"I see." The older woman looked from Penny to Mack and then at the baby. "How did you get in here then?"

"The nurse assumed because of our color that we were somehow involved with the young woman," Penny stated, and then she thought for a moment and added, "it was an honest mistake. There aren't many of us living here, and we were at the scene."

Carol Young's face grew concerned. "First, I'm sorry the nurse took it upon herself to assume you were in some way connected with the young woman. The nurse should have asked for identification. I know you're right; the nurse just assumed and that can be a bad thing. I'll speak to her about it. Now we have to deal with a motherless child and no identification to find her family."

Penny and Mack nodded.

"I'll have to put her in a foster home until we can either find her family or a good home for her to go to." She sighed heavily. "I was so hoping we wouldn't have to do that."

"You don't," Penny stated definitely. "I could take her for a couple of weeks or at least until you find her family. The right family."

Mack stared at Penny. Their gazes met. She could feel the consternation from him but she had given her agreement to the dying woman and she didn't want little Aurora to go to just any home. Ms. Young smiled at the couple. "I'm afraid it's not that easy. If you knew the mother and were part of her family, we could place her with you temporarily. But we know nothing of you, and it would take at least a month to get your home licensed." She held the baby out to Penny. "Would you mind holding her while I make a few calls?"

Penny held out her arms and gently took the baby. Her stomach was knotting to think the child who'd been halfway entrusted to her would soon be with strangers, probably a White stranger. She'd never considered herself racist, but never in her life had she felt as she did at this moment. "Carol?" she asked, when the woman was between phone calls.

The older woman looked up. "Yes?"

Penny chewed on her lower lip, then stole a look at Mack. An uncertainty crept over Mack's face; his eyes were saying leave it alone. She shook her head. She couldn't leave it alone. Even as her mind clouded with doubts and fears Penny knew she had to be there for this baby. She turned back to the older woman who was thumbing through her address book. "I would really like the baby to go to a home where there is a person of her race." There, Penny thought. I've said it and I have no idea how I'll make it happen.

"Ms. Hart, Penny," the older woman's voice was filled with compassion. "I do understand your concern but I don't have any African-American foster homes here, and I hate to send her down state until we discover who her family is."

"Couldn't I be a temporary foster home? There has to be a way to do this. If you could've seen the terror in the mother's face, you would feel the obligation that I do." Penny's voice was filled with entreaty.

An earnest tear ran down the caseworker's cheek. "I do feel that obligation. That's why I do this job. You have to understand there are rules I must follow or I won't be able to help anyone." She swiped at the unwanted display of emotion running down her cheek.

Mack paced the floor with his hands clasped behind his back and his head bent in total concentration. He sure has been a lot of help, Penny thought. she was mildly irritated with what seemed to be his cool and aloof manner. Sighing heavily, she conceded to herself that it wasn't as if Mack could have done anything anyway. She masked her inner turmoil and shot a meaningful glance at Mack.

Mack stopped pacing and came to stand beside Penny. "We can't just turn our backs on her. That young woman trusted us with her dying breath to do as she requested. Maybe you could see your way to helping us keep that pledge." His voice carried depth and authority as he took charge with a quiet assurance.

Frown lines creased on Carol Young's tired face and then lit as if a new day had dawned. "I think I have the answer." She quickly dialed a number without looking in her book.

Penny placed her hand on Mack's arm and whispered, "Thank you." She felt his forearm tighten and then relax under her touch. He placed his hand over hers and offered her a supportive smile. His touch was reassuring, and the warmth seemed immense. Penny relaxed a little knowing this man, her father's friend, was on her side.

"Paige?" Penny heard the caseworker speak into the phone and then listen closely. "How are you tonight?" Carol Young paused to listen and then said, "And Linc?" Another pause and then, "Yes, I know it's the middle of the night. But I have a problem that I think only you can solve." She asked whomever she was speaking with to meet her at the hospital.

Penny looked at her expectantly. The caseworker smiled back and answered the look. "Paige Cross is Black. About a year ago, I asked her to sign on to be an emergency foster care home. She completed all of the paperwork and subsequently she received approval. At the time, Paige had a new baby so I put her on the backburner. People like Paige and Linc are the best kind of foster home. They don't need the money.

They do it for the love of children." The caseworker realized she was rattling and ended her statements with, "Anyway they are the kind of home where a child can be taken for, overnight or a short time, until the court places them elsewhere. You know what I mean?"

Penny had no idea how the foster care system worked. Her family had always been together and although she had known kids in school who'd been in foster homes, she'd never asked about how it happened.

Carol waved her hand. "Well, that's how it's done," she said matter-of-factly and then asked, "Why don't we get coffee and wait for the Crosses to arrive. I think they'll meet your approval and for that matter mine too." She walked to the coffeepot and continued talking more to herself than to Mack and Penny, "I just knew someday the Crosses would come in handy. They are such sweet people, and their children are so well cared for."

Penny accepted the cup of coffee handed to her by the older woman. "They have more than one child?" she asked, wondering if they would have the time to care for a new one.

"Oh yes, "Carol Young bubbled. "Turner is two and Brook is almost one." The older woman smiled as she thought about the family. "Lincoln Cross is an architect and a member of the Ottawa/Chippewa Tribal Council and Paige was a model but gave that up to be Mrs. Cross and raise her children."

"It's good that some women can give up their careers to raise families," Mack stated.

Penny glanced at Mack who was smiling at her. She

boldly met his gaze, wanting to impress upon him she wasn't going to do that. His smile grew wider; he seemed very pleased with himself. See, she thought, you let him get under your skin and he knows it.

Penny dismissed Mack's grin and asked the caseworker, "With two small children, will they have time for another one?"

"Oh, Linc's mother lives with them and helps with the children." She smiled in self-satisfaction. "This is a match made in heaven."

Just then, the door opened and the smiling, but sleepy couple walked in. Penny felt an instant relief as Paige and Lincoln Cross greeted all of them. They had an aura of warmth and love that seemed to spread over the room and pull in everyone who was there. The caseworker introduced the couples as she made fresh coffee and played hostess to the people in the room, pouring coffee for everyone.

Paige was tall and a bit on the heavy side. To Penny she was one of the most beautiful women she'd ever seen. No wonder she'd been a model, Penny thought. She couldn't help thinking how the weight gain must have been part of the reason the woman had given up her modeling career. She could identify with the weight thing; she was on constant vigil against packing on the pounds. She watched as Carol hugged Paige and then Lincoln. They all genuinely liked one another. Penny's relief turned to joy as she watched the couple. She wouldn't have to spend time in jail or go to court because she refused to give up Aurora.

Paige sipped her coffee and then set the cup on the table.

"Penny?"

"Yes?" Penny answered the woman with whom she had an instant rapport .

"Could I hold the baby?" Paige held out experienced arms to take the infant.

Penny turned over the baby without a doubt in her mind; she was impressed with the obvious confidence Paige inspired. "I named her Aurora. It seemed the right thing to do being her mother died under the Northern Lights and she was born under them."

Lincoln Cross stepped beside his wife. "Aurora is her name. I can see she'll have the brilliance of color and light in her life forever."

"I hope so." Penny looked at the handsome man who was Paige's husband. He was obviously Native American. Looking at them made her wonder what their children looked like. How could they be anything but beautiful?

"Oh, she will. Spirit guides are never wrong." Lincoln Cross winked at Penny, dropped a kiss on his wife's head, and poured himself another cup of coffee.

Penny smiled at the loving relationship and the self-assuredness of the man who seemed to be one with himself and nature. She glanced around the room to see where Mack had gone. He was standing staring out the window.

Mack had been silent other than the initial hello when the other couple had entered the room. Penny knew he wasn't being rude; he was assessing the people and the situation. Once an investigator, always an investigator her father had said many times. Now Mack gave a huge smile to the couple and held out his hand to Linc. "It's good to meet you."

Lincoln accepted Mack's hand. "It's good to meet you too. I haven't seen either of you around. Did you move here recently?"

"I've been here for a couple of months, and Penny just arrived today." He looked at his watch. "I should say yesterday." Mack smiled at the other three and then continued, "We were on our way home from dinner when we witnessed the accident."

Penny scowled at him. He was telling the truth but it made it sound as if they were a couple. She thought about denying it but that would make it sound as if she protested too loudly. Besides, she was there to make sure Aurora had a good home, and she could deal with Mack later. She turned her attention to Paige, who was cooing over the baby. "If you need anything for Aurora, just let me know."

Paige looked up from the baby and smiled. "Brook, our daughter, is just a year. She has doting family and more than enough of everything to share with Aurora."

Penny smiled in relief. The burden of the baby had been given into capable hands; now she could get on with her life before the accident. All of the adrenaline Penny'd been riding on waned. The baby would be safe with this couple and she would visit as often as she could. Her knees grew weak and she slid down to the chair behind her.

She looked to where Mack was standing and talking to Linc. "No," he was saying, "I'm between jobs now." That was odd, she thought. Why didn't he say he was an FBI agent on a sabbatical or something at least to let them know he did have a job? Her coffee cup slipped from her hand and seemed to float to the floor with a loud crash as it landed. "Damn it," she uttered before she knew what she was saying. Heat filled her face as all heads turned toward her. She dropped down and began wiping up the coffee with napkins.

Mack was beside her before she could finish the cleanup. Affectionately, he smiled at her. "Tired?"

Penny nodded; she was too weary to speak. Allowing Mack to help her to her feet and guide her toward the door, she offered a weak smile in apology. The other couple hugged her and told her to visit anytime. She hoarsely whispered, "Thank you."

Mack dropped her coat over her shoulders and led her out of the hospital. She breathed deeply of the cold morning air and felt the sun of the new day. She shivered and he pulled her to him. Penny didn't resist. Last night had been a life-altering experience and she needed time to decide how much change had taken place. She'd wanted to be on her own but it sure felt good to have a friend close.

Mack smiled at his sleeping traveling partner. He'd been surprised and proud when Penny fought for what she believed, but he knew she couldn't have won if she'd tried. He wondered why Carol Young had listened to Penny at all. The caseworker had the upper hand, she had to know that, he ruminated. The older woman didn't have to listen and she surely didn't have to grant Penny any concessions. Just a nice old broad, he concluded.

He had his second wind and wasn't ready to return to the cabin. He had to admit to himself that his curiosity had been piqued at the accident scene. Mack thought about the young woman's last words and shrugged. He was there to discover the actual events surrounding his partner's death but it wouldn't hurt to look into Nikki's allegations. Having her name made it even more personal. She'd been running like hell to escape. But, escape what?

He knew he'd seen the sign for Sugar Moon close to the cabin where he lived, but he hadn't paid attention to what it was. Now as he drove along I-75, he spotted the sign. The Harts' cabin and the home for unwed mothers were on the same road.

He glanced at Penny. After he got her back to the cabin, he might just have to do a little investigating.

Chapter 4

Penny rolled over as the bright spring sun seeped through her eyelids. She thrust her arm over her face in an effort to stay asleep but the warmth urged her out of bed. Clang, clang, clang, the sound of metal on metal. She stretched lazily. A week ago, that sound had jolted her out of bed while she'd been trying to catch up on the sleep she'd lost the night before. After a week, the noise was more comforting than disturbing.

Smiling, as she listened to Mack lifting weights. A hot flush shot through her body. She pictured his large, sinewy black chest heaving under the strain of the weights. "Damn!" She cursed aloud. The thought of sweat beads rolling off that beautiful body caused her to jerk inward. And those thoughts were more disturbing than comforting.

Her mind and body had been at odds with each other since she'd arrived and she saw no way it was going to change unless she moved out or insisted Mack did. Penny knew she was attracted to Mack and felt he might have some feelings for him too. She sighed heavily. Her original plan had been to get rid of him, but the longer he stayed, the more difficult moving him out became.

It had been a long week. During the days that followed

the young girl's death, Mack would disappear for hours. She assumed he was investigating but she never asked. For some reason she felt it necessary to tell him where she was going. Well, she told herself, that is going to end. I don't have to report to anyone.

She'd called Paige and Linc every day checking on Aurora and was planning to visit the baby later that day. But she wanted to do it without Mack, just to keep some distance from him and the ever-growing attraction.

Penny dragged herself out of bed and pulled on her jogging clothes. The only way to calm her wild hormones was to run, and she'd need to run a marathon for this one. Quietly, so he wouldn't hear her, she padded down the loft stairs. Tiptoeing across the hardwood floor to the solid oak door, she smelled the aroma of fresh coffee. Inhaling deeply she thought, damn, he's good: fun, considerate, works out, cooks like a chef, looks like he just stepped off the front of a modeling magazine, and makes the best coffee I've ever tasted. She shook her head trying to rid her mind of thoughts that she felt were hers alone. Thoughts of him would be the death of her and her plans for the future.

Mack had given no indication he was interested in being anything but a friend. There were those times when she was sure he was feeling something more than friendship but then it would leave so quickly. Still, she was undeniably attracted to him and she didn't want to be. She paused at the door, thinking of grabbing a cup of coffee to take on her run.

"Good morning." Mack's deep voice boomed with liveliness.

Penny whirled around. "Will you stop sneaking up on me like that?" She couldn't help smiling as his golden-black gaze danced with the sheer delight of being alive.

Mack pulled his look from her and poured coffee. "Want some?"

Penny shook her head. That *want some* thing again. He had to quit asking her that. She stepped around him into the small kitchen and filled the water bottle she carried in a sling on her hip. Snapping the bottle in place, she moved quickly to the door. Her need to run was increasing with every second she was with him.

She glanced back at Mack's smiling face. He held up his cup as if to salute her. "I'll fix breakfast while you're gone."

"Thank you, but I don't really eat that stuff." Her hand swept over the counter filled with eggs, bacon, sausage, and all of the fixings to clog arteries. "I'll grab something when I come back," she added, hopefully sounding less ungrateful as she pulled open the door.

"No problem." Mack reached in the refrigerator and held up bagels. "Will these do?"

Penny nodded and stepped outside. If Mack was competing for roommate of the year, she was sure he would win. Somehow, the things he did for her made her feel grateful and irritated at the same time. She'd made no effort to cook, clean, or do anything special for him. Shaking her head she uttered to the forest as she began her run, "I can't think straight."

Pulling a long breath of fresh, late April air deep into her lungs, she felt a tug of urgency. The aroma was sweet and new but it was also dry. Warm, arid winds had been severe-ly drying the fields and forests. The snowstorm of a week ago was only a drop of moisture to the parched woods. The month of March had been the driest on record and now April had followed suit.

Gravel and sand crunched and parted as she ran along the side of the road. She searched the depths of the Hiawatha National Forest. The snow had disappeared as if overnight. Penny listened as she ran. Drying debris crackled on the woodland's bed as the wind and small animals made their presence known. The troubling sounds only added to the recipe for disaster.

Warily she assessed the majestic maze of trees. Deep green jack pine leaned into softer green spruce and white pine and in the mix were a few poplar and maples straining to bring on their leaves. Penny knew that over the next month the moisture would gather in the new growth producing green-up that would reduce the threat of fires but right now, it was serious.

She ran faster as adrenaline pumped through her body, making her alert and aware of her surroundings. As she passed the entrance to the forest rangers' station, she read the sign. Just as she had surmised, the fire danger was very high. Penny had no idea when she'd made the decision but within minutes, she found herself inside the empty station.

She walked to the wall with the map of the forest. For the past week, she had gone to sleep with the layout of the area woodlands on her chest. She had studied it and now as she perused the map, she recognized the areas that were marked as potential risks. Inhaling deeply, she couldn't help thinking how she loved her job. The woodsy aroma mixed with the scent of paper, ink, and coffee. She was home! This was her work, her love, and that was why she was here.

"Can I help you?" Penny started and spun around as the gruff male voice reverberated in the empty office. The uniformed man was tall with close-cropped black hair. His long face reminded her of Lincoln Cross. She'd been relieved when she met Paige Cross and now she would be working with a man who was obviously Native American. Inwardly she breathed a sigh of relief. When she'd made the decision to transfer, the lack of Blacks in the area had been a concern, but then after much consideration, she'd decided the forest and advancement in her career were her reason for relocating and she'd worry about the people later.

Penny smiled broadly and stuck out her hand to the man. "Penny Hart. I'm to report for work here in a couple of weeks but looking at the forest this morning I decided to offer my help early."

"Dan Ryder," the man said as he shook her outstretched hand. "Pleased to meet you, Penny." He smiled broadly. "I knew from your former supervisor that you'd be reporting in early. Hard to ignore the warning signs in our forest." He smiled knowingly as he reached in the side drawer of the large desk and pulled out a folder. "In here are all of the forms you have to complete and a beeper that is programmed for you already." His smile grew wider as he pulled the beeper from the folder and handed it to her.

Penny flicked the on switch and snapped the beeper on

her belt. Accepting the folder, she said, "I'll complete these and report for work on Monday morning."

"Sounds like a plan to me," Dan answered. "Would you like to meet the rest of the crew?" He plopped his hat on his head and continued, "If you have time we could do that now and then when your beeper goes off you won't be with strangers."

"I have time," she said, eager to be working again. She could feel the adrenaline pump, in anticipation of strapping the bladder bag on and rushing to fight a fire.

"Here." Dan handed her the familiar yellow jacket and hardhat. Quickly she slid into the gear. It was as if her body and mind equated the color, the rough texture of the fire-resistant fabric, and scent of the gear with urgency. Penny tucked her hair under the hardhat and tapped it. "Ready."

Dan knowingly smiled at her. "Is there anyone you should call? I sure wouldn't want you to be put on the missing persons list." He chuckled as he pulled on his boots.

"Phone?" For the first time since she walked into the station, she thought of Mack. "I should let my roommate know." She reached for the phone and then hesitated about calling him. Hadn't she promised herself that she wouldn't report to him? She told herself this was only common courtesy as she punched the cabin phone number on the keypad. Later, when they were together, she would have to lay down the new rules but until then, she wouldn't want him bringing the whole FBI looking for her.

"We aren't available, leave a message." For a brief instant her heart leaped for joy and then Penny could feel the blood drain from her face and a mist grow in her eyes. The answering machine message was still her father's voice. His rich melodic tones wrapped around her, reminding her of how much she missed him. His message was so him, direct and to the point. Her heart trembled with the pain of loss.

She shook her head to ward off the gloom and left a message. "I'm at the rangers' station. I'll be back later." There, she thought, that wasn't as if I was giving exact details of my whereabouts. She replaced the receiver and briefly thought of changing the message before her mother heard it. But then she knew that after five years her mother knew her father's message was on the answering machine and hadn't had the heart to change it.

The fire horn sounded, shocking her into action and removing thoughts of anything but the fire. Dan located the area on the map and hurriedly motioned her to follow. Within seconds, they were bouncing over the rough two-track until they saw smoke billowing over the trees. Penny slid on the fire boots and gloves and shoved safety glasses on her face. She checked her radio and the headlamp on the helmet. Her equipment was ready and so was she. Her heart pumped rapidly as she steeled herself for fighting the fire.

Dan pointed east. "There, in the meadow before the jack pine." He turned the wheel of the Jeep and headed down another two-track that led deeper into the forest.

Penny grew more watchful. Graceful meadows were struggling to cast off their dead and dried growth of last year and grow green again. Jack pine surrounded the meadows and the smoke swelled from that area. Her heart gathered speed. Jack pine fires were one of the hottest and fastest if not contained quickly. In the distance, they could see the roaring fire and soon they were encompassed by billowing smoke. She felt her body jerk forward with the abrupt stop of the vehicle. As her eyes adjusted to the darkness, she could see they were right at the edge of the control line.

"Penny?" Dan hollered as he threw his water can over his shoulder and moved forward.

"Here!" Penny yelled back quickly, knowing time was more important than conversation.

"The holding crew won't know you're here so follow me, and I'll call back." She nodded and fell in beside Dan. Her bladder bag was full and ready to spray on the fire. Spot fires had crossed the control line. She and Dan fell in beside each other, spraying the fires and waiting for the bulldozer to run along the line again.

Ahead of her, the yellow jackets moved rapidly against the orange-red fire. Every time she saw the yellow against the orange-red, she marveled that the color did not blend in. It seemed the fire suits should merge with the color of the fire but she was glad they didn't.

Other firefighters joined them on the line. They fell in beside Penny as if they'd worked with her for years. Her mind and heart grew at ease as she felt the camaraderie of the others.

She glimpsed the sun and decided it must be getting late afternoon. It was always a shock to her how time flew when she was fighting a fire. Yes, she thought as she looked around at the others who'd been working beside her, I'm going to be happy here.

"Penny?" Dan called as the line moved forward.

"Here!" she responded loudly.

Penny shot a spray of water at an errant flame. "Looks like we have it under control," she hollered to him.

Dan moved along the line handing out assignments for containment to the fresh group of firefighters who had just moved in. When he finished, he came to where Penny and the rest of the tiring crew were beginning to relax. "You guys want to grab a bite at Dunn Inn?"

"I would but I left my truck at the cabin." She smiled sheepishly.

"No problem." Smoke dust crinkled on Dan's face as he smiled. "Ride with me and I'll give you a lift home later."

Penny accepted gratefully. She really hadn't meant to leave home for the day but after meeting the fire crew she was glad she had. It was good to be back with people who would understand her.

⋘⋙

After Penny left that morning, Mack had gone for a run. He'd stood on the road looking in the direction she'd sprinted and then turned the other way. He was troubled when she wasn't at the cabin upon his return. In fact, he worried for half of the day until he reached to make a couple of phone calls and saw the answering machine blinking. He hesitated to take the messages. The communications could be for Penny and he didn't want to invade her privacy. On the other hand, he argued with himself, they hadn't discussed the answering machine and he was the one who'd been there for a month so he deduced the messages were probably for him. His finger hung over the message button for what seemed forever. Finally, he punched it, deciding he'd waited long enough.

Listening to her message he released a long breath and slumped against the wall. Until he heard her voice, he hadn't realized how concerned he'd been. He couldn't help worrying; after all, he'd promised her mother he'd watch out for her, and there were some strange things happening. But was that all there was to his concern? Mack had to admit he was more than a little interested in the beautiful woman with whom he shared a cabin.

The next message was for both of them. Paige and Linc were inviting them to dinner Saturday night. He smiled. Guess that'll put us together tomorrow night, he thought.

The last message was from Cavine Eastman, a friend and fellow agent who worked closely with forensics at headquarters. "We did get the clothes of the young woman who was killed. The outfit came from a rather upscale store in Chicago. Either she got them from someone or the kid has some money. Oh, and I am running a missing persons on Nikki M. with the description you sent." There was a slight pause and then she added, "What have you got your sweet butt into this time?"

Mack smiled. Cavine was one beautiful woman. They'd dated for a while but their careers had taken priority over their relationship. Since then, they'd worked together and ignored what might have been. Neither agent had been willing to let their work suffer for a relationship. He listened to her message again and couldn't help grinning at that sultry voice with the British accent.

Since Penny's arrival, he'd done very little on the investigation. The week since the young woman's death had flown past. The only thing he'd done was send the evidence from the accident to the crime lab and ask them to use their powers to get the victim's clothing. Now his curiosity was piqued. He'd thought the way the dying girl pronounced her last words was not only with a Chicago dialect but as if well educated.

He paced in the cabin, first thinking about the investigation and then turning his thoughts to that of his roommate. Subconsciously he poured a cup of coffee and glanced at the clock as the grumbling turned to a roar in his stomach. "Six o'clock." He whistled aloud. "She must be having a great time at the rangers' station." Thoughts of rangers and anyone else who might be occupying her time gave him a feeling he'd never experienced. Pangs of jealousy crept over his body. "Don't be stupid," he berated himself. "That's it! I'm going to dinner."

On his short drive to Dunn Inn where he'd eaten almost nightly since his arrival, he mulled over his situation. He'd been entertaining the idea of moving. The promise to Penny's mother was becoming harder to keep and that couldn't compare with the honor-bound feelings he had for her father.

Thoughts of his late partner always gave him tugs of guilt. If only he'd accepted Cliff's invitation to spend a couple of weeks fishing. In the back of his mind he'd had a feeling his mentor's fishing trip was more than had been verbalized. Yet, he'd rationalized at the time, he'd allowed no time for play during his internship and wanted to make up for it. A hot flush swept over him. While he'd been playing, someone had killed his partner and closest friend. He swore he'd never make that mistake again.

Gloomy thoughts swarmed his mind as he entered the inn. Laughter rang out from a dimly lit corner where someone was pounding out "Great Balls of Fire" on the piano. Some of the men surrounding the piano were in uniform. On closer inspection, he could see they were with the National Forest Service. He turned toward the table he'd always sat at when it dawned on him that these were Penny's coworkers.

Mack twirled on his heel and joined the crowd at the piano. Perched on the edge of the piano bench his roommate's feet rapidly tapped the pedals and her hands flew rowdily over the polished ivory. Well shit, he thought. I've been home worrying about her and she's been at the bar having a great time. Again, he felt the green-eyed monster twinge. Before he did something he would be sorry for, he stepped back and went to his table.

Ordering his dinner, he took the time to settle down. What she did was no concern of his. If she wanted to play, that was her business. The music stopped and loud conversation filled the air. Mack listened and learned they had been fighting a fire and had contained it before it took out a jack pine forest. He didn't know exactly what that meant but he knew it must be good from the way their excitement grew as they talked about it.

He shoved his fork into the pile of mashed potatoes and gravy and ate without tasting it. He'd had the meatloaf dinner several times and loved it. But today it seemed to lose its flavor. While he ate, he listened. Penny's voice filled with life as she recounted her fight against the fire with the others. Pulling his wallet from his pocket, he stood and laid the money on the table. Mack needed time to sort out his new feelings, and this was no place to do it.

"Mack?" Penny's breathless voice called across the room.

Mack's shoulders slumped. He stopped in his retreat. It wasn't as if he could say she'd mistaken him for someone else. He was the only Black man in the room and probably within a hundred miles. He turned and forced a smile. "Hi. I see you've found the local watering hole." He tried to sound good-humored but wasn't sure he was pulling it off.

"Why didn't you join us?" Penny asked as her coppery eyes filled with questions.

Mack shrugged. "It looked like a private celebration."

"Hey Penny?" Dan hollered. "You leaving the party now?"

Penny glanced at Mack and then back at her fellow firefighters. There was something in Mack's demeanor that demanded attention but she wasn't sure what. Maybe something was wrong with her mother or maybe with the baby. Whatever it was she instinctively knew it was time to go.

Dan moved to her. "Thanks for pitching in today." His easy gaze moved over Mack.

"I loved it! I can't think of a place I would rather be than fighting the fires." Penny felt heat rise to her cheeks as she realized how silly that might sound to someone who did not fight fires.

Dan smiled. "I know just what you mean. Fighting fires seems to get in your blood." He glanced at Mack and then back at Penny.

"Oh, I'm sorry. Dan, this is my…a family friend, Mack Holsey. Mack, this is Dan Ryder, my supervisor." For some reason she wanted to let Dan know Mack was just a family friend. Not that it mattered to Dan, she was sure he didn't care, but it mattered to her. And if she introduced Mack this way, it kept them on a more casual relationship. Not that he wanted it differently but she didn't want him to think she did either. It was a defensive move and she knew it, but she wasn't going to let her runaway physical desire mess with her career.

Mack shot her a look but then turned and offered a smile to Dan. The men shook hands and greeted each other. She watched as Mack pushed his lips into a grin and cordially greeted Dan but she knew his smile and this was not it. After a week with this man who smiled all of the time, she just knew there was something wrong.

"We'll see you on Monday morning?" Dan tapped Penny on the shoulder, bringing her from her musings.

"You sure will." She smiled warmly at Dan.

"Oh and a bunch of us are going to Nun's Creek smelt

dipping later. Do you want to join us?" Dan asked, smiling at Penny.

"That sounds great! What time should I be there?" Penny loved smelt dipping. She knew it was one of the biggest parties of the year and the fish were great too.

"About midnight?"

"I'll be there." Penny's heart filled with the new joy of her job and fellow rangers.

She watched as her new supervisor returned to the crowd of celebrating coworkers. She was going to be happy here. Today had made her decision come to life and lessened any fears she might've had.

Other rangers hollered over the bar noises. "See you later on."

Penny waved and smiled at her new friends. "I'll be there."

Smiling, she turned her attention to Mack. "Do you think I could hitch a ride back to the cabin?" She'd almost said home but caught herself just in time. It was her home, she reasoned, but it wasn't their home. Fighting the fire had left her physically exhausted but her perception of Mack's mood change had her mentally awake.

"Sure," Mack answered in a neutral tone.

"Thanks." Her stomach knotted as she let her imagination run wild. His normally bright golden-black eyes clouded and his smile stopped at his lips instead of taking in his whole face. Something terrible had happened, she just knew it, and he was waiting to tell her.

Chapter 5

In Mack's truck, Penny waited for him to speak but he was silent. She fidgeted in her seat, wondering what could have happened to the happy man she'd left that morning. She wanted to ask him but then if she was letting her imagination run away with her, she didn't want him to know. She stared out the window until just before they turned into the driveway of the cabin. "How was your day?" she asked, trying to find out what was going on without asking.

Mack turned toward her. Their gazes met and held. Shaking his head and averting his gaze, he answered. "It was okay. How was yours?"

Penny tried to read past the cloudy wall in his look. Could she have been wrong? Was this just her imagination? Well, she wasn't going to play any games. "My mistake. I thought something had happened to Mom or something." Penny let her words drop off as she watched him shift uncomfortably in his seat.

His brow furrowed deeper as he answered. "No, Penny, I would've told you something that serious right away." He paused and continued. "I was just surprised to see you there...I mean, of course you can be where you want, but I was surprised."

"Oh," Penny uttered as she thought of how truly inconsiderate she'd been. "I'm sorry. When the fire horn sounded, I didn't think of anything but the fire and doing my job." She was sorry for her thoughtlessness but his attitude irked her. If she lived alone as she'd planned, this would be a non-conversation, a non-problem.

"I..." Mack began and then stopped as he turned the truck into the driveway and noticed a car parked in front of the cabin. "I forgot the housekeeper would be here today." His brow furrowed as he studied the housekeeper's car.

Penny followed his gaze. A late-model sedan was parked in the drive. "Now that is one clean car." In the past week, she'd grown used to seeing the vehicles Officer Finney had described, and one that was not muddy where you could read the license plate was indeed rare. She applauded herself for becoming one of the Yoopers. It would take a Yooper to realize a car was too clean for the area. Or an investigator, she thought.

Penny glanced in Mack's direction and noted his face was a watchful fixity. His stare seemed to be boring into the car as if to read where it had been and why it was clean. In her mind, she could hear her father say, once an investigator, always an investigator. She poked him in the shoulder. "I was only kidding." She laughed lightly. "I'm sure not everyone's vehicle is a muddy mess, even if Officer Finney thinks so."

Mack turned slowly toward her, a glimmer of a grin growing on his firm mouth. "Penny Hart the mind reader. Now that could come in handy. Could you tell me why the housekeeper is here on Friday instead of Thursday?" His strong but velvet-edged voice held a challenge.

Penny's first reaction was to be snide but then biting her tongue she said, "Obviously she was having her car cleaned yesterday." She laughed as she climbed from the truck. "Now I'm going to meet the woman who keeps house like my mother does."

"Oh, no you don't." Mack jumped from the truck and caught up to her quick stride. "I know your kind. You are going to make friends with her and I'll have to fend for myself." Amusement flickered in the eyes that met hers.

Mack held the door open for her and then hollered. "Mrs. Rowe?"

They listened for an answer but could only hear someone humming.

"Mrs. Rowe? Is that her name?"

"Yeah. Why?"

Mack quirked his eyebrows questioningly and looked down at her. His gaze dropped from her eyes to her shoulders to her breasts. He was so disturbing in every way she drew in a deep breath to throttle the dizzying current running through her. She couldn't tell but she thought she saw a glimmer of interest in his gaze. Penny looked away to gain control and answer without sounding as if she was about to have an orgasm. "Nothing, it's just that I can't imagine humming and cleaning the bathroom, it seems like such an odd behavior." There, she told herself. I can control myself around him. I just have to pretend he is a fire and I'm the one who will put it out.

His eyes grew openly amused. "I know just what you mean." He leaned against the doorjamb and placed his hand on her shoulder. "Remember I saw her first." His eyes sparkled.

"Sure," Penny answered. The heat from his hand shot right to her hormone pool and activated the desire she'd managed to control a few minutes ago. She couldn't believe how this man kept her emotions in a constant whirlwind.

"Mr. Holsey?" Penny and Mack whirled around as if they'd been caught doing something they shouldn't. The woman's face broke into a huge smile.

"Mack," he addressed the older woman. "Just call me Mack."

Penny watched Mack as he studied the housekeeper. She wondered if he ever met anyone he didn't want to investigate. Good thing he knew her or he would check her out too.

"Of course, Mack, and why don't you two call me Stella. I would feel much more comfortable with that." The housekeeper subconsciously wiped her hands on her apron. "My poor husband has been dead for more than twenty years and I really don't feel like Mrs. Rowe anymore." Her head hung when she spoke of her husband, evoking sympathy from Penny as she'd watched her mother go through the same thing.

Penny placed her arm on the older woman's shoulders. "Of course we will, Stella. Now I have to let you know that you aren't only caring for Mack here." She smiled at her roommate. "I've moved into the loft bedroom. And I'll be here after he's gone." This time she shot a meaningful look in his direction. Mack smiled and this time his smile lit up his eyes as she'd seen for the past week. She felt her insides calm. He affected her in ways no one had before.

"Oh, I thought Mr.- I mean Mack, was here for quite a spell." She smiled at her employer. "I would be glad to care for both of you and when you have to leave, I would like a chance at getting the job with you." She turned her attention back to Penny.

"Of course." Penny gave the housekeeper's shoulders a friendly squeeze. The woman, who was so caring and needed to have people to care for, had stolen Penny's heart.

"And," Stella began and then blushed furiously, "I noticed the loft had been used by a female. I cleaned it. I thought Mr....I thought...you know what I thought." The older woman shifted her stance and looked past the couple.

Mack and Penny laughed. Penny started to explain but Mack beat her to it. "I'm a long-time friend of Penny's family. I'm on vacation here but Penny has decided to become a Yooper."

Penny looked in his direction as he took charge with quiet assurance. He sure is a keeper. Before her thoughts went farther, she turned to the housekeeper. "Of course we will pay more now. You let us know what you think is fair."

"Oh dear. Mack gives me a fair wage and neither of you is that messy."

This time Mack and Penny laughed loudly. They both knew they could get the slob of the year award.

"Are you done for the day?" Mack asked and then

looked again at her car.

The housekeeper nodded and followed his gaze. "I just had it painted," she explained quickly. "Trying to keep the rust away; you know how the winter salt is on vehicles."

Mack nodded. "Nice job. Who does your work?" He walked with the housekeeper to the car and held the door for her as if he weren't interrogating her. Penny had to admire his charm or maybe that was his training. She didn't know when he was Mack Holsey or an FBI agent.

"Oh, the caretakers from Sugar Moon cleaned, painted, and did some minor repairs for me. They had it yesterday; that's why I wasn't here."

"Do the caretakers work on vehicles on the side, or is that part of the service at Sugar Moon?" Mack asked.

Stella laughed. "Oh, no, Fred and Phil are friends of mine. We all work there and help one another as much as we can." The older woman stared at her hands on the steering wheel for a moment and then added, "We don't get much pay for working at Sugar Moon, but the reward of helping young women is more than enough. I was in their shoes as a young woman and I had no help."

Penny leaned down to the car window. "I would love to volunteer some of my spare time. Is there room for volunteers there?" She looked at Mack whose eyes had clouded. Returning her attention to Stella, she urged, "Is there?"

"Oh, my goodness yes. In fact we are beginning a literacy program and need volunteers to help the young woman learn to read, which we hope will help break the cycle of teenaged pregnancies." Stella shook her head. "It's a shame what happens to them."

Penny grew excited. She had volunteered at shelters before and loved working with people who truly wanted the help. "I'll stop in after work on Monday, if that would be convenient."

"That would be perfect." Stella beamed. "I work until seven on Mondays."

Penny patted the older woman on the shoulder and then leaned away from the car. "It's a date then."

Stella Rowe smiled brightly at Penny and then turned her smile toward Mack. "By the way, Mack. Have you heard how that baby is doing?"

"Baby?" Mack asked, his voice carefully colored in neutral tones.

"You know, the young mother who was hit by the car." Her hands played over the steering wheel. "Well, I heard that you were the last to see her alive."

"You did?" Mack acted as if he were surprised.

The housekeeper let out a little laugh. "News travels fast up here."

"I see that," Mack stated as if he wasn't interested in what she might have heard.

"And I also heard that she spoke to you." The older woman looked at him for confirmation but he didn't answer the unasked question. She shrugged. "I guess we're all wondering what the poor thing had to say before she left this world."

Penny noticed a mask drop over Mack's features. She knew he was suspicious, but she also knew natural curiosity would make anyone wonder what the young woman said. Penny moved beside Mack. He gave her a look that was fleeting but it was there and she knew he didn't want her to tell the older woman anything that the girl said before she died.

"Well, that's what gossip does for you," Mack said with a smile.

Stella Rowe's expectant look changed to obvious disappointment. "Yes. It's just that I think the young woman was from Sugar Moon." She turned the key in the ignition. "It could be my imagination but one of our girls left rather unexpectedly that night. At first, I thought she was the poor little thing from the accident, but the manager of the home said no one was missing. Well, I have to get back to Sugar Moon." She smiled broadly at Penny. "We'll be grateful for your help."

They watched in silence as she backed the car out of the drive and sped away. When she was out of sight, Penny asked. "What harm would it have done to tell her what was said?"

Mack shrugged. "If the baby's mother had wanted to tell Stella or the whole town she wouldn't have chosen us." Penny remembered how the young mother searched the crowd and connected with only them. "You're right of course, but it wasn't as if she said anything that others couldn't hear."

"I know that and you know that, but she was out there under less than normal conditions and it has to make one wonder." He held the door of the cabin open. "And if there was something illegal going on, I wouldn't want what she said to get back to the perpetrator. If he or she thinks we know something, it could bring them out."

"Oh, great." Penny felt a chill run through her as she thought someone might want to find out what was said. "What makes you think the girl wasn't just out there? Or that she isn't a runaway as the police suspect."

Mack poured coffee from the carafe. "I don't know, and neither do you. That's why we have to wait and see." He held the carafe and a cup and raised his eyebrows.

"No thanks." She plopped in the wooden rocking chair next to the phone.

"I'm not sure I think it's a good idea for you to be volunteering at Sugar Moon," Mack said as he sipped his coffee.

Penny eyed him carefully. "What problem could you have with me helping young mothers to learn to read?"

Mack shrugged. "I'm just not sure running a home for unwed mothers is all that is going on there."

"What would make you say a thing like that?" Penny couldn't believe how suspicious he was of anything and everyone.

"Just a hunch."

"I don't think I'll run my life or make my decisions based on one of your hunches if you don't mind."

Mack shrugged again. "I guess I wouldn't make decisions based on someone else's hunches either." He paused and then said, "Oh, by the way the Crosses called. They want us to come to dinner tomorrow night."

"Oh shoot." Penny jumped up and looked at the clock.

It was almost nine. "I was going to go see the baby today." She dropped back in the chair and set it rocking fast. "Good thing that caseworker didn't let me have Aurora. I would have gone off to fight a fire and forgotten I had her." The speed of the chair picked up as she chastised herself.

"I don't think you would forget her if she were here." Mack sat on the arm of the overstuffed chair next to her and stretched out his long legs. "You almost forgot I was here but…"

Penny shot him a glare. "I left a message. We are both adults and don't need anyone to hold our hand all day." She shot from the chair and headed for the loft. She could hear the chair rocking wildly and Mack roaring with laughter.

She spun around. "And what is so damned funny?" Her heart was pounding so loudly that she could barely hear herself speak. He mocked everything she did and she was tired of it. She wasn't going to take it anymore. She pulled on her reserve strength. "Well, answer me."

Mack smiled broadly at her, drew in his legs, stood, and in one long stride parked in front of her. She stepped back and bumped into the wall. "Damn it," she cursed.

"You, my little naïve lamb, are cute." He reached out and brushed the hair from her cheek. "That's what's so funny." His compelling eyes riveted her to the spot.

Her cheek burned from the imprint left by his fingers. The smoldering flame she saw in his eyes shocked her. Until that moment, she'd thought she'd been the only one with hidden desires. It could be just the moment, she told herself.

The touch of his hand was suddenly almost unbearable in

its tenderness. Her breath caught in her throat as he moved so close they were breathing the same air. He leaned forward, placing his hands on the wall on either side of her, trapping her. The heat from their bodies mingled as they stood in fixed tableau. Lamb? she thought as her mind tumbled and twirled between desire and anger. He thinks I'm naïve. Penny struggled to hold her anger but her resolve to let him know where they stood was melting with their body heat.

❧❧*

Mack leaned in closer and inhaled deeply. The smell of the forest fire mixed with her body perfume only made her more attractive to him. Gazing into her fiery coppery eyes misted with passion, he could see her confusion. As if compelled by some outside force, he brushed her soft, full mouth and then claimed it hungrily.

He'd wanted to do this since the first time he saw her a week ago. But his promise had kept him in check.

"Mmmmm," he groaned as he pulled her into his arms and pressed kisses over her forehead and cheeks before reclaiming her soft lips. He felt her body go limp against his and knew if he didn't stop, they would be making love within a heartbeat.

He shuddered as she laid her head on his shoulder and snuggled into his neck. Mack wanted to make love with her more than Penny would ever know, but he'd promised her mother and he just couldn't do this to her or her parents, even if one was deceased. Loosening his embrace, he gently pushed her away. "I'm sorry, I don't know what came over me." Oh, he thought. I know what came over me but I'm not here to seduce my deceased partner's daughter. I'm here to restore his good name, and this is no way to do that.

Penny stood motionless, staring into his eyes so deeply that he cringed. "Damn it." He cursed at her unspoken words. He pushed away and moved quickly to the kitchen, removing himself from the accusation in her eyes.

The silence from her was deafening. He'd blown it and he knew it. How to fix it was the next thing. Should he offer to move? He'd considered that already just to avoid this kind of mistake. But then he wouldn't be there to take care of her. Not that she wanted to be taken care of, or needed him for that matter. She let him know in many ways that she was capable of taking care of herself and didn't want or need him.

To Mack's relief the phone rang. He waited for Penny to answer but she turned her back and started up the loft stairs. He didn't answer either and soon they were both hearing a new message on the machine. "Hey you guys, are you coming to dinner tomorrow night or not?" Paige delivered her message with a laugh. "When you didn't answer the earlier message, I had to consider that you might be gone for the weekend. I know you're busy. If you don't call tonight then I'll assume you're not coming." She paused and they could hear her talking to Linc. "If not tomorrow night call and let us know when."

Penny walked back down the steps and picked up the phone. She glanced in Mack's direction but then looked away. Her pride was suffering greatly. She'd spent years working on her weight and her ability to deal with men.

Now with one kiss and then a rejection she felt as if she'd gained a hundred pounds and lost the five years of confidence and self-esteem she'd amassed. She was sure the kiss was just because he was lonely and she was there. Somehow, she had to get on top of the situation. She could feel his stare boring into her back. But she had to get hold of her emotions before she turned to deal with him.

Okay, she told herself. Face it head-on. That's the way you have been successful in the past and that's how you will do it now. Penny swallowed hard, lifted her chin, turned, and boldly met his gaze. "I'm going to accept the invitation." There was defiance in her tone as well as a subtle challenge.

Mack winced and his shoulders slumped. "I guess you mean without me."

"You got that right." Triumph flooded through her when he grimaced at her words. "I don't take crap from anyone. I don't care if you are on a self-righteous mission that involves my father. You have no right to...to..."

Penny felt tears gathering at the back of her eyes, and she fought to withhold them. She wasn't sure exactly what he didn't have a right to do but she wasn't going to let it happen again, whatever it was. She kept telling herself, Don't let him see you cry or sweat.

Mack moved to her but held his arms out wide to show her he wasn't going to touch her. "I'm sorry, Penny. I wish I could explain. But I don't think you would believe me if I did." He held his hand out for the phone. "Please don't do this. I would like to be at dinner with you and see how Aurora is doing."

She shrugged to hide her confusion. His dark eyes showed the tortured dullness of disbelief. She replaced the receiver in the cradle and tapped the plastic with her nails. Her bearing was stiff and proud, but her spirit was in chaos. Penny couldn't believe how she felt. She was frozen in limbo where all decisions and actions were impossible.

How could she let this man do this to her? Mack's face said please forgive me but she wasn't sure she wanted to. He had hit at the very center of her innermost feelings of inadequacy. How could she know he wouldn't do this again? She did not intend to let herself fall under Mack's spell. That was for weaker women. With one last drumroll of her nails on the receiver Penny lifted her hand from the phone and said, "You do whatever you think is right."

Mack stared at her as if seeing her for the first time. She watched his face as he considered the situation. There was an almost imperceptible note of pleading just under his mask. Sighing heavily, she spoke in appeasing tones. "I guess you're right. We both promised to take care of the baby, so we should both go." She turned toward the loft and then looked back at him. "Oh, and about the other thing." Her hands turned out in a gesture of nonchalance. "It was only a kiss and not that great of one anyway." She put her foot on the first step to the loft and threw back over her shoulder, "So don't worry about it." She climbed the stairs to the loft without another word.

Chapter 6

Penny's last comment about the kiss stung. He considered retorting that she'd seemed to enjoy it, but then knew he had to leave the situation as it was…for now. After his seeming rejection of her, he felt she deserved to have the upper hand, even if it did hurt. Mack confirmed dinner with the Crosses and yelled up to Penny to let her know and all he heard back was a grumbled, "Yeah, okay."

He knew she was planning some kind of fishing thing around midnight. He decided to wait until she came down. Somehow, he was going to go with her. He sat patiently watching the clock. At eleven-thirty, he heard her coming down from the loft. Mack braced himself for more of the cold shoulder he deserved.

Penny alighted the stairs dressed in fisherman's waders with a small net on her belt and a big net over her shoulder. She glanced in his direction and then continued to the door.

"Penny?" Mack didn't know what he would say next but he wanted to stop her from leaving without him.

"What?" her cold word echoed in the cabin.

"I was wondering if you'd mind if I go with you." He paused and rushed on before she could answer. "I mean, I've never been smelt dipping and I'd love to learn if you don't mind." Mack thought any activity that could bring him closer to the people and earn their trust could aid in his investigation. At least he was giving that rationale to himself.

Penny glared at him for a minute; then an easy smile played over her lips. "Of course you can come along. I don't think the others would mind and I don't really care what you do."

"Ouch!" Mack acted as if he'd been hit.

Penny glared at him but ignored his fake injury. "What are you going to wear? I'm sure you don't have this equipment." She looked down at herself.

"Is there any reason why I can't wear my jeans?" He looked her over carefully. "Would you by any chance have another net?"

Penny nodded and threw him the large net. "I have another one in my truck." She looked him over and then added, "It gets cold on the creek. You might want to bring your jacket."

Mack smiled. He knew he wasn't making much headway but he was making some. He grabbed his jacket and looked at her. "Do I need anything else?"

Penny slowly shook her head. "No, I think that will be just about fine."

Mack had a gut feeling he was being taken on a snipe hunt but it was his idea and he wasn't going to turn back now.

✠

Penny loaded her nets and buckets in the back of the truck and waited for Mack to get in. She knew she wasn't being very nice but she hadn't asked him to come along and he deserved whatever he got. If he jumped in the creek as all smelt netters did, then he would freeze in those clothes. Not only would he have to stand in the cold water but also if the smelt run was hard enough and fast enough it could knock him down. She glanced in his direction. She didn't believe in physically hitting anyone but if Mack landed in the cold water, it would make her feel a lot better about the rejection he had delivered earlier.

Penny drove Mackinac Trail to a two-track road and maneuvered the truck over the rolling logging trail. She could see Mack was holding on to the door grip but could also see his jaw was set not to say a word. In a few short miles, she could see the blazing campfire and knew the party had begun.

She whipped the truck over a steep embankment and then rolled along the rugged creek bank and parked next to the other vehicles. Penny jumped from the truck and headed to the campfire. She greeted the rangers she knew and they introduced her to the rest of the group. Penny in turn introduced Mack.

All around the campfire, the anglers sat on beer cases and munched on huge sausages from the grill. Every once in awhile someone would lean back far enough to pull a brew from their seat and pop the top.

Penny looked at Mack. His wide-eyed expression was topped with a furrowed brow. She didn't know whether to laugh at him or comfort him. She watched as one of the men threw his arm around Mack's shoulders and led him to the edge of the creek. "Mack," she hollered and when he turned, she threw him a net. "Catch a big mess of smelt and we'll have them for supper soon!"

Mack smiled at her. "Only if you are doing the cooking."

"No problem," Penny hollered louder as the crowd began to chant, "They're comin'! They're comin'!" Everyone jumped in the cold creek. Penny could feel the onslaught of little fish all around. She fought to keep her balance as the swift current drove the onslaught of thousands of smelt past her. She scooped, rapidly filling the buckets she'd placed on the edge of the creek. People were elbow to elbow as the run kept coming. Smelt were everywhere.

Penny glanced around to see Mack in the creek like the rest of them. His jeans were soaked but he was laughing as hard as the rest of the people. Mack scooped smelt and filled any bucket he could find. Dan threw him another container and he filled that too. Penny hated to admit that she was slightly disappointed. She'd thought he would get cold and wet and then become discouraged, but instead he was having the time of his life.

When the run was over they all cheered and crawled up the creek bank back to the warmth of the fire. The cheering and laughter filled the night air. Penny felt her spirits lift. The sting of Mack's earlier rejection was still there, but she knew she could deal with it now. Her friendship base was rapidly growing and they all enjoyed the outdoors as much as she did.

Penny reached in one of the case seats, pulled out a beer, popped the top, and drank it fast. She hadn't realized how thirsty she'd been.

Mack came sloshing up the creek bank and stood by the fire. Dan threw him a dry pair of sweatpants.

"Here, put these on until the next run. There should be one more good one tonight."

"What the hell do you do with all of these fish?" Mack asked as he glanced around at the hundreds of buckets.

"We eat 'em!" came the chorus of voices from the creek and the campfire.

Mack stepped behind her truck to drop his jeans. She could see smelt falling around his feet as he peeled his wet jeans from his shivering body. She giggled; her head was feeling light. Either she was happy or the beer was getting to her. Whichever it was, she didn't care. Mack had gotten at her ego a bit tonight and she knew, even though he was enjoying himself now, this fishing trip was a big surprise to him.

Mack strolled over to the campfire in his bare feet. His shirt was drenched. Penny knew he had to be cold. "There's a big sweatshirt behind the seat of the truck if you would like to wear it."

Mack shook his head. "Mind if I sit on the case next to you?"

Penny shrugged. "Not my case. You could be evicted when the owner comes crawling back over here."

Mack laughed as he took in the party scene. People were cooking on grills and sharing stories of how that run had taken some of them off their feet. Dan sat down next to them. "You know I believe that was the biggest run I've ever seen. Mack, I don't know how you stayed on your feet." He stuck a long stick in the fire and pushed the coals around. "That was damned sporting of you to help fill my buckets. Most of the fish I get I take to the reservation. We have some fairly poor folks and this helps to feed them." Dan smiled broadly at Mack, "I'm not sure I'd go out there in my jeans. Hell, you could have frozen the family jewels off." Everyone around the fire roared with laughter.

Penny felt her cheeks getting very warm. She pushed back and blamed the bonfire but she wasn't sure her heated cheeks were from the fire warmth or the thought of Mack's family jewels. She popped another can open and began to drink it. Damn, she thought, not only did Mack have a good time, now he is a damned hero for feeding Dan's tribe.

Mack leaned closer to her. "I think you'll need a designated driver tonight."

"I think," Penny said slowly, trying with all her might to sound reasonable, "I'll call a taxi." She held her can in the air, "To the smelt!"

Everyone lifted their cans, joined the toast, and then roared in laughter. "Mack, I think it's about time to take your roommate home before she gets herself blasted," Dan offered.

Penny stared blankly at them. What were they talking about? She'd only had two beers. She stood and steadied herself. "Ima fline." Her slurred words sounded funny to her. She giggled, and the others joined in.

Mack led her to her truck and dumped her into the passenger seat. Penny offered little resistance. She was sure it was fatigue. She wasn't a big drinker, but she'd had more than two beers before, and walked away just fine. Mack loaded the buckets and the gear into the truck and then hopped into the driver's seat.

"I can drive," Penny insisted.

"No, you can't!" Mack was just as adamant.

"Fine, I hope you get lost."

"I won't."

Mack drove out the same way Penny had driven in, almost. He was sure he'd made the right turn but for some reason they seemed to be going farther into the woods.

Penny felt the darkness of the woods engulf the truck and sat straight up. "Where the hell are we?"

Mack shrugged. "Not where we're supposed to be."

Penny felt less giddy as she surveyed her surroundings. Finally she shook her head. "It's not your fault. If you aren't familiar with the forest, it's easy to get lost. I get lost in the city just as easy." She did a studied survey and then said, "turn toward the moon; it will take you to Mackinac Trail."

Mack did as she said. Penny studied his jaw as the muscle along it flexed. She wondered what he was thinking but sure wasn't going to ask.

When they got home, Penny pulled one of the buckets of smelt from the back of the truck and half dragged and half carried it to the springhouse. Mack grabbed the other one and followed her. She sat them inside. "We can clean them tomorrow and then I'll show you how to cook them," Penny said.

Penny walked quickly to the house. Mack stayed close

behind. She turned just after they entered the cabin. "Night, Mack. I hope you had a good time."

"Night, Penny. I did."

Penny climbed the stairs to the loft. As she showered the fish odor away, she wished the earlier part of the evening had not happened. His rejection was so loud and so clear that she held no doubt he was no more than a good friend.

As she towel dried, she had to smile. Mack had taken what she'd handed out, all in good humor. Penny wasn't sure she would've been such a good sport about being led to a cold creek unprepared. She knew and she was sure he knew that she had led him into the situation hoping he would fail. It was probably all an act, she told herself. What man would want to look bad in front of all the other men? The cold of the evening and the warmth of the shower made her very sleepy. She rolled into bed and tucked her pillow under her head. He was fun though and damned sexy, she thought as she drifted off to sleep.

Mack had felt the cold of the springhouse, but it wasn't that chill that cut to the bone. He knew she'd allowed him to go with her to Nun's Creek only to throw at him what she felt he'd thrown at her. He shivered. He'd damned near frozen in that creek. But he had to admit it was fun. They'd had a great time smelt dipping, yet he could see the events of earlier that evening were still with her and would be for some time.

As the night hours ticked away and the red dawn of a

new day was showing in the sky, he felt as if this was the worst stakeout he'd ever done. Except on those watches, he hadn't been personally involved on the job. And this wasn't a keep-under-surveillance assignment! This was real, his reality! He'd spent many hours cursing her mouth and the same hours wanting to devour it. If it hadn't been for his losing control and kissing her, everything would be as it had been. Tossing and turning, sleep didn't come for Mack until the moon slipped below the horizon.

When he woke, the sun was in his face. He jerked awake. Damn it. He knew it had to be past three in the afternoon because his bedroom was on the west side of the cabin.

He listened but couldn't hear any noise. Either Penny was sleeping or she was gone. Throwing on his boxers, he moved quickly through the hall to the kitchen, stopping at the bottom of the loft stairs to listen. No, she was gone. "Now where is she?" he protested loudly as he padded to the kitchen to make coffee.

Sleepy eyes glanced around the kitchen and then blindly reached for the coffeepot. His hand wrapped around paper on the handle and then stared at it as the sticky note fixed to his hand. Turning it over he couldn't help smiling. At least she knew him well enough to know right where to put a note. His smile dropped when he read the evenly printed script. *Gone shopping, see you at the Crosses tonight.*

He dropped the note. "I suppose she plans for us to drive in separate vehicles," he mumbled as he jabbed the start button on the coffeepot. She's going to play this to the end, he thought. And in a way, I guess I deserve it.

Coffee in hand, Mack sat down with his notebook and began putting clues together. He couldn't help wondering about Stella. He hadn't sought her out. She'd come to the door asking for a job and he'd needed a housekeeper. How did she know he was living there? And why come to his door?

The cabin was off the main road and a person would have to be watchful to note that someone was there. Stella Rowe had shown up the day after he moved in. Was that a coincidence or was she at the cabin for another reason? He'd parked his truck out back for unpacking on the day she came to the door. At the time, he'd a passing thought that it was odd but then shrugged it off.

Now as he recollected the scene, she'd stood in the door fumbling with her car keys. And she hadn't knocked because he'd seen her and gone to see what she wanted. She could've been nervous, he told himself, because she needed a job. Whatever it was, she had moved from the back of his thinking to the front.

He punched in the numbers to Cavine's home phone, knowing she wouldn't be at the office on Saturday. But he had questions she could answer. After four rings, her machine picked up and again her sultry voice made him smile. "Someday that voice alone will get her in trouble."

"I don't think it will."

Mack spun on his heel and clasped his hand to his back where his revolver usually was. "Cavine? What the hell?"

The beautiful woman he was face-to-face with laughed

until tears fell from her eyes. "And you would be searching for what in those sexy boxers?"

Mack felt the heat grow to his neck and face. All he needed was for her to take this back to the other agents. He'd never live it down. Shaking his head, he thought Cavine would never change; she was not only good at her job but also strikingly beautiful and self-confident.

"Ah, comic relief after a month of working my butt off." Cavine walked into the kitchen and grabbed a cup. "Mind if I do?"

Mack shook his head. "No, go ahead." He chuckled. "And while you're at it, make yourself right at home."

"I think I will. Thank you." Her face lit as she poured a full cup. Cavine added cream to her coffee and studied it. She held the cup up to her face as she always did. "Does it match my face?" Mack nodded. "Good. Then it's perfect."

Mack moved to the door left open by his uninvited guest, he looked out, saw no vehicle, and then turned back to her. "How did you get here? And more importantly, why are you here?"

Cavine took her cup and plunked herself in the rocking chair. "Ah, the serenity of home sweet home," she said as she began rocking. "It's like this, my good friend." She shifted to see him as he stood in the small kitchen. "I had some vacation days left. Some of my friends were coming up to spend time at the casino, so I caught a ride and decided to help you."

Mack smiled on the outside, but on the inside he was wondering how he was going to explain her to Penny. Not that he owed Penny an explanation, but after the point he'd made yesterday of them letting the other know what was happening, he knew finding another woman in her home would not be something Penny would appreciate. He cleared his throat and tried to act as normal as he could under the circumstances. "What is it that you plan on doing to help me?" He chuckled deep in his throat thinking of how Cavine had reacted when he'd reached for his gun. "I'm sure you don't want to help find my gun." He patted his hip and smiled sheepishly at her.

"No, I know where your gun is." She laughed seductively and then her face went serious. "I brought the forensic test on the fibers you collected at the accident scene and a few other goodies from the lab I was sure would interest you." She smiled as if she had the secret to the universe.

Mack looked down at himself. "Would you excuse me while I get dressed? I feel uncomfortable doing business in this." He grinned, snapped the elastic on the waist of the boxers, and then headed to his room.

"It's not like I haven't seen you in your boxers before," Cavine shouted out to him as he moved down the hall.

Mack had stopped and turned to issue a snide answer when he saw his biggest worry standing at the door. Penny's face was unreadable but he was sure her thoughts were not nice, especially toward him. "Hi," he tried to say as nonchalantly as he could. "Thought we were meeting at the Crosses tonight."

Penny smiled sweetly. "We are." She moved to the loft stairs but stopped at the rocking chair and stuck out her hand to Cavine. "Hi, I'm Penny Hart, the owner of this cabin."

Cavine stood and shook her hand. "It's nice to meet Mack's roomy. I'm Cavine Eastman. I work with Mack."

Penny offered a bland laugh. "I heard that as I walked in."

Mack watched as the women sized up each other. He was in more hot water in the past week than he'd ever been working for the FBI. He didn't want Penny or Cavine to get the wrong impression but he was at a loss as to how to make either believe what was really happening. "You ladies get to know each other while I get dressed." He tossed his words into the air, hoping someone would hear him.

❧❧

Penny stared down the hallway after him. Her breath had caught in her throat when she'd walked in on the intimate scene. She'd held back until she could draw in a deep, fortifying breath. Now she could understand Mack backing off the kiss when he knew this gorgeous woman would be there today. On one hand, she had to appreciate his loyalty to Cavine and on the other, she wished he'd told her there was someone else. Rejection would've been much easier to take if she'd known.

But then, they hadn't discussed their private lives this past week. They'd talked about their jobs, the baby, the cabin, and the weather. They seemed to have an unspoken mutual agreement not to discuss his investigation or their personal worlds. God, she felt like a fool but she'd be okay, she told herself. Well, she'd be okay as soon as she could breathe again.

She turned back to his houseguest. "Cavine?" The years she'd spent covering her true feelings were actually working for her now.

Cavine nodded. "Beautiful cabin you have here. It's so sweet." Her face split into a big grin. "I would bet you're sweet too. It would take someone like that to live with that big oaf."

"Thank you." It would take someone like me to live with him? What was she talking about? I don't live with him. She wanted to scream but instead bit her lip and said, "My mother is responsible for the sweetness you see in the cabin." Penny moved to the kitchen. "Can I get you something?"

"No thanks, Mack took good care of me." Penny glimpsed the woman's smiling face.

"I bet he did." As soon as she uttered the ugly comment, Penny wanted to suck the words back in. "What I mean is, I know he is a great host."

"He is that for sure." Cavine's gaze shot down the hall.

Penny was fast sensing she was the fifth wheel and she didn't like the feeling at all. She grabbed her pager from the counter and snapped it on. "There, I knew I had forgotten something when I left this morning but I couldn't think what it was." The truth was when she'd left she'd been so upset that she couldn't think. She smiled at Cavine as she walked quickly to the door. "Gotta go. You two have a great day."

"Thanks, I'm sure we will." Cavine stood as she spoke. Penny couldn't remember ever seeing another woman that perfect except for models. Everything fit perfectly, even her voice.

The sugar-covered tones of her husky voice with a hint of a British accent set Penny's nerves on edge. As she almost ran to her truck, she couldn't help thinking there should be something wrong with that package. Being perfect was not normal. But then, Cavine didn't seem normal. She was perfect. Then she let out a long sigh. "Some have it and some don't."

Glancing at the clock as she drove away, she talked to herself. "In a few short hours, I have to be with him again." Only this time it would be different. She now knew he had a significant other and significant didn't even seem to fit that woman. Cavine had been wearing more gold jewelry than Penny owned. How could she compete with a woman like that?

"What the hell is the matter with you?" she chided herself. You don't have to compete. You don't want to compete. Her fingers feathered over her lips, still remembering the heat of his kiss and the warmth of his embrace. "No, I just won't go there," she told the windshield. She would go shopping and show up at the Crosses as Mack had planned when he returned Paige's phone call. She'd given tacit approval to the plans. If she'd known about Cavine, she would never have agreed to dinner at the Crosses with Mack. She would have gone by herself and spent time with Aurora. Penny inhaled deeply. It was going to be a long night.

Mack's heart was heavy when he discovered Penny had

left again. He could imagine what she was thinking and he would have thought the same things. A week wasn't long enough to know you were in love with someone. He knew that; he was too practical not to know. Maybe it was that he felt so protective of Penny because of her parents. Whatever the reason for his feelings or his actions; he didn't want her believing he'd kissed her out of some instant passion thing. He would make this right with her.

"Mack?" Cavine's voice had softened in concern. "Is everything okay?"

Mack struggled and then pulled himself back to the task. "Yeah, everything is fine." He picked up the packets she had brought. "Now what is it that you think I will find so interesting in these?"

She eyed him carefully for a minute and then shrugged. "If you ever want to talk about it, you know I am a good listener among other things."

"Nothing to talk about. Now let's have it." He was interested but not as interested as he was pretending. His mind was with Penny and for him having someone else on his mind and not being able to concentrate on work was a new experience. He tapped the pile and checked his watch. "Let's get started. I have a dinner date."

Cavine smiled broadly. "Yes, sir."

Mack laughed and punched her in the shoulder. "Don't start that sir stuff with me." He let out a long breath. He was back on track...almost.

"See these fibers?" Cavine pulled a plastic evidence bag from the manila folder. "These are the ones you got at the accident scene."

"And?" he questioned.

"See these?" She held up another bag.

He nodded as his curiosity grew. He took the two bags and held them up under the sun from the skylight. "They look a lot alike."

"They came from the same carpet. All of the properties are identical." She pulled out the written reports and handed them to him.

His eyes grew wide as he read. "Oh, my God. How can this be?" He dropped the papers on the counter. "They couldn't have known each other...Cliff has been dead for five years now."

"Maybe so, but they were both on the same carpet at sometime before their deaths." She leaned over the papers. "It's an old shag and wasn't hard to identify. The lab also noted that it is on a cement floor and hasn't been cleaned in years." She moved the fibers around. "When you study them you can see some of the same dust elements." She considered them with him for a minute, then added, "The dirt particles were aged and found to be there for more than a decade."

Mack whistled. "I knew it!" He poured another cup of coffee. And I would bet anything that it has something to do with that home for unwed mothers."

Cavine looked at him questioningly. He swallowed the coffee and explained. "It's a home called Sugar Moon. Everyone around here thinks the home is there for the welfare of young women with unwanted pregnancies. These girls are there to give up their babies for adoption. My suspicions were born the night the young woman was killed and she asked Penny and me to make sure they didn't get her baby." He paced the small area for a moment.

"Was she living at that place?" Cavine asked, her voice filled with the curiosity of an investigator.

"They say she wasn't. The police think she is a runaway. She told me something while no one else was around. She said that they were delivering healthy babies and saying they were dead. But even if she hadn't said that, think about it. She was Black with a dialect right out of Chicago, and she spoke as if she'd been fairly well educated." He stopped and stared at the fibers. "The question is, why was she here? And how do these seemingly unrelated deaths connect?"

"I can take a month off to help if you'd like," Cavine eagerly offered.

Cavine's enthusiasm to help was that of an investigator wanting to solve the conundrum. Mack knew it but there seemed to be something underlying her eager attention. He'd known her for years and today she seemed to be flirting more than usual. Or was it just his imagination? And how could he ask her to help and then stay at some other place? He rubbed his hand over his hair while he was thinking.

Cavine placed her hand on his arm. "I'm not asking to move into the little bungalow here." Her hand swept over the open cabin. "This is like camping to me. I need a hotel where they bring my food when I pick up the phone and gather my laundry and return it without telling me how I waste money." She laughed. "I don't know how you do this. I thought you were more city than this."

"I did too." Mack smiled broadly as he glanced around the homey place. "I'm sure it will wear off."

Cavine studied his face. "I know you don't want me to say it but...but are you falling for the country bumpkin?"

Mack scowled at his long-time friend. "Quit acting like a private eye. Penny and I are roommates, and I don't know for how long that will last."

"Oh, has she discovered what a pig you are?" Cavine's lusty laugh filled the air. She glanced around as if she'd had an afterthought. "Oh, Mack."

"What?" His scowl grew deeper.

"This place is too damned clean for you to be doing it. Are you taking advantage of her?" Slapping him on the back she added, "You chauvinist, you."

"Cute! I'm not taking advantage of anyone." But last night, he thought, he'd come close to letting his raging body take another kind of advantage. "We have a housekeeper." He sat on a stool at the counter in deep thought.

"What about the housekeeper?" Cavine asked knowingly.

Mack glanced at his watch. "Tell you what. I only have a few hours before I have to be at dinner. Why don't you and I take a long hike, maybe around Sugar Moon?

"In the daylight?" Cavine asked incredulously.

"No," Mack said thoughtfully, " better yet the river runs through the estate. Let's take a canoe trip and scout the place."

"I don't know how to canoe." Cavine stuck her lower lip out in a pout.

Mack's eyebrow quirked. "When did not knowing something ever stop you from doing it?"

They laughed as they drove to the canoe rental Mack had put on his list of possible uses when he'd first arrived. He loaded the canoe and drove to the river; he dropped the canoe in and helped her into the front. Mack sat at the back knowing he had to propel the craft.

"While I paddle and guide us I want you to pay attention to the surrounding area." He pulled the canoe around and headed downstream toward Sugar Moon.

"You say the sweetest things," Cavine cooed.

Mack scowled at her. "We are conducting an investigation here."

"I know that, sweetie, but that doesn't mean we have to be all business, does it?" Her face lit in a beautiful smile.

Mack had known Cavine for years and after they'd quit dating, they'd had a long and successful working relationship. But all of a sudden, he felt as if she was coming on to him and it wasn't a dream, he told himself. A couple of months ago he would have welcomed the advances but right now he had to sort out his feelings for Penny. The last thing he needed was another woman to deal with.

The beautiful spring day lent itself to an easy drifting trip down the river. The Sugar Moon estate seemed to be just what it was purported to be. Not once did either investigator have a revelation about anything they'd seen. Cavine spent her time complaining about the bugs and the brush from the banks of the river that scratched her as they paddled by.

Mack stared at her. "You are usually much tougher than this. What's your problem today?"

"I don't have a problem. I'm in the middle of a romantic boat trip and bugs are biting the hell out of me." She swatted at something that landed on her arm.

Romantic? Mack thought. He must have missed something. He glanced at his watch. "We will be at the canoe pickup in about ten minutes. That will give me time to get home and get ready for dinner." He looked at her as her face dropped into a pout. Ignoring that he asked, "Is there anyplace I can drop you?"

"I guess if you have to run off to dinner with the country bumpkin you wouldn't want to be late."

Mack wasn't sure this was the same agent he'd known all of these years. As he pulled the canoe into the livery he said, "I do have to run off to dinner with other friends and I don't want to be late."

"Well okay," Cavine answered, as if she hadn't been pushing him to stay with her. "What would you like me to do tonight? That is, if I don't become otherwise occupied," she added with a huge smile.

As Mack pulled the truck around he thought, I'm sure she will find something to do, she always does. He gave her orders as she climbed into the truck. "Here, take my notes tonight, and if you aren't partying too much, read them."

Cavine laughed as she accepted the notebook. "Okay, hon. You go get yourself all gussied up for your date. I'll read and then when you're ready, we will work on the investigation."

Mack was more than happy to drop off his partner. Maybe she was one of those women who only wanted a man when he was interested in someone else. Whatever it was, he wasn't happy that she was pushing the issue now. But he was pleased with the investigation. At least there was one thing going his way. Somehow, he would make up with Penny. She had to understand how important discovering the surroundings of her father's death was to him.

He stepped into the shower. As the warm water poured over him, he could almost feel Penny's breath on his neck from the night before. "Ohhhhh," he moaned and leaned against the shower wall. "This is going to be a long night."

Chapter 7

Penny drove toward the shopping mall trying to decide how she wanted to present herself. Did she want to be cool and aloof or did she want to be warm and understanding? Without thinking, she picked up her cell phone and dialed her mother.

"Hello." Diane Hart's soft voice brought instant relief to her daughter.

Penny smiled, feeling the reprieve. "Hi Mom. I'm sorry I haven't called. How are you?"

"Hi, sweetie. I knew you were busy and would phone when you had time...or a problem." Penny could hear the concern in her mother's voice.

"I have time," she said to put her mother's mind at ease. "In fact at the moment I am on my way to a new friend's house. Paige Cross, you would love her. She is one of those natural-born mothers."

"Yes, dear, I know." Penny could hear the smile and the approval in her mother's voice. But she had no idea how she knew. Penny had not phoned home since she'd arrived a week ago.

"How do you know?" she asked curiously.

"Oh sweetie, Mack phones a couple of times a week to

let me know how the investigation is going. He told me about the accident and the baby." She heard her mother take in a deep breath. "I'm so happy you were not injured and I am very proud of the way you handled yourself. Mack told me how you fought to keep little Aurora from going to just any home."

"Oh," Penny said. She wasn't sure she liked Mack reporting everything to her mother.

"Now Penny," Diane Hart's voice grew softer but firmer. "Mack and I have been talking for months. He does not tell me anything about you other than something he knew I would be proud of, and of course he let me know you'd arrived safely."

Penny sank in her seat a little. "I'm sorry, Mom. I won't let that happen again. I guess I just got all involved in my job and the surroundings and just didn't call." Oh, I was involved. I was so busy lusting after Mack that I totally neglected my mother.

"I understand, sweetheart." Diane paused for a moment and then continued, "Why don't we make a date to phone Sunday mornings after church? If you don't call me, I'll call you."

Penny knew that was her mother's subtle way of reminding her to attend church. She smiled. "That sounds like a great plan, Mom."

"Now, I know you wanted to check in. What was the other reason for phoning me?"

Penny laughed. "Mom, you should be a detective. I don't know, I guess I've just been feeling kind of lost and I needed my mother to ground me."

"Okay," Diane Hart began and then she let out a long breath. "Penny, some things are discussed more easily with people your own age. Of course I am open to listening to anything you have to say but I was young once too." Diane paused, but Penny didn't pick up the conversation so she continued, "I suggest you go speak with Paige. If she is as great as you say then she will be the one who can help you through...shall we say this little crook in your road?"

Penny's heart felt light. As always, her mother knew without being told that there was a problem and as always, her mother had a solution. "Mom?"

"Yes, dear."

"I love you."

"I love you too. Now go take care of your problem and if you need to talk later, you know where I'll be."

"Thanks, Mom." Penny flipped the cell phone closed and laid it on the seat beside her. Her mother had a way of making her feel as if there was no problem too big to solve. And Penny knew she would work out her feelings for Mack too. I wish I were more like my mother, she thought as she turned the truck on the road to the Crosses' home. She'd felt a connection with Paige the first time they'd met and now she just needed to talk.

She turned into the long driveway and followed the twist and turns until she came to an enormous log cabin. She wasn't even sure that a three-story structure could be considered a cabin but it was certainly a home made of logs.

Standing in front of the massive oak door with

etched glass windows, Penny suddenly felt dumb. What was she going to say? I've known Mack for a week and I really want to get with him?

She'd turned to run down the steps when a little voice said, "Hello, lady." Penny turned to encounter the most adorable child she'd ever seen. His face was long and surrounded by straight blue-black hair like his father's, his lips were full like his mother's, and his eyes were so dark they looked like black marbles.

Penny couldn't resist him. "Well hello." She searched her memory for his name. She knew she'd heard it. She smiled broadly as the name came to her. "Turner?"

His eyes grew wide. "Yes, ma'am?" he said as if she had addressed him for something bad. Penny laughed softly. "No, honey, I mean your name is Turner. Is that right?"

His face lit proudly. "Yes, I'm Turner Lincoln Cross." Turner reached behind the small bush beside the porch and tugged, pulling the toddling cherub that Penny knew had to be Brook. In his sweet voice, he said softly, "This is my sister Brook Mara Cross."

"I'm happy to meet both of you." Penny could feel her spirits lifting. She really did love children, she told herself, and someday she would have her own but not right now. She knelt down to be on their level. Their smiles were so adorable she just wanted to scoop them up and hug them.

"Penny?" Paige asked as she stood at the door. Then she looked at her wayward children and said, "I don't think this looks like your playroom." The children giggled and rushed behind Paige and then off to another room.

"Sorry about the greeters here." She laughed lightly. "I swear Turner is running for president."

"He has my vote." Penny smiled and then continued. "I know I'm early but I just…well…when we met I felt that sister connection and I …well, I was wondering if you have time to talk."

Paige smiled broadly and hugged Penny. "I felt it too. Of course I have time to talk, I'm glad you're here. Come on out to the kitchen and we'll talk while we work."

"We work?" Penny teased.

Paige's laughter was infectious. Penny was glad her mother had suggested coming to see Paige. She felt better already. "Before we do that, could I take a peek at Aurora?"

"Sure," Paige said and motioned Penny to follow. Opening the door of the nursery, Paige put her index finger to her lips.

Penny nodded and tiptoed to the crib. The baby curled contently as if she knew she was safe, even without her mother. Penny released a long breath, and then tiptoed back out. It amazed her how providence had brought her and Mack to the accident site and then Paige and Linc to care for the baby.

In the kitchen, Paige handed her a paring knife and potatoes. "I think women say what they are actually feeling with a knife in their hands. Don't you?" Penny looked at her. She truly looked serious until the laughter broke out. Both women laughed as if they'd known each other for years. When the laughter settled Penny began peeling potatoes.

"So girlfriend," Paige began, "when did you realize your

feelings for Mack were not just friendship?"

"Do you believe in love at first sight?" Penny answered the direct question in a way that surprised even her.

"I'm not sure. When I first met Linc I know I was in lust at first sight." Paige's face glowed in remembrance.

"Now that, I can identify with." Penny laughed softly. "Damn, I think he is so sexy and he hardly knows I exist. To top it all off he has a girlfriend who is drop-dead gorgeous. She looks like a model."

Paige looked up from the piecrust she was rolling. "Penny, you are beautiful."

"Thank you." Penny answered quietly because she'd heard that for years from her mother and other relatives but she knew they were being nice just as Paige was.

"Don't even go there, girl. I have no reason to lie to you and feeling sorry for yourself will get you nowhere," Paige said sternly. "I've been there and done that. You have to look at yourself as others see you, not as you think they see you."

"Yes, but you were a model at one time. Doesn't it bother you that your career is over because of having a family and…" Penny was going to add, and now that you've gained weight, but her sensitivity to the subject kept that unsaid.

"Oh, Penny, my career isn't over." She smiled knowingly at her. "I think you should come up to my studio with me and see my modeling pictures." She wiped her hands on a towel and tossed it to Penny.

"Come on. First, let's make sure the kids are behaving." Paige smiled at Penny and led her through the house decorated with African-American and Native-American art. Penny stopped to stare at the photo over the fireplace. It was Linc and another man who was definitely not Native American. "Who is this?" she said, wondering who would deserve such a prominent place in their home.

Paige smiled. "That's Linc and his brother Jack."

"His brother is White?" Penny had a hard time hiding her surprise.

Paige laughed. "I should've said half-brother. Linc and Jack have the same father but different mothers."

"Oh," Penny uttered, embarrassed she had asked such a personal question.

"Penny, are you uncomfortable with interracial marriages?" Paige had stopped and stared at her.

Penny laughed. "Oh, my gosh, no. Where I come from, mixed families are the norm."

"Good," Paige said as they looked through the playroom window. She waved at an older woman, indicating they were going upstairs, and the woman smiled and nodded.

Penny followed Paige up two flights of highly polished hardwood stairs and marveled at each new area. This cabin was more like a small palace. The floors were a mixture of hardwood and marble. The ceiling vaulted in the center of the house, and a skylight let the sunlight drift warmly over the rooms below.

When Paige opened the door to her studio, there was light everywhere. Only one wall graced the room; the rest were all windows. Hanging over the white marble fireplace was a recent portrait of Paige. Penny turned slowly and looked at all of the pictures of Paige. In every picture, she was beautiful, stunning in fact, but she was not a pencil-thin model.

"They are beautiful." Penny began, "You are beautiful." She wanted to ask where the modeling pictures were but didn't want to hurt Paige's feelings.

Paige pointed to the portrait over the fireplace. "This one was taken when I was in Milan doing a shoot just before I met and married Linc." She went on to point out pictures and tell a story about each picture.

As if someone had turned the lights on in her mind, Penny asked, "Oh, you're one of the larger-sized models?"

Paige looked at her and smiled. "Yes. I was like you. I thought I was fat and ugly until I began modeling. Now I know you can be a beautiful woman no matter what size you are. And Penny, you are a beautiful woman. In fact, you are not only beautiful, you are smart. Those two attributes can take you a long way."

Penny dropped to a chair where the sun was brightest. "I was really huge five years ago. I'm down to a size twelve and I have to work to stay here. I still see myself as a hundred pounds heavier."

Paige sat in the chair next to her. "And you probably always will. You just have to accept yourself as you are and move on. I can't tell you how great life has been for me since I did that."

"Yes, but, you were a model," Penny said quietly as she pondered her new friend's words.

"Penny, you're a firefighter. I think that is a heck of a lot more important then walking down a catwalk. I really admire you."

"Thank you," Penny said sincerely.

"Now, we have to discuss this lust or love at first sight thing you have going."

Penny laughed at how abruptly Paige turned the subject back to where they'd been in the kitchen. She let out a long breath and told the story of her week with Mack. How their friendship was great and getting better all the time. How she loved his sense of humor and couldn't stand his being such a great roommate. And how she'd originally wanted him to move out and still did, but didn't. She had to admit that living with him was more difficult all of the time, because of her feelings. "And now," she finished, "I have a beautiful woman like Cavine to deal with."

Paige scowled at her. "I thought we got over that beautiful woman thing."

"That's easier said than done," Penny answered wistfully.

"How do you know Mack and Cavine are an item? Has he talked about her this week?"

Penny shook her head. "No, but if you saw her, you would know what I mean."

"How did he introduce her to you?"

"He didn't introduce her. She did it herself."

"Well, what exactly did she say?"

Penny thought for a moment. "She said, 'I'm Cavine Eastman, a coworker of Mack's,'"

Paige burst out laughing. "She probably is just that."

"But when I walked in, Mack was headed down the hallway to get dressed. I heard Cavine tell him that she'd seen him in his boxers before."

Paige thought for a moment. "Mack looks like a model; is he?"

Penny laughed. She'd thought the same thing. But shook her head. "No, he's an FBI agent on vacation here. He was my deceased father's partner." She wasn't going to tell anyone that he was on a ghost hunt of some kind.

"Cavine and Mack are both agents," Paige said thoughtfully.

"Yes, well Mack is, I'm not sure about Cavine," Penny answered cautiously. "But I'm not supposed to tell anyone."

Paige smiled. "Then the secret is safe with me. And about the other woman; have you considered they were on a job together and that is how she saw him in his boxers?"

Slowly Penny shook her head. She was remembering the first time she'd seen Mack in a towel after his shower and how he had apologized for his appearance. "I know he's been on stakeouts with female agents. He mentioned that." She paused thoughtfully.

Paige laughed. "Girl, quit buying yourself trouble. Just go with what you feel. I saw the way he looked at you the first night we met."

"That was the first night Mack and I had met too."

"I'm sure I saw that spark in his eyes," Paige said thoughtfully and then continued. "Okay, let's give him one hot woman to look at tonight. If there is any interest, you'll know by the time the night is over. If not...nothing ventured, nothing gained."

Penny glanced down at her jeans and T-shirt. "I guess part of it could be the way I dress. But I've never felt the part of a diva and I sure don't know how to play one."

Paige jumped up and tugged Penny's hand. "You know, when I was dating Linc I was having all kinds of troubles. I almost lost enough weight to lose my job." When Paige laughed at that Penny had to join her. She couldn't imagine having that problem. "Come, let's see what we have."

Penny held back. "I don't want to be something I'm not."

"Don't be silly; besides you don't have to be a diva. All you have to do is show off what you already are. Every woman has many facets. One minute we're feeding a child and the next, we're mowing the lawn. And after we finish those chores we are entertaining VIPs from God only knows where." Paige pulled on Penny's hand. "Forget all that you thought you knew and follow me."

Penny stood in front of the mirror staring at her transformation. Her dark copper hair that normally hung in reckless waves around her face had been changed to spiral curls. Paige had pulled some of the spirals forward to cover Penny's cheek.

The tight-fitting fuchsia crocheted knit clung to her full breasts and pulled in at her waist. She turned to look at her backside and could see the soft knit hugged her butt. The muscles she'd been working for definition showed in the dress more than anything she'd ever worn. At least something she'd done was working for her. She sighed heavily, worried that this was all for nothing. Pushing up the three-quarter-length sleeves just a tad, she added the gold necklace to the jeweled neckline of the dress, the matching bracelet, and a couple of rings.

She looked down at the matching heels and wondered for whom she was doing this. Was she really interested in Mack or was she just jealous of the gorgeous woman who had his attention? Her mind tumbled with countless thoughts and emotions. Since the breakup with Cooper, she hadn't dated much. Her job was her first priority and first love. For the past year she'd wondered if she'd ever truly been in love with Cooper, or was it, she thought, he was the only man who would be interested in a woman of her size?

Penny drew in a deep breath. Whatever it was, she was in a new place with new people and she was starting all over. One last look in the mirror told her she was ready to meet the future no matter what it was.

"Penny?" Paige opened the door of her dressing room and called. "Linc and I have to feed the children and get them ready for bed." She smiled as she looked at Penny. "Wow, you look great. See, I told you women have many facets."

Penny smiled in return. "I'm not used to this one but I think I could learn to like it." She twirled around. "I hardly know me."

Paige smiled broadly. "Anyway, Linc and I have to do our nightly ritual with the children and I was wondering if you would entertain Mack when he gets here so he won't feel unwelcome."

"I don't know." Penny answered, biting her lower lip. "The last time I saw him he was in his boxers with another woman."

"I know, hon, and I wouldn't ask you but we're running late." Paige squeezed Penny's shoulders. "You'll be fine, and we won't be long."

Penny couldn't help thinking this was a put-up job but then Paige had spent so much time with her in the last couple hours that she was probably the reason they were behind. "Of course I'll do it. What am I saying?" She moved to the door. "Just don't leave me to my own devices too long or I might make a mess of your whole evening." She laughed lightly, trying to conceal the turmoil she was feeling. Inside, her stomach was knotting and her heart rate was at a runner's pace as she thought of spending time alone with Mack after today.

By the time the women alighted from the stairs they could hear Mack and Linc talking by the front door. Paige spirited Penny around a few corners and led her to a candlelit screened-in deck with an intimate table set for four in the corner. "I thought we would enjoy the warm April evening," Paige whispered. Penny smiled at her knowingly. "Now I'll show Mack out here and Linc and I will hurry through our nightly rituals with the children."

Penny's stomach knotted thinking of being alone with Mack in this very romantic setting. Paige had obviously gone to a lot of work while she had dressed for the evening. She turned to go back in; she just couldn't do this. Paige caught her by the hand and led her to the subtly swirling mist of the water fountain filled with water lilies. "I find this area very soothing." She smiled and left Penny alone.

Just before Paige disappeared through the door she pushed a button and music floated through the air. Penny smiled and then laughed to herself as she recognized Tracy Chapman's "New Beginning." Paige had thought of everything.

Mack was standing on the patio before Penny had a chance to consider running again. The soothing nature's melody that played as the water meandered over the fountain rocks calmed her. When she saw him, her first emotion was relief. After walking in on him earlier, she wasn't sure he would show. She'd thought he might be upset with her for her quick exit or maybe even on a date with Cavine. The fact that he came communicated more to her than any words he could speak. Penny wasn't sure what it said but she was sure if Cavine and Mack were in a relationship, he would not have left her for a dinner with people he scarcely knew and his partner's daughter.

Her heart turned over at the sight of him in his chino pants, open neck shirt, and sports coat. He looked as if he'd just stepped off the cover of *Luscious Men* magazine. Think about something else, she told herself. Steadying her shaking hands and body, she took in his reaction to the scene around him.

She watched as he stood in awe as she had. His gold-black eyes flashed brighter as he surveyed the festive area. The lines in his face relaxed as the ambiance soaked in.

Patio lights that looked like candles surrounded the deck and cast soft shadows over everything. Real candles in hurricane lamps burned softly in the center of the table. Red and white roses mixed with baby's breath formed a ring around the base of the lamps and were the table centerpiece. Napkins matching the flowers stood folded precisely in the crystal stemware at each place setting.

When his gaze finally drifted to Penny, he let out a low whistle. She wasn't sure if it was for her or for the elegant decorations. She smiled. "I know, Paige really knows how to entertain." She could feel the sexual magnetism that made him so self-confident and turned her knees to water.

"Yes, she does know how to entertain but the whistle was for the beautiful woman by the fountain." His voice was soft and low while his gaze bathed her in admiration.

Penny bit her lower lip and turned to look over the valley. "Thank you," she murmured, trying not to read too much into those few words. "This view is breathtaking," she said as she watched day's light quietly drift behind the horizon. Her voice had muted into a hushed whisper. She cleared her throat. She'd floundered under the brilliance of his look, and she needed to gain her ground again.

Mack walked to her and stood looking out into the valley as she was. From a side-glance, she could see his hands clasped behind his back but she also could feel his gaze on her. He seemed to be peering at her intently as if waiting for the right moment to say something.

Summoning courage, Penny wanted to be like the other sophisticated women he knew. She drew in a deep breath, squared her shoulders, and looked up at him. "Mack, I'm sorry I walked in like that today."

"Penny…" Mack half-groaned as she put her finger on his lips to stop his protestations. His steady look bore into her in silent expectation.

"No, Mack. The fact is we share a living space and we need to set up signals so that neither of us makes that mistake again."

"But…" Again, she hushed him and in his eyes, she could see the humor returning she'd grown to love.

"And," she said with authority, "I was wrong not letting you know how long I was going to be gone the other day. I could've called when we were done fighting the fire." She took another deep breath and continued, "I'm well aware that we do not need to report to each other but it is difficult when we live in the same house…and well, share some of the same past not to have some consideration for the other." She edged away from him just a bit so that his intense body heat did not melt her reserve to be the mature one.

"Okay," Mack said thoughtfully as his gaze traveled over her face and searched her eyes.

Penny felt her hard-fought-for resolve draining out of her toes. She wanted to start all over with Mack as a mature adult, not as his partner's little girl. Her heart jolted and her pulse pounded as he studied her. Averting her eyes, a sense of urgency drove her to speak again. Say anything, she told herself, just get out of this.

"Well good then." She forced herself to smile at him. "After we finish here tonight maybe we can sit down and make an agreement to cover our problems." She forced her gaze to the valley below to avoid looking at him. If she looked at him again, she would have to fight the longing to be held in his strong arms.

"Okay," Mack said again but his voice carried a hidden chuckle.

Everything she did seemed to amuse him but this time she wasn't going to buy into it. She was going to be a refined woman and ignore his jibes. The music had changed to Luther Vandross' "If Only For One Night." Penny moaned inside. Darn that Paige, she was making it hard for Penny to remain detached.

Mack touched her fingers lightly to gain her attention. "Beautiful night, beautiful song, beautiful woman; it would be a real shame to waste it. Would you care to dance?"

"Here? Now?" Penny looked up at his face. His look was as soft as a caress. Okay, Ms. Sophisticated, what are you gonna do now? She looked around him to see if they were still alone. He followed her search with his eyes.

"There's no one here but us. They are busy with the children and we have the night in front of us." His deep voice seemed to rumble through her.

A warning whispered in her head. If you dance with him, you will be lost to him and you aren't even sure he's interested. She dropped her lashes quickly to hide her confusion. She wanted to come off as a person who was confident and secure in what she was doing.

Mack gently pulled her into his arms and moved slowly over the deck. Penny was lost forever just as she'd feared.

The warmth of his body, the woodsy aroma of his aftershave, and the strength of his arms took her far away from the woman who was fighting to be in control.

Mack released the breath he'd been holding since Penny had left earlier today. He'd hoped against hope that Penny's misconception of the scene she'd walked in on earlier had not damaged the relationship he'd felt was growing between them. He held her just close enough to let her know they were dancing but far enough so she didn't think he was pressing her for anything. They needed to start their relationship again. He loved the way he could talk and joke with her and truly loved her innocent reactions. The women he knew were laid back about the simple things in life. Penny seemed to be in awe of everything. It was as if she were seeing the world for the first time and she was allowing him to see it again, through her eyes.

He thought of her standing by the fountain. She looked so different with her hair curled and hanging loosely over one cheek. She was one of the sexiest women he'd ever met and he'd bet she had no idea of her sensuality. Her fresh aroma was soft and stimulating. Everything about her was warm, comfortable, and extremely exciting. He glanced down at the dazzling copper vision in pink and knew their mutual paths were set in motion for something he hadn't known he wanted until that day.

"Thank you," he murmured in her hair.

"For what?" she answered huskily from somewhere in a

dreamy world.

"For being you," he answered as if she should have known. Mack smiled to himself. She really didn't know how desirable she was.

"I don't know how to be anyone but me." She leaned back and gazed at him. He felt her eyes were inviting him to move forward, but with caution.

"They sure take their time with the kids, don't you think?" Mack thought if Paige and Linc didn't come soon they would have to throw cold water on him. When the song ended, he returned her to the fountain and stood beside her. There they stayed in a peaceful silence watching the sun lazily slump into the night sky. Until Paige cleared her throat, it felt as if they were the last two people in the world. Mack liked it that way.

They twirled around in unison and stared at their hosts. Mack couldn't believe he'd been so self-involved that he hadn't heard them approach. He glanced at Penny and could tell she'd been in the same world with him.

"We get lost out here too," Linc said as he patted Mack on the arm. "You'd better watch it, old man. The moon, music, a warm night, and a beautiful woman can make a man lose his way."

"Lincoln," Paige scolded playfully. "So, you think you lost your way." She smiled warmly at her husband.

"Haven't I?" he questioned with a smile.

"Oh!" Paige motioned Penny to follow her. "Come, let's see if they enjoy it as much without us here."

When the women left Mack asked, "How's Aurora?"

The unusual and untimely death of her mother kept the baby on his mind.

"She's well," Linc started and then looked at Mack. "I hope the authorities find her family soon or I fear Paige will have a difficult time giving her up." Linc leaned to see where the women were. "They'll be a few minutes. Come with me to check on the baby."

"I was going to ask to see her, so sure." Mack followed Linc across the hardwood floors, trying to walk as quietly as his host did. When they got to the baby's room, they spoke softly as they looked down at her.

"What do you think?" Linc whispered.

Mack shrugged. "She's a pretty one." He spoke in hushed tones.

Linc smiled. "I'm not sure Paige will be the only one who will have a difficult time giving her back."

Mack placed his arm around Linc's shoulder. "Just remember that somewhere people who are true family to Aurora are praying that someone like you and Paige are the custodians of their cherished family member."

Linc's face lifted in a brighter smile. "I wish I knew how the investigation was going."

Mack stared for a moment, wondering if he should share his concerns with Linc and the fact that he was the investigator for the FBI on the case. "It's going as well as can be expected."

"How do you know? What have you heard?" Linc asked eagerly.

"I'm the lead FBI investigator on the case. I have several leads and I am working on them as hard as I can."

Linc's eyes widened. "Then you aren't here on vacation?"

Mack shrugged. "Actually I was on a year's leave to investigate the untimely death of my partner, who just happens to be Penny's father. The pieces of the puzzle are coming together but it seems one leads to the other."

Linc let out a long breath. "If there is anything I can do to help. Please let me know."

They shook hands. "Thanks, man, I'll do just that."

"Showing Mack the house?" Paige asked as the men joined them.

"Yes, and he wanted to see the baby so we stopped in and admired the Great Spirit's handiwork." He held Paige's chair for her.

Penny watched Mack as he moved to the table and pulled a chair out and nodded to her. Something had changed between the men, and she wasn't quite sure what it was but she wasn't sure she would like it if she did know. "She is a beautiful baby. It's so sad she will never know her mother. Her mother was such a brave little thing," she said as she accepted the seat Mack held for her.

Paige nodded as she bowed her head. If you don't mind...we say grace." If Penny had had a doubt about this woman as a friend, Paige's taking time to thank God erased them all. She smiled in agreement.

When she finished her prayer, Paige passed the salads and picked up the conversation right where Penny had left off. "I know every time I hold her or feed her or just look at Aurora I offer a prayer for her mother. The poor little thing, I sure hope the authorities find her family soon."

"I'm sure they will." Penny glanced at Mack for confirmation.

Mack nodded at the women and then turned to Linc. "The design of this place is unusual. Who was the architect?" Mack looked around appreciatively and then continued, "I was thinking if I ever settle down to raise a family, this quiet place would be perfect to do it.

Linc smiled. "I'm the architect."

"Whoa." Mack's eyes flew open in total amazement. His hand flashed toward the house. "This is a work of art."

Linc laughed and smiled at his wife. "We worked it out together."

"Well, I know where to come when I want to build," Mack said, still amazed at the talent of this unassuming man.

"No problem, friend. Whenever you're ready."

Penny's ears perked when Mack indicated he might want to build. She knew so little about the man she was living with. Okay, she told herself, the man who is my roommate. The conversation over dinner never stopped. Penny didn't want the evening to end. Her heart filled with pride at being with Mack. Even if she wasn't really with him, it felt like it and the feeling was great.

As Mack and Penny were leaving, the women arranged to meet and shop at the mall in Ontario. Or as Penny had learned, what the locals called going into Canada, going over the river. Linc and Penny walked them to their trucks. The men were talking vehicles and the women were talking flowers. It all seemed so surreal to Penny. She hadn't been this happy in a long time. It had to be Providence that she and Mack were the ones at the accident scene. If they hadn't been there, Aurora would not be with Paige and Linc and more importantly to Penny, she and Mack would not have had a bond to hold them together. She might have kept her original plan to get rid of him and would have missed the companionship of this wonderful man.

Penny heard Mack's truck start. She watched the other couple as they walked back into their home and then she turned the key to start her truck. All she heard was a click. Penny tried a couple more times and then threw her arms in the air. "Darn it!" she yelled as she tugged the lever to the hood and heard it pop. She jumped from the truck, opened the large toolbox, and pulled out her tool kit. From the console, she retrieved a flashlight and studied the engine.

Mack stopped when she didn't back out and hopped out to help her. He looked at her and asked, "Want a ride home?" He grinned and the corners of his eyes crinkled, the gold shimmering with mischief.

Penny moved the light over the engine to the battery cables. "Hmm," she muttered and then looked down at her dress.

"Here let me fix it for you," Mack offered. "You will ruin that nice-looking dress if you do it." Mack's eyes drifted over the dress as if seeing it for the first time. "You look nice tonight."

"Thank you," Penny said politely. She opened the truck

door pulled out coveralls and tugged them over her dress. "There, now we don't have to worry." She looked up at his face; his eyes were filled with merriment. She ignored his unspoken jibe and handed him the flashlight. "If you could hold this, I'll fix my truck."

Penny plunked the toolkit on the engine and snapped it open. She searched for the battery brush. When she found it, she cleaned the battery post and the cable connection. Penny replaced the brush in the tool kit and searched for another tool. Standing back, she muttered, "Now where the heck is my open-end wrench?" She thought for a moment and then said, "Oh yes." She went to the console of her truck cab and pulled out the cell phone, makeup, mirror, and finally the wrench. She smiled at Mack. "I used it the other day." With the wrench, she snugged the connection securely back on the post. "There." She brushed her hands together. She turned to Mack. "How do you suppose that cable got loose?"

Penny was sure she saw a glint of mischief in his laughing eyes. He shrugged and turned his attention to her toolkit. He snapped it shut and then couldn't resist. "Pink? You carry a pink toolkit?" He shook his head in wonder.

Penny jerked the box from his hand and returned it to the back of the truck. "It was a gift from my dad. I like it." Her stubborn chin set as he chuckled. She shot him a withering glare. "And you of all people, Mack Holsey, should know that you can't judge anything by its cover or color." She slammed the big toolbox in the rear of the truck and opened the driver's side door. "I'm going home." She turned the ignition and it fired right up. She sure would like to know what happened to that battery cable.

All the way home Penny struggled with her feelings for Mack. He was fun, helpful, and so handsome she could hardly control herself around him yet he seemed to think everything she did was funny or just fluff. Nothing she did was important. That was it! She had put her finger on it; he had no respect for her or what she stood for.

Oh, Penny Hart, you are running a double standard. How can you think poorly of him for having no respect when you are totally enamored with his looks? If he wanted her for her looks, she wouldn't have much respect for him either. But he doesn't know what I think of his looks. But then he might know. It wasn't as if she could keep her feelings secret. If only he'd conducted his investigation from his desk in Chicago, she wouldn't be going through this right now.

She turned onto a side road that led to Mackinac Trail to avoid the expressway. It was so dark out there and she hated being on the highway at night. She liked being where she could see a house and friendly lights occasionally. Glancing in her rearview mirror, she could see Mack had not seen her turn or had just decided to get home the fastest way.

Sighing heavily, Penny thought about that evening. He'd certainly seemed interested but then who knew what turned a man on or off? He ran as hot and cold as she did. Or was it just her perception of him? She would be glad to be at work on Monday morning and then at Sugar Moon in the late afternoon. Both jobs would give her the needed relief from Mack and her own feelings.

She saw the Sugar Moon sign and wondered if it was too late to visit Stella Rowe and see what she would be doing next week. She shook her head. "You are just trying to avoid setting the rules with Mack. And how mature is that?" Her voice sounded loud in the truck. She laughed. "Now I'm talking and laughing all by myself. I'd better get a grip on myself soon or the men in the white jackets will be carrying me off to a place for safekeeping."

Penny slowed to a stop in front of Sugar Moon. She'd seen nothing sinister at all. The place was cheerful and she was sure Stella kept it spotlessly clean. She laughed again as she thought how her mother would give it her seal of approval.

Mack hadn't said it but Penny had the feeling that he suspected something disturbing was happening at Sugar Moon. What is it that he sees that I don't? she wondered. The walls were high but then maybe they had to protect the young women. New babies were a premium and people might try to kidnap them. Penny could imagine how hard it was to keep some of the young women's boyfriends away. No, if Mack was thinking there was something sinister at Sugar Moon, then Mack was wrong. There was a reason for everything. And these reasons were logical to Penny.

She edged her truck up to peek through the gate. Penny strained to see, but the whole place looked at peace. Glancing around she could see she was alone and this wasn't a good idea. A woman alone at night was never a good idea, no matter where she lived. She could just pretend to be visiting Stella Rowe but then she would have to ring the gate bell and that might wake half the residence. Besides, how would she explain her presence so late at night?

She leaned her head against the back of the seat. She'd seen the way Mack had questioned Stella Rowe about Sugar Moon. Mack's suspicions were spilling over on her. This was crazy. There would be a logical explanation for the high walls, the caretakers who doubled as mechanics on a car that could've been the hit-and-run car, and the housekeeper who seemed to want to know too much about the dead young mother and her baby.

On Monday, Penny would see for herself what Sugar Moon was all about when she reported for her volunteer work. Slowly she drove away from the scene wondering what it was, but reassuring herself that Mack's suspicions were really nothing.

Chapter 8

Mack paced the small kitchen waiting for Penny's arrival. The back roads she'd taken would've put her behind him by five minutes at the most. He glanced at his watch. "Damn, twenty minutes." He didn't know whether to wait or look for her.

He all but slammed his coffee cup on the counter. "That's it! She's ticked off over that toolbox comment I made." He slapped his forehead with the palm of his hand. "How was I supposed to know it came from Cliff? That was a stupid thing to say, but it was so cute and so feminine." He smiled thinking of her working on the battery cable he'd loosened. He'd wanted her to have to ride back with him. Independent women, he thought. Can't live with 'em and can't live without 'em.

He perked his ears as he heard her truck pull in. Mack quickly grabbed his coffee, went to the living room, and sat down in the easy chair with his feet on the ottoman. He wasn't going to let her see he'd been worried.

"Hi." Penny strolled in as if she'd been right behind him. He watched her move to the kitchen and grab a Diet Coke. She turned after a minute and asked, "Now, should we set some rules for our comings and goings?" Mack considered her demeanor and wondered if this new casual woman was performing or if this was the real Penny. Whichever it was, he liked this one too.

"Have more trouble with the truck?" he asked, wanting her to explain why it took so long, but unwilling to ask her. His gaze followed her as she moved like a seasoned princess to the rocking chair. Something about her had changed. There was a thoughtful look just behind her eyes, and he was curious to know what had put it there.

"No. I was just enjoying the warm evening as I drove." She sipped her soft drink and then added, "I thought about stopping in to see if Stella was still at Sugar Moon but then decided it was too late." She offered him a smile that said go ahead and tell me how bad that place is.

For a moment, Mack thought he saw a shadow of hesitation in her eyes when she mentioned Sugar Moon. He was worried about her working there but he would discuss that with her again, when and if he ever got more evidence. "Guess you'll have to ask her how late visitors are allowed."

Penny briefly frowned at him and then her features relaxed. "I don't think it's a matter of allowed hours. I think it's a matter of common courtesy."

Mack swallowed hard. She was trying his patience and he was sure she knew, but he wasn't going to bite. He didn't want to argue with this gorgeous woman. On the contrary, he wanted to pull her into his arms and make love with her. The lovely vision in fuchsia standing by the fountain kept tripping through his mind. His pulse quickened as his thoughts wandered to what if. With a great deal of effort, he turned his thoughts to their project for the night. "Weren't we going to set some guidelines for our comings and goings?"

"I think we have to, don't you?" She rocked a little faster. She smiled but he could see a pensive shimmer in the shadow of her eyes.

Mack nodded. "Penny, about today..."

She held her hand up. "No explanation needed. This is your place too. After all, you are paying rent." Abruptly she stopped rocking and looked Mack in the eye. "We began on an awkward note." He wanted to speak but she held up her hand again. "I don't agree with the investigation of Dad's death. I think when you're done you'll prove the original findings correct and Mom will have to live with the disappointment again."

Mack leaned forward to listen. Now he was going to hear what she'd been thinking for a week. He studied her, trying to decide if he was talking to the grieving girl or the young woman of reason.

"I know..." she began and then clasped her hands in her lap. "I know I have not been nice or cooperative with you. But now I think the more cooperative I am, the sooner we'll be able to put this behind us and move on with our lives." Her fingers twisted in her lap. Mack wanted to pull her into his arms and comfort her but instinct told him to just listen.

"First...," she offered him a timid grin, "for occasions like earlier today." She looked down at her hands. "We will find something to hang on the door so if the other one comes back and it's there, then we'll know not to disturb."

Mack nodded but wanted to protest there was no reason

for her to ever stay away. Her twisting fingers moved to her hair and pushed the sexy curls behind her ear. Everything about her was disturbing, in every way. Her nearness shot fire through his body. If not for that damned promise to her mother, he would be trying his damnedest to have this little firefighter extinguish his flames. He tried to make himself see her as a little sister but that would take a veteran actor and he wasn't that. His inability to act like someone else caused him to lose all of the undercover assignments.

"Now," she said as she bit her lower lip, "I know I was remiss in not letting you know where I was the other day. That won't happen again." She started the chair rocking again. "Because we are living in the same place, it would be difficult for either of us to not worry if the other didn't show up when expected. So as a matter of socially acceptable practices and just out of consideration for each other, we will make the other aware of our whereabouts."

Mack smiled inside and thought, Socially acceptable practices? Penny's speech sounded reasonable but the way she delivered it was so sweet he could hardly contain himself. She was the most pleasant, independent, and beautiful woman, both inside and out, he'd ever met. In many ways, she was her father's daughter. Cliff would never have let anyone see him sweat. Even his last request to Mack had been very casual, and now Mack was sure it had been anything but chance appeal. Her mouth was still poised to speak so Mack waited.

"We agree then." Awkwardly she cleared her throat. "We will post a sign for privacy and check in when we'll be gone longer than we thought."

Mack tried to look her in the eye but she dropped her long lashes as a shield. He was almost positive she didn't want to worry about another woman here any more then he wanted to worry about another man. But when it came to women, he'd been wrong before. Cavine was a good example. He and Cavine had never progressed past that one night of frenzied passion when on assignment in California. They both knew their sexual act had been just an act of comfort, solace, and yes, even release. The chemistry outside the sheets was all wrong. Cavine was not the type to settle down with one man. She loved them and left them faster than a bee flew from one honeyed flower to another.

He shook off the urge to ask if this was what Penny really wanted. What if he asked and she said yes in such a definite way he knew he didn't stand a chance? No, I think I'll ride this one out.

"Mack?" Penny's soft, sweet voice brought him from his internal conflict.

"Yes?" His voice was just above a hoarse whisper.

"Is that enough rules?" She smiled. "Making rules for adults to live by sounds silly, doesn't it?"

Mack smiled in relief. He really didn't like confrontation, especially when there was no need. "Ummm, I have one more."

Penny's eyes grew wide. The heavy lashes that shadowed her cheeks flew up. "Did I leave something out?"

"It's nothing major." Mack chuckled at the woman who thought she had it all under control. He looked at the answering machine. "How can either of us know when to take the messages? There could be personal communications."

Penny looked at the answering machine. "I really hadn't thought of it." She paused, remembering her father's message. She should change that soon. She looked at Mack. "Well, tomorrow I'll go shopping and buy one of those answering machines with different mailboxes for each of us. All your friends will have to do is push star and then number two and they'll leave the message for you." She brushed her hands together, stood, and stretched.

Mack stared at her as her full breasts pushed against the snug fitting dress. He averted his eyes so she wouldn't notice him staring at her breasts, and he wouldn't do something like drool. Instead, he put the matter away with his usual humor. "Why do I have to be mailbox number two?" He chuckled as she turned around in thought.

"You don't." she stated firmly. "I'm positive you will receive many more personal phone calls then I will, so you can have box number one."

"I was thinking I would like box number three." He jibed as he let his gaze rove lazily over her.

Penny stopped and stared at him for a moment. Her eyes were wide; she looked like a deer caught in headlights. "And that's another thing. I think you should preface everything you say with, this is a joke, so I know when you are serious and when you aren't." She folded her arms over her chest and firmly held his eyes.

Mack stepped closer and ran his finger over her cheek,

releasing the strands of hair she had shoved behind her ear. "What makes you think I'm joking?"

Penny sucked in air and stepped back. "Because," she said breathlessly, "that's the way you are."

Mack moved back and looked at her. He wanted to tell her he wasn't that way but knew it was not a good time to press anything. "Penny, I was teasing about the toolbox. I'm sure when Cliff gave it to you, it meant as much to him as it did to you."

"Thank you. It does mean a lot to me and I think it meant a lot to Dad. He'd spent the year before my sixteenth birthday teaching me how to work on cars."

Her eyes misted but she held the tears in check. Now Mack was sure why she didn't want the investigation. For Penny this would be living her grief all over again. He placed his arm around her shoulder and gave her a squeeze. "If you ever want to talk about your dad, I loved him too." He released her with a nudge to the chin and moved to the kitchen to keep himself from doing anything that would bring on more hurt or tears. And to keep his animal instincts under control. She was no ordinary woman, she was special, and he would show her that.

Penny had to conquer her involuntary reactions to that gentle loving look of his. She was sure Mack was being nice because of his remark about the toolbox. She was sure he felt guilt over her father's death, or why would he be spending his own time and money to investigate something that happened and was settled five years ago. She didn't want to be anyone's charity case.

She had to change the subject, but to what? Pondering their dinner at the Crosses, she knew she couldn't bring that up. The evening had too many romantic suggestions for a conversation about that right now. She didn't know if his amorous feelings were from the evening Paige had set up, or his feelings for Cavine, or his guilt over her dad's death. A couple of times, especially when they'd danced, she was sure she felt chemistry from him, but how would she know?

Her drive home and her brief stop at Sugar Moon had reaffirmed her feelings that Mack was wrong about the place. She knew if she brought this up it would move the conversation from her. "Mack." She hesitated, torn by conflicting emotions. If she told him what she thought about Sugar Moon, he might get angry. On the other hand, it would take the subject in another direction, and she could relax a little.

"Yes." He turned all his attention to her.

"You know when I told you I was going to stop to see Stella at Sugar Moon?" She noted his brow lift as he nodded. "Well, I looked the place over good, and I know in my heart there is nothing wrong there. It's just as it seems. A home for unwed mothers."

As she'd mentally predicted, Mack glared at her. "You can think what you like. Why don't you leave the investigating to me?" His censure of her caused her mood to veer immediately to anger.

"Because, damn it, I'm sure there is a logical explanation for everything you suspect. I didn't expect you to go off on me." Penny swallowed hard and squared her shoulders. Now that felt good. She complimented herself on returning to the way she would normally react. And if nothing else, it certainly removed the yearning she'd had to be in his arms.

A warning cloud settled on his features. "Penny, I don't want you going there at night. Especially when no one knows where you are."

Penny was afraid to speak or she would say more than she wanted. She busied herself with gathering the few dishes on the counter and setting them in the sink. Wiping the counter with a sponge, she watched as he grabbed his black jacket and slipped into black pants.

Penny stopped suddenly and smiled in exasperation. "What are you doing?"

"Something I should've done long ago. I'm going to set up a surveillance of that place. Crooks don't show themselves in the daylight."

Penny openly stared at him. He was seriously thinking some of the people at Sugar Moon were crooks. She glanced around the cabin. With him gone she would be alone, and at the moment she felt uneasy about that. "You aren't going without me!" she stated adamantly.

"Don't be silly. You aren't an agent and you have no idea what to do." He pulled a black cap on.

"Oh, I see." She walked to the phone and handed him the receiver. "Why don't you call Cavine? I'm sure she can sit and watch nothing with you. You couldn't expect a forest ranger to know the forest and to know what might be just ahead...could you?"

Mack eyed her with a calculating expression as he took the phone from her and replaced it. "I thank you for the offer but I'm just not sure."

"I understand that. I wouldn't want to take you into a forest fire. But I would take you on fire watch with me." She hesitated as a faint light twinkled in the depths of his black eyes while he looked her over seductively. "Stop that! You know what I mean. Rangers do surveillance, too, and we are watching for arsons as well as other fire starters. And believe it or not, arsonists just hate the daylight." She took a deep breath; she had to throttle the yearning that was welling up again. Every time he looked at her, her heart turned over in response. Anger works so much better for me with him, she thought.

Amusement flickered in eyes that met hers. As he spoke, a wide grin spread over his face. "And does the ranger carry a sidearm?" His brows rose inquiringly.

"She can and she is a marksman. The ranger you are inquiring about was taught by her father." Penny straightened herself with dignity and smiled confidently at him, daring him to challenge her ability.

Mack nodded knowingly and said, "Then get dressed for night work. Oh, and your complexion is too light, so put some charcoal on."

Penny was dressed within minutes and back down. "Ready."

Mack's approving smile deepened into laughter. "Guess we are partners for tonight then. Hart and Holsey doing duty again. I like that." His smile changed and almost became somber. "This Hart will come to no harm." With a light squeeze of her shoulder he said, "Let's go."

Penny offered him a reassuring smile.

꒰ঌ�꒱

They pulled into a secluded spot in the woods Penny recognized from the maps she'd studied. "The woods here are dense pines with a dry forest bed." She spoke quietly, more to herself then to Mack.

"I've parked here a few times before and yes, it is dense." He smiled his approval at her.

Penny turned to him as if surprised he'd heard her. She waved her hand. "Oh, I was thinking of the fire conditions." She felt the heat in her cheeks. She'd wanted to act as if she could be his partner here and not a firefighter but that was so in her blood.

"I know you were, and I also know you don't believe there is anything at Sugar Moon but it's a gut feeling for me more than evidence right now." He paused to look and listen, then continued. "Have you ever had a gut feeling about, say, a fire? You know all the conditions are there, all you have to see is that one spark that lets you know your gut was right." Without waiting for an answer, almost silently he opened his truck door. "Slide out this way. One door closing is enough."

Penny did as she was instructed, all the while thinking of the question he'd just asked. The answer was yes; she'd had that feeling yesterday when jogging. She guessed his trained eye was seeing something she wasn't. But then a fire and illegal activities were different, weren't they?

Without a sound Mack led the way through the heavily wooded area. They crept through the moonlit night along the perimeter of the brick wall until they came to the place where the wall changed to wire fencing. Mack motioned Penny to stand back. He pulled a rectangular tool from his backpack that Penny knew was a Power Probe. He positioned it over the fence where they stood. The Probe gave a digital reading of the voltage. "Whew." Mack let out a low whistle and gave her a look of total disbelief.

Penny could feel her eyes grow wide as she saw the high voltage going through the fence. That wouldn't just shock, it would do harm…possibly kill. She shook her head in disbelief and Mack nodded his agreement with her thoughts.

Mack ran the Probe over a long length of the fence to see if there was a fault area where he could climb over. There wasn't. Dropping to his knees, he crawled along the bottom edge of the fence and pointed to the embedded wire in the ground. She turned her palms up and gestured in question.

He smiled at her, stood next to the fence, and measured himself. It was waist high. He pulled her up and stood her in the same spot. It was breast high. He took long strides back and looked again. Shaking his head, he backed up until he ran into a pine tree.

Penny put her hand to her mouth to suppress a giggle. She was sure he was going to try to jump the barrier between them and their goal. His even white teeth stood out like a neon sign, as his responding smile grew wider.

He dropped his black backpack and indicated to her to

get it when he was over. She shook her head and started to walk toward him. Penny had to protest the jump; it was dangerous. But before she got to him Mack sped off in a dead run. His leap was as graceful as that of any Olympic athlete she'd ever set eyes on.

He stood proudly on the other side, his eyes gleaming like glossy volcanic rock. Mack crooked his index finger for her to come to him. She grabbed the bag and moved quickly to the fence. Mack held his hand out for it, but Penny shook her head. He spread his arms and mouthed, "What now?"

Penny wanted to giggle again; he looked so earnestly baffled. "Not without me," she whispered.

If he could jump that fence, he could lift her over, she reasoned. Then smiled to herself. Five years ago it would've taken him and five more like him to lift her. Her other self said this would be a big job and she shouldn't ask, but she wasn't going to let him discover anything without her by his side. And she wasn't going to be left by herself.

After all, they were investigating the way her dad died. A shiver ran through her. For the first time since her father's death, she was admitting something might be wrong with the way he died and now she was in a position to help prove it. A flash of wild grief ripped through her as she realized how she'd been fighting the possible truth. The revelation shook her so much that she stood and stared blankly at Mack.

Mack snapped his fingers, breaking her stare. She could see him frown, his eyes leveled under drawn brows. The gold in his black eyes shimmered unspoken questions. Penny filled her lungs with the fresh night air and her heart with the new knowledge that she was now part of this investigation.

Lifting her gaze to meet Mack's she watched as he pointed to her and held his arms out straight. She held her arms out straight and stepped forward. Mack locked his strong hands under her arms and began lifting, holding her away from the dangerous voltage. Penny knew he had cleared the fence with her and started to lower herself. Mack held her tightly, looking around.

Penny held her breath. What had he heard? Slowly he lowered her and held her closely. "You look like you need a hug," he whispered in her ear.

Penny had to admit the warmth and strength of his arms wrapped around her made the pain of a few seconds earlier much easier to take. Gently she pushed away and managed an unsteady smile. "Thanks."

"You okay with this?" Mack whispered hoarsely.

She nodded as she saw the heart-rending tenderness of his gaze. His look spoke volumes. He understood what she was going through and would be there for her. No wonder her dad had liked his partner so much. He had a good heart. But just because she finally admitted her dad's death was suspicious didn't mean she thought Sugar Moon was part of it.

Her courage and determination were like a rock inside of her. Penny wanted to be part of solving her dad's death but she had to prove to Mack Sugar Moon was not the place to start. Not that she knew where to start, but she was sure it wasn't there. She felt the providence of everything that moved her to this place, at this time. And that fate was for her and Mack to solve the mystery of her dad's death.

She grabbed his hand and tugged him in the direction of the large house. Ahead of them was a large stand of old maple trees. She stood on her tiptoes and whispered to Mack. "It's sugar time so be careful, they might have lines running from the tapped maple trees to carry the sap to the vats."

His brow creased in question and his eyes glimmered. "Sugar time, huh?"

The double meaning of his words did not escape her but she had other things on her mind now. She tapped him on the chest. "Maple sap for syrup."

A flash of humor crossed his face. "Could we discuss this later?"

Penny stared at him. "Discuss what?"

"Sugar time." His mouth quirked with humor.

"Stop that!" she whispered.

She turned and pushed a path through the heavy brush before the hardwoods. Stealthily she picked her way through the sugar maples. Suddenly she heard a thump and a quietly uttered curse from Mack.

She spun around. Mack was lying on the ground his feet tangled in one of the sap lines. She had the urge to laugh and say I told you so but instead crept back to where he lay and began untangling him. "This might have an alarm on it."

"Why?" His brow creased. "Are they afraid someone will steal their sap?"

Now Penny placed her hand over her mouth to suppress

the laughter. When she gained control, she whispered. "No, silly, so that they know when they are losing sap."

"Oh." Mack hung his head in feigned embarrassment.

Her lips trembled with the need to smile. She leaned closer. "If you don't get serious, I'm going to do this by myself and you'll be left to the wolves."

Mack drew himself from the ground, stood in front of Penny, and saluted her. "Yes, ma'am."

"This time follow my trail and don't go off on your own." She spoke with authority but the laughter was in the soft ring of her voice.

They covered acres of trees and underbrush before they came to one of the utility buildings. Mack leaned against it and brushed the debris from his shirt. Security lights shone over the estate grounds, forcing the couple to stay behind the small building. Penny pointed to an area a short distance from them. "See how peaceful it is here?" She cleared her throat. All of the whispering was making her throat sting.

Suddenly Mack grabbed her by the shoulders and pressed his fingers to her lips. Penny's heart hammered against her rib cage, making her gasp for air. Mack held her tighter as she now heard the noise that had alerted him. Mack pressed them against the small shed to keep their shadows out of the bright moonlight.

They listened to the conversation of people walking close to the shed.

"How are we going to get that kid now that the mother is dead?" a male voice asked.

"I guess we'll have to give the buyers their money back if

we can't get the baby," a female voice answered.

"They don't want their money back, they want a baby," the man snorted. Did you contact the prospective parents of the other baby?" The man again, Penny thought.

"No, we have a month before it's supposed to be born," the woman answered.

"What will you tell them?" The man's voice grew anxious.

"Maybe we won't have to disappoint them. There's a chance I can get her back," the woman said.

Then silence fell on the walking couple. Mack held Penny tightly to him, pressing them flat to the shed. She shivered as sheer fiendish fright swept through her. She felt her breathing go rapid and then slowing, almost stopping. She could feel Mack's warmth next to her, and she sensed he had frozen in place as she had.

Then from a distance they could hear voices. Mack slowly peeked around the shed to see where they were. Two people had entered the back of the house and were now standing on the glassed-in porch talking.

Mack let out his breath and sagged against the building. He looked down at Penny, took her by the hand, and led her back to the thick underbrush. There he held her tightly as she shivered. Her stomach still clenched in a tight knot, she pressed herself against him for safety.

"Okay," he whispered, "let's get out of here so we can discuss this."

Penny nodded. She wanted to run but she knew they had to be inaudibly careful on their retreat or their investigation would be over. She still wasn't positive something was going on at Sugar Moon but she wanted to find out and she wanted to know why Mack thought it tied in with her dad.

She stared at the back of the man leading them the same way she'd brought them. Massive muscles flexed as he twisted and turned through the heavy brush. Penny was so happy they'd reached a mutual agreement on their lives together. She was by no means immune to his magnetism but she was clear in her own mind that she would wait and see how their relationship developed.

Mack stopped dead in his tracks, causing the musing Penny to run into him. She looked up at him as he reeled around. "What's wrong?"

Mack pointed to a strange greenish glow in the forest not too far from where they'd parked the truck. "You stay here and I'll go ahead and see what that is."

Penny smiled as she caught his hand and tugged him back to her. "You don't have to protect me from that."

Mack scowled at her. "How would you know?"

"It's foxfire," she stated with confidence as she stared at the glow.

"What the hell's that?" Mack grumbled to her.

"Swamp gas," Penny answered.

"Are you sure?" Mack thought for a moment. "Swamp gas glows?"

"Under the right conditions it does," she answered expertly.

Mack released a long breath and smiled broadly at his companion. "You sure were right about bringing my own private ranger along." A devilish look came into his eyes as he whisked the loose curl from her cheek. He scanned her critically and beamed appreciation.

Flattered by his approval, Penny knew she was gaining the respect she desired. She met his gaze and a vaguely sensuous light passed between them. Heat rose to her cheeks as she realized he was thinking what she'd been thinking.

Mack stepped back to make room for Penny beside him in the heavy brush. He bounced on the ground. "Why is this so soft?"

Penny's eyes grew wide and she pressed her hand to her mouth to squelch the scream. Just after he spoke, the earth swallowed him.

Chapter 9

"Oh, my God. Oh, my God. Please let me know what to do." Penny uttered a prayer as she dropped to her knees to avoid falling in herself and felt her way to Mack. She moved gingerly over the area until she felt where it turned soft. She pulled the tie from her hood and secured her ankle to a small tree. "Hurry," she repeatedly whispered to herself worried Mack might smother under the dirt that was falling in the hole.

Carefully she inched her way to the opening. "Mack?" she called down. A moan was her answer. "Can you give me your hand?"

She heard him spitting and coughing. He added a curse as he expelled the dirt. "I'm not sure. I think I'm stuck." His voice carried no fear. She felt reassured that only one of them was scared to death. Studying the gap in the earth for a minute, Penny decided what she must do. "I'm going to go back to the truck and get that come-along I saw in the bed of your pickup."

"Penny?" Mack sputtered the word as he spit out fresh dirt.

"Yes?" she answered, listening intently to hear his muffled voice. She froze in place as she heard a twig break in the near distance. "Shhh." She issued a warning to him. While she held her breath, she silently prayed Mack could breathe.

Penny released the air she'd captured in her lungs when she saw a deer walking away from her. She stuck her head back in the opening. "It's okay." As Penny whispered that, she heard Mack groan and heard him plunge through the earth, leaving a gapping empty hole.

Penny drew in air to keep from screaming. Now she'd even welcome help from the people they perceived as crooks. Tears of frustration and fear streamed down her face. In her mind she was trying to sort through all of her training. What kind of hole would be here? The area wasn't right for quicksand. Penny had reached down to untie her ankle so she could run for help when she saw a light in the gapping hole.

Scrambling back to the entrance, she peered through the dust particles caught in the flashlight beam to see Mack standing at least ten feet underground. She leaned as far down in the hole as her tied ankle would allow and called out. "Mack?" Her whispers had taken on a fevered pitch.

Mack looked up. His face was covered with dirt and his eyes were red from wiping at them, otherwise he seemed okay. "Penny, you aren't going to believe this," Mack said in a loud whisper. She could hear the dismay in his voice and wondered what he'd found that would take his mind from their predicament.

"What?" she asked anxiously.

"There's a tunnel system down here. The only problem I have is how to get out." He turned in every direction and then looked back up at her. "If you can help pull me out, we can cover the opening and bring the right equipment back to search the area."

Penny nodded and hoped all of her strength training had worked. She knew she was stronger now but she wasn't sure she was this strong. Knowing she had to try, she stretched her arms down in the opening as far as she could. Mack extended his arms as far as he could and stood on his tiptoes. They were within a couple of inches of making contact. "Look around for a rock or something down there." Her fevered whisper was almost a command.

Mack left her view but she could see the light as it bounced around. The light grew fainter and Penny's heart beat faster. Maybe the batteries in the flashlight were dying. Or maybe...no she didn't want to think of the alternatives.

After what seemed like hours, she saw the light bobbing up the hole again. She all but cheered as she saw Mack drop a huge rock on the bed of the hole and climb onto it. He held his backpack up for her to take. She pulled it out and thought how much heavier it felt but didn't have time to consider why. Again, she stretched to reach him. Their hands met and clasped tightly. "If you can pull, I'll use my feet to push on the side of the dirt wall that I'm closest to." He smiled up at her. She could see he felt nothing but confidence in her ability to do her share.

Penny thought for a moment and then issued another order. "Let me do the pulling and you just hold on, no matter what. If you try to push with your feet, you might cause a cave-in. If I can't pull you out this way, I'll go get the come-along."

Mack nodded in agreement. Without talking about it, they wrapped their hands around each other's wrists. Penny tugged her anchored leg making sure of her security and then she began pulling. Every muscle in her body strained. Pain shot through her arms, her back, and her chest. She knew she'd never felt this kind of strain even with all the weight lifting.

When she got Mack almost out of the hole, she paused to rest but held tightly. She began again; sweat beads rolled off her forehead and plopped into her eyes. The salt burned. Her eyes blinked uncontrollably to stop the stinging. "Damn it," she cursed and pulled so hard that he popped out of the opening as if she'd birthed him from the bowels of the earth.

She fell back, exhausted. As she lay there, her arm and leg muscles began to cramp. Penny knew that if she didn't move soon she would be too stiff to do anything. She watched as Mack rolled over, stared at the stars, and then back at her with a glint of wonder in his eyes. "Sweetness, you are some partner."

"Thanks," Penny answered halfheartedly. Inside she was blaming herself for not noticing the soft ground. If she'd been paying closer attention she would've seen or felt the possible danger and avoided it. Stiffly she reached down, untied her ankle, and rose to stretch the pain away.

Mack dragged himself up and moved alongside her. Placing his arm around her shoulder, he spoke with quiet assurance. "You did a great job. I'm glad it was you at the top."

She smiled. "I think I need to study the area better. I

should've known something about the possibility of break-through places in the forest." She stood staring at the hole in disbelief.

"There is the chance that not many people know about the tunnels." He playfully tapped her on the chin. "Let's cover the opening so no one else will find it. When we return, we'll be prepared for a painless exit." He gave her a tight squeeze and then released her.

After they'd covered the hole and walked back to the truck, Mack opened the door for her and kissed her lightly on the cheek. "I don't usually kiss my partners, but none of them have ever gone that far to save my life."

Penny winced in pain as she pulled the seat belt and snapped it in place. "This partner should have known better then to tromp through the woods without knowing the area better." She folded her aching hands in her lap.

"Oh no, you aren't going to blame yourself for this. When I felt the soft area under my feet, I should have stepped off and examined it. Nope, little one, you will have to find something else to feel guilty about." Mack climbed into the truck and turned the key. "As far as I'm concerned, if you are willing, I sure would love to have you with me on this case. Even if you don't believe there is anything to work on."

Little one? she thought. He had no idea how sweet those words were. She glanced at him. His ruggedly hand-some features softened as he met her gaze. "Sorry, I get all caught up in a case when the lead is hot."

"No problem," she answered tiredly and thought of her

own feelings. She hadn't wanted to believe her father's death was anything but an accident. And she still wasn't sure, but now she had a gut feeling something strange was going on. She leaned her head back and closed her eyes. "Let's talk about it in the morning," she mumbled.

"That's a good idea. I'm going to take you home and get you into a hot shower. I'll even fix you one of my famous after-the-job snacks. After what you've been through you deserve pampering, and I know just the guy to give it to you."

In the short ten miles to the cabin, Penny relived their escapade. The whole day had been a test of her emotional and physical endurance and as far as she was concerned, she'd passed. All, she thought, except that damned hole in the forest. Who would've thought there would be a tunnel out there? What was it doing there? Her mind filled with questions as her body screamed for relief.

She thought about crawling into a hot tub of water and then remembered the tub was in the downstairs bathroom. I'll just wait until he goes to bed, she thought, as she yawned widely and felt the ache in her jaw too. Relief flooded her as Mack pulled into the driveway. She couldn't remember a time in her life when she'd felt this glad to be home. The tub and her bed were calling her and she was going to answer that call.

Mack's arm went around her waist and steadied her as they walked into the cabin. He guided her to the couch and then busied himself in the kitchen. "You just relax and I'll whip up my special hot chocolate and peanut butter and jelly sandwiches."

"Oh, that is special," Penny said drowsily.

"You'll see, young lady." He glanced in and smiled at his new partner. He gathered the items he needed to make his special hot chocolate. He knew she'd love it. "You know," he hollered from the kitchen, "when I build my own house, I'm not going to have a kitchen. I'll have a room filled with vending machines."

He heard her laugh softly and thought how he loved just the sound of a murmur from her. The promise he'd made to take care of Penny didn't mean he couldn't fall in love with her, did it? It meant she would come to no harm. In just a week, was he in love or lust? If it weren't love, then he would be doing her harm.

Mack loaded the snack on a tray and took it to Penny. He glanced down at her and realized she'd fallen asleep. I bet she'll hate waking to find herself that grimy, he thought. But he wasn't going to rouse her. He set the tray on the end table and pulled the afghan from the back of the couch over her. Staring down at her, his heart swelled with affection for the woman who was so determined to be independent. She had the face of an angel and tonight she'd been his guardian angel. He took the tray back to the kitchen and stood watching her while he unconsciously ate the snack.

Mack heaved a long sigh. He smiled as he studied her dirt-speckled face. He stopped his gaze from drifting below her neck. If the FBI needed a test of will and strength, they should use this one. Except, he wasn't sure he would pass the final test.

He stacked the dishes in the sink and grabbed his backpack. While underground, he'd found some interesting items that he wanted to examine further. In his bedroom, he caught a glimpse of himself in the mirror. If he hadn't been working on staying quiet, he would've burst out laughing. His tightly cropped black hair was a few shades lighter as was his face. His clothes looked as if he'd rolled in the dirt. In a sense, he thought, that's just what he had done. "I need a shower," he muttered to the image in the mirror.

He tiptoed back to the living room. Curled in a ball under the afghan, Penny slept like a newborn baby. He checked the locks on the doors and windows and then tiptoed to the bathroom.

The hot shower poured over his tired and aching body. He leaned his head against the shower wall and thought of the beautiful woman sleeping in the other room. Mack wondered what it was about him that made her so reticent to be even casually interested. Sometimes, he could swear she was attracted to him but most of the time she acted as if anything more than a friendship would be hard to come by.

She ran so hot and cold he didn't know which way to turn. Was it him? Or was it because of the investigation? Was it something in her past? Or was it just that she didn't feel the same chemistry that he did? Maybe he should consider moving out, but then if he did she would be alone and unprotected. When this thought came, he had to laugh. Penny was the one who'd saved him tonight, not the other way around.

Mack climbed from the shower, towel dried, and slipped on the boxers he'd brought into the bathroom with him. When he'd packed to come here, he hadn't thought to throw in a robe. Why would he? As far as he knew, he'd be spending the summer alone. Maybe when Penny went to buy that new answering machine he'd go along and get him something more, as she would put it, socially acceptable to wear around the house. He chuckled to himself as he checked on her before he went back to his room. He needed to study the items he'd collected in the tunnel and make notes on the surveillance. He peeked in the living room and saw she was dead to the world. He frowned. She is going to hurt in the morning.

Penny's body jerked and her eyes popped open. She had no idea how long she'd been sleeping but it was still dark out. Her body ached as she tried to move. Slowly she rolled to her side and moaned in pain as she pulled herself up. She listened. Mack must have gone to bed. The afghan that had been covering her fell to the floor. Puzzled at how the afghan had gotten over her, she picked it up and threw it back on the couch.

She needed to soak in a hot tub. As quietly as her aching body would allow, she crept down the hall and listened at Mack's door. When she heard no noise, she tiptoed to the bathroom and shut the door gently to avoid making a sound.

She glanced in the direction of the shower. It was obvious he'd been there; water still dripped from the curtain. She felt to see if the water on the curtain was cold. It was.

161

Confident Mack had showered a while ago Penny moved around the divider wall between the tub and the rest of the bathroom and began to remove her clothes.

Her fingers ached as she unbuttoned her jeans. Throbbing muscles restricted her movements as she undressed and threw her clothes in the corner. Slowly she let her aching body down to sit on the edge of the cold porcelain. Penny shivered as her butt made contact with the tub. Her hand flew to her mouth to hold back the screech. Adjusting to the ice on her butt, she reached to turn on the water and winced as a new muscle tightened in pain.

The steaming tub looked so inviting but Penny held her breath and listened closely before she slid in. She didn't want any naked incidents with Mack—at least not tonight. Stepping into the steamy bath, Penny pulled the curtain to keep in the heat. The warmth of the water swathed her sore body. As the pain subsided, she rolled a towel, stuck it behind her head, and leaned back.

With her toe, she reached the switch for the whirlpool. She sighed heavily as the hot humming water whirled around her. Her eyes drifted. Mack sleeping in the next room brought her hard put-away desires fully to the front of her mind. Images of his steamy body in the shower grew and brought her body full awake.

"Whoa," she whispered. "You have to stop thinking about him, like that anyway." She glanced at the door as if her thoughts would wake Mack and bring him to her. Not that she wanted him there but she had to admit she wanted him...sometime.

The humming of the whirlpool and the hot water that had lulled her minutes before seemed to be adding to her physical needs. She poked her toe at the whirlpool button, turning it off as if it and not her own mind was the cause of her growing desire. Now she'd need a cold shower she told herself. Damn! What was wrong with Mack? One minute he was all over her and the next, he was throwing ice water on their relationship. Maybe he really did have a thing for that Cavine. There are other men, she thought.

Penny looked at her pruned toes and fingers, placed the soap on the edge of the tub, and began to push herself up. I'll just go to bed and sleep it off.

The door opened as she stood. Through the shower curtain Penny could see Mack's clouded image in the mirror. Mack stepped to the sink and put toothpaste on his brush. His brow creased in deep thought. He hadn't noticed she was in the tub.

She stared with longing at him. The muscles in his arms flexed as he brushed his teeth. Her toes curled thinking of those arms wrapped around her wet, naked body. Mack leaned in to inspect a tooth and she saw the sinewy muscles of his legs contract. Oh, she moaned inwardly.

The dividing wall between them wasn't wide enough. If he looked in her direction, he'd see her. She carefully slid down without making a ripple and covered herself with the water. I know I was thinking about him but it's not as if I really wanted him to see me like this. If I just hold my breath and am very quiet, he'll leave and I can get to the loft.

Her eyes moved to the soap that was slowly sliding over

the porcelain. No! Her mind screamed. The soap didn't hear her fervent plea because it slipped into the water with an echoing plop! Oh, damn, she thought, as she slid farther under the water.

Mack reeled about and stared in the direction of the noise. He leaned to look around the wall at the tub as if he wasn't sure of what he was seeing. His eyebrows shot up in surprise. "Oh." He moved to the door. "I didn't know you were in here. I really didn't."

Penny watched as he stood with his hand on the door-knob staring at her. She hadn't laid out a towel so she could-n't wrap herself in it. "I know you didn't." She tried to ease his embarrassment as well as hers.

Her voice had grown husky, and she knew that came from her ever-present desire for him. "If you could throw me a towel, I'll get out of here and go up to my own bathroom," she whispered to hide the sultry inflection she was hearing in her own voice.

"No, I know you're hurting and you don't have a tub. Stay as long as you need to. I'll just go back to my room." His voice broke with hoarseness. "Would you like a cup of hot chocolate?"

Penny giggled. "Well I'd really rather have a towel but if you insist." The levity helped the awkward moment pass.

Mack threw his head back and let out a great peal of laughter. "I guess that would work better than hot chocolate for this." He chuckled as he opened the linen closet.

Penny let out a breath but was still in the throes of her fantasy. If it's hot chocolate he wants... She scolded herself for being so single-minded. If he knew what she was think-ing he would run, she thought.

Mack brought her a towel and held it out to her. "Need anything else?"

Oh, she groaned inwardly, don't ask that. His gaze searched her face reading into her thoughts. Penny shivered as his mercurial black eyes clouded to smoky gold. "Well," she said in a voice she could barely get above a whisper. He looked at her with genuine interest in what she wanted or needed. "You could turn around so I can get out."

"Oh," Mack said as if he was dumbfounded that he still stood there. Featherlike laugh lines crinkled around his eyes. "I guess...I think...I'll go fix us a snack."

Laughter echoed in the small room as Penny lifted her fingertips and accepted the towel. She stared at him. "Mack?"

"Hmmmm?" He stared back.

"Just what kind of snack were you thinking?" Penny flushed at the brazen innuendo.

"Hot chocolate?" He answered with a question, looking her over seductively.

She didn't miss the double meaning of his question. Penny tried to throttle the dizzying current running through her as she saw the smoldering flame in his gaze. Her heart danced with excitement as the very air around them became electrified.

Pulling the towel to her chest, she stood and expertly wrapped it around her without revealing anything. Mack stared for a moment and then held out his hand to help her from the bathtub. Penny placed her hand in his and immediately felt the sexual magnetism flow from his body to hers. A delightful shiver of wanting ran through her as her eyes held his.

Mack's arms encircled her with one hand in the small of her back, holding her firmly to him. The brush of his thigh against her hip sent tingling shivers through her. Her blood raced upstream to keep up with her rapidly beating heart.

"I can't do this," he whispered against her ear. His words said one thing but his body pressed against hers said otherwise.

"Okay," Penny whispered as if she hadn't heard him.

He looked longingly into her face and gently brushed his lips over hers. His large hand gently took her face and held it. "Are you sure?"

Penny nodded. She'd never been more sure of anything in her life but she didn't have the voice to say it. Mack claimed her lips ravenously. Any calm she might've had left shattered with the hunger of his kiss. Without another word, he swept her into his arms, carried her to his room, and laid her gently on his bed. Mack tugged at the towel and sucked in air as her body revealed to him.

Penny held her breath, wondering what he was thinking. He looked at her as if photographing her with his eyes and then lifted his gaze to hers, beaming approval. Penny's haze of passion had totally consumed any reservations she might have had. Her fingers traveled up the muscle of the front of his leg and tugged on his boxers. To her surprise, they dropped immediately. A thrill ran through her as she saw the evidence of his passion and the object of her desire. Her steamy gaze met his. They didn't need to talk, they both knew where they were going.

She swallowed tightly as he dropped beside her and pulled her into his arms. Penny moved toward him involuntarily, driven by her own passion. Their kisses came fast and furious. His tongue sent shivers racing through her as he traced the soft fullness of her lips and then explored the deepest recesses of her mouth. She felt her soft curves molding to the contours of his lean, muscular body and pressed to become one with this man she admired so much.

✖

Inhaling deeply of her fresh scent, Mack hesitated for a moment. How could anything that felt so right be wrong? That thought ran dimly through his mind as he traced a path from Penny's nipples down to her sweet spot. His body jerked involuntarily as the syrupy aroma of her fresh honey drifted into his senses. He brushed his mouth over her sweet bundle and moaned as he traced his way back to drink from her full breasts. Penny held him in her arms and pressed her breast to his hungry mouth, urging him to take her fully. Her fingers trickled down the center of his body until she reached his proud manhood and enveloped the physical evidence of his passion. Tenderly she squeezed and caressed him. "Oh, my God," he whispered hoarsely against her breast. He grabbed her hand and held it tightly. "Wait, baby."

Penny knew he wanted to prolong their pleasure. Unwillingly she trailed her fingers away from his rock-hard shaft. Mack's tongue licked a path over her breast, down her stomach and then drank of the honey she had produced just for him.

She pressed her passion-filled body to him as he brought her to life. Her body arched and twisted as she sought the relief a woman can only feel from having a man inside. Slowly Mack made his way back to her lips and nipped at them as he looked into her expectant face. He felt her legs spread, and he could wait no more. He entered her slowly and then plunged to the depths of her body. Penny whimpered and then clutched his back to hold him close.

Mack watched her sweet face as her head tipped back in total ecstasy. The thrill of pleasing this marvelous woman drew his excitement to the peak. Her rhythm met his, and together they moved into the passionate world of a couple discovering love for the first time. They soared their way to the top and rumbled to the bottom when their carnal needs were satisfied. Mack fell on top of Penny and shuddered as the last of his passionate fluids exploded into the hot, contracting cave of the woman he knew would be more than his partner in investigations.

When he could breathe normally, Mack rolled beside her and pulled her into his arms. He didn't know what to say. She'd been a willing participant but was that enough to rationalize breaking his promise?

He felt her snuggle under his chin and drop kisses on his neck. Her hot lips moved over his neck to his chin and then to his lips. Misty coppery eyes gazed into his. She stopped and lay silent in his arms.

Guilt and remorse filled him. It was too soon! Now he'd blown it completely. How could he forgive himself for this? What would Mrs. Hart say if she knew how he'd broken the promise he'd made?

"Penny?" he whispered.

"Hmmm?" Penny responded.

"I'm sorry. I know this changes things and I didn't really want to do that."

Penny studied his features for a long time. Mack began to feel uneasy. He could see her face as the thoughts came and went. Finally, she answered him. "Now can we have that after-the-job snack?" Her smile moved from her sweet lips to her eyes as if she'd just decided how she wanted to handle the issue.

Mack couldn't believe his ears. He was sure she'd want to talk about their lovemaking—he thought all women did that. But this little pixie wanted to eat. His deep, rumbling chuckle turned into a full laugh. There was probably more to her thought pattern than what she'd said, but the relief he felt overwhelmed him. "No more hot chocolate, then?" he said half seriously.

Penny smiled. "We'll discuss that some other time. Right now we have to see what we can find in the vending machines." Mack smiled. So she had been listening when he was in the kitchen. Yet, with all her levity he was sure he could see shadows in her smile

He stared at her for a moment wondering what she was really thinking. Was she hungry or was she looking for a way out of the situation. He decided to play it her way and see what happened. He really was left with little choice. If he asked right now, it might not be what she wanted to answer or what he wanted to hear. A well-thought-out answer would be much more to his liking. With his decision made, he leaped from the bed and pulled her with him. "Damn, sweetness, you are my kind of woman." He pulled on his boxers and led her to the kitchen. Mack picked her up and plunked her on the stool at the counter. "You stay awake this time, and you'll have one heck of a snack."

"How are you going to top the last one?" She smiled.

Mack studied her. He wanted to believe she was speaking her true heart but her eyes were saying other things. "I don't think that's possible. But I'm willing to try."

Penny laughed softly. "You could be cooking all night."

Mack flipped the calendar page on the counter and glanced at his watch. "It seems I'm free to cook—or do whatever—all night."

Chapter 10

Penny bounded off the stool. "While you operate the vending machines I'm going to find my pajamas." She glanced down at the sheet she had grabbed when he pulled her from the bed. She glanced at the kitchen clock as she was leaving. "You know it's five in the morning. I would think you would be fixing breakfast." She glimpsed his wide smile as she turned the corner to run to the loft.

Plunking on her bed she let out the emotion she'd held inside. Tears of joy and sadness flowed onto her pillow. The whole day had been so emotional. Realizing her father's death might not have been accidental had shocked her and sent her mind whirling. Pulling Mack back to freedom had drained her physically, and making love with him had taken the last of her emotional strength. She'd been vulnerable at that point, and she knew it.

Of course, making love with Mack was precious to her. And his lovemaking was certainly everything and more than she'd fantasized. Yet, in her mind, he was having casual sex and she wanted to keep up the facade that she was too. She was never going to let him know how badly she wanted him. Or, how in ten short days she'd found the man she wanted to be with for the rest of her life. But she was not going to lay her heart on the table.

"Just because I'm love struck does not mean Mack is," she reasoned with herself. "We are both consenting adults." She lifted her chin and squared her shoulders. "Nope, nothing or no one is ever going to take me down again."

With her resolve to be mature about their relationship firmly back in place, Penny dried her tears, took a quick shower, dressed, and returned to the kitchen. She would show Mack and herself that she could be mature about a relationship. She knew he still had Cavine and wondered exactly what their relationship was or had been. She shook her head to clear her thoughts. That is none of my business. Mack and I are a completely separate issue, she lied to herself. Penny's defenses were coming up as years of training dictated and she was feeling much better.

"I don't have any change for the vending machine," she joked as she joined Mack in the kitchen.

Mack reached into his loose-change bowl on the counter. "This one's on me."

"I think we should go Dutch," she said as she grabbed her purse and threw change on the counter. Penny could see the questions in Mack's eyes but for now, they would be unanswered. She had to be sure of his feelings for her and of her feelings for him. She wanted to know exactly what was happening so she could react appropriately. And knowing how unsure she could be about emotions, it would take a while for that to happen.

Their gazes met and held as they sized each other up. The ringing phone finally brought Penny from the pensive stare. Dropping from the stool, she took the few steps to the phone, wondering who it was and still feeling Mack's stare fixed on her.

"Hello?" Penny could hear the fatigue and vulnerability in her own voice. She made a mental note to work on that as she listened to the caller.

"Yes, he's here. One minute please."

She held the phone to Mack. "It's your partner," Penny said with disdain.

Mack's features creased instantly as he took the receiver from her. "Hey, you're up early. What's up?" Mack listened; his eyes flashed as he answered. "I'll be over in a few minutes." He listened again and then said, "Yeah, sounds like something we should look into."

Penny's heart sank. Just a quick call from Cavine and everything they'd been doing came to a screeching halt. She'd promised herself to stay mature about all of this but she wasn't sure she could keep that promise. She drew in a deep breath and asked, "Is there anything wrong?"

Mack shook his head. "No, not wrong...I have to go." He stared at Penny. "I don't know how long I'll be gone."

Penny's heart plummeted to her toes. "I understand."

"Cavine has discovered some evidence that we need to look at." He let out a long breath and ran his fingers over his hair. He paced and then turned to Penny. "I know the timing isn't great, but duty calls."

"You do what you think you have to do," Penny said dully.

Mack stared at her for a long moment. "I meant the timing because of..." He paused in thought for a long moment, "Never mind." Mack dropped his hands to his sides and turned away.

Penny could feel her heart trip over his words. She'd wanted him to say because of them and what they'd been doing but he hadn't, and now she knew where she stood. In a way, it was a relief, she told herself. After all, this is what she'd wanted from the beginning. Wasn't it? She'd wanted to be alone in her cabin. Just her and her career.

Mack walked quickly down the hallway. When he emerged, he was dressed and carrying his duffel bag. He looked at her and then at the bag, "I don't know how long I'll be."

"Okay," Penny said slowly not really knowing what to say. She sounded normal but inside she was hovering a step above foreboding. In her heart, Penny knew with Mack leaving, he wouldn't be back...not the way he had been. Grow up! she reproached herself. Like you said, it was only sex.

Mack walked to the door, turned as if to say something, and then left.

Penny dragged herself to the loft and got dressed. When she came back down, she considered going to church so at least she could make her mother happy. But she wasn't in the mood to hear that prayers were answered. Until Cavine called, she and Mack were in their own little heaven but Penny could see the writing on the wall. She was fine until Mack's coworker snapped her fingers. Then he was gone.

What was she to do? "This is stupid!" She grabbed her gear and drove to the rangers' station. She knew there would be a crew in on Sunday because fires didn't use calendars.

She entered the still empty office and went to the desk with her nameplate on it. Folders of reports were stacked neatly with notes from Dan to complete and send to the head office. She scowled. Paperwork already? Completing reports was the one part of the job she didn't like, even though that's where she began her career as a forest ranger.

For the next hour, she worked diligently on the forms. Penny wanted to get the job done. She always did what she liked least first, to get it out of the way and move on to more pleasant activities.

"Hey, you." Dan spoke as he entered the office. "I don't want my staff so dedicated that it makes me look bad." He laughed and poured himself a cup of coffee.

Penny scrunched her face. "I think that's yesterday's coffee."

Dan took a drink and shuddered. "Wow, that's as good as having caffeine intravenously fed."

Penny smiled. "Tomorrow I'll remember to put the coffee on when I get to work."

"That could get you a raise," Dan said as he made a fresh pot. "So what are you doing here so early on Sunday? I thought you weren't reporting in until tomorrow."

Penny shrugged. "I rather figured I would have paperwork to do. I knew you'd been shorthanded and you knew I could do it. And I like to get it done so I can do other things. I'm almost done with the folders you left. Would you mind if I spend some time in the fire tower today?"

"Actually," Dan said as he delivered her a cup of coffee,

"that will work out great. I need one of the guys scheduled to run to the supply warehouse downstate today."

Penny accepted the coffee. "Thanks."

She watched Dan sink into the chair at his desk and delve into his paperwork. It was obvious, like her, he accepted the bad with the good. And the good was the time when they were out on fire duty like surveillance, prevention, or fighting a fire.

Amazingly, within an hour, all of the rangers were out of the office and into the field. The station was left empty but for the dispatch operator. As Penny left the office, she stopped at the dispatch desk. "Hi, I'm Penny."

The young woman smiled up at her. "Cindy." She held her hand out.

"It's great to meet you, Cindy," she said as she shook her hand. "If anyone needs me I'll be out in fire tower three today." Cindy wrote the information on the calendar. "Thanks." Penny smiled as she left the building.

The drive to the fire tower was over two-track roads, a couple of rickety bridges over streams, and finally she had to park and walk a mile through dense forest and brush to reach the tower. Penny climbed the circular stairs and at the top, she turned slowly to take in the panoramic view of the forest, lakes, rivers, and hills. She drew in a deep breath. Penny knew others would not understand, but for her the forest and all that it held was the best place in the world.

"Hi, there."

Penny jerked around to where the voice came from. She'd completely forgotten she was replacing someone.

Penny smiled. "Hi. I think I met you on the fire line the other day." She thought for a moment. "Bob?"

He shook her hand. "Yep, and you're Penny, our newest staff member and the only one of us who can play the piano," he laughed. "We can't wait to have something to celebrate again just to hear you play."

"I won't wait that long," Penny said. "When a piano and I are in the same room there is music."

Bob plunked his hat on his head. "And that is music to my ears." He turned to leave, "I'm off to the big city to pick up supplies. Need anything?"

Penny smiled and shook her head. The only thing she needed was to work and regain her sense of priority.

She reported every hour but there was really nothing happening. The forests were serene today. She'd spent the day watching the deer, squirrels, and other forest creatures as they hunted for food and then found their way home.

When her replacement arrived, she gave him the daily report sheets and wound her way down the stairs and out into the open. Even the mile walk back to her vehicle was enjoyable. Having a job she loved so much seemed almost illicit. But she sure wasn't going to complain.

By the time she'd checked out it was six-thirty. Instead of going home, she went to Sugar Moon, eager to check in with Stella a day early too. Penny drove up to the spiraled steel gate and announced herself as a volunteer. After a couple of minutes, the gates opened and she drove up the long drive of the walled complex.

The three-story stone building stood majestically in front

of her. It looked like something out of a Tudor architectural magazine. Penny could see the gardens were being prepared for summer and in the daylight, she noted the sap lines ran through a hole in the base of the house. She couldn't help thinking of Mack tangling himself in the lines after she had warned him.

Penny climbed the stone steps to the enormous double doors and rang the doorbell. Stella Rowe greeted her with open arms and led her into what Stella called the great room. In keeping with the Tudor theme, the vaulted ceilings had exposed beams.

"I'm so happy you decided to volunteer with us and a day early, too; I like that kind of dedication," Stella was saying as she took Penny's hand and literally pulled her through the great room.

"I'm glad too," Penny said honestly. She loved to help others. Working with women in a shelter was the kind of volunteer work she'd done when she lived at home. And this was the perfect escape from her constant thoughts about Mack and Cavine. She let her glance rove over the room. She'd never seen a shelter as nice as this one.

"If you will wait here for a minute, I will find Mr. Proctor and introduce you to some of the young women you will be working with." Stella unconsciously wiped her hands on her apron and scurried away before Penny could do anything but nod.

With Stella gone Penny continued her scrutiny of the room. The highly polished hardwood floors were all made of bird's-eye maple that Penny knew was very rare and used mostly to make musical instruments. Whew, she thought, this is one expensive floor. She stared at the tightly knit swirls in the wood and admired the workmanship that went into making the swirls match at the joints. She was sure this floor was one that had been down for at least a century. No one could afford to use that wood to walk on now.

Penny's examination went from the floor to the bright-papered walls. The great room was homey, warm, and friendly. Relief flooded through her. Her fears that some-thing nefarious was happening at Sugar Moon were leaving much faster than they had come. Whatever she and Mack had heard in their late-night-trip at Sugar Moon must have a logical explanation.

Women in various stages of pregnancy were entering the room. Laughter and chatter filled the air. Penny turned and smiled at them. They all greeted her and welcomed her to the fold. Penny realized they thought she was a young moth-er in trouble as they were.

"Thank you," she addressed them all, "but I'm here to volunteer."

"Volunteer at what?" A blond headed pixie not much into her teens, asked bluntly.

Penny shrugged. "Anywhere they need me but Stella thought I could help with the literacy program."

"What's that?" the young woman asked.

Penny smiled. "Stella thought I could help some of you to learn to read and write."

"I sure want to learn that," the young woman answered.

"I can read but I sure need to know how to fill out job

applications," another chimed in and asked when they could begin.

Penny's heart went out to them. It still baffled her how people could go to school and not learn to read. "As soon as they let me, we'll begin," Penny said confidently.

Stella hurried back into the room with a man in tow. She smiled brightly at Penny. "I see you have met some of your students."

Penny nodded and wondered if this man had the voice she'd heard the other night.

"Mr. Proctor," Stella said, "I'd like you to meet Penny Hart, our literacy volunteer."

Mr. Proctor held out his hand to Penny. "I think it is very nice of you to volunteer. The literacy program is our hope to stop the cycle. We feel an education is the key to a better life."

Penny nodded and listened closely. No, this wasn't the voice she'd heard the other night. That voice was deeper and didn't speak as plainly or as concisely. She smiled as she took his hand. "I couldn't agree with you more."

Mr. Proctor continued. "As you can see the spirits are good here. Our young women are bright, good people. All they need is someone who is willing to help them with the fundamentals of reading and math." He shook his head. "After the babies are born these young women will return to where they were if we don't give them a leg up."

Penny's heart leaped. This was what she wanted to do. "I'd love to be part of helping in any way I can." She smiled at the young women who had encircled her.

"Well then, it's a deal." Mr. Proctor shook her hand and said, "Welcome aboard, Penny."

Stella hustled everyone away and smiled at Penny. "Would you like to see the rest of the facility?"

"I would love to," Penny said sincerely.

"First, you just have to see the babies." Stella led Penny a short way down the hall and opened the door to a bright nursery. Penny walked in and couldn't help smiling. Three newborns were snuggled into bassinets.

After Penny and the older woman tiptoed back out Penny asked, "Are they all up for adoption or do some of the mothers keep them?"

Stella's face saddened a bit. "Most are up for adoption. Only rarely does a young woman come up with the means to support herself and a child," she said wistfully.

Penny glanced back at the closed nursery door. "It is such a shame that this has to happen." Her heart ached for the babies and the mothers who would be separated forever.

"Yes, dear, but when our new programs are in place, and with volunteers like you, we can make a difference." Stella's voice filled with the joy of hope.

Penny was beginning to trust Stella and knew if there was something going on at Sugar Moon this woman was not part of it.

Stella led her through the bedrooms, recreational rooms, library, and finally the birthing rooms. "As you can see we have everything to operate a wonderful shelter for our young women," Stella said proudly.

Penny was in awe. "I can see you have an impressive

home for the young women. But I'm wondering a couple of things."

Stella turned and looked at her. "Feel free to ask anything."

"It is so beautiful and well kept and I can see you are responsible for the upkeep but who pays for all of this?" Penny asked, still amazed.

Stella smiled. "I am in charge of the housekeeping but the young women do their share. We tell them it's their home and they have to share in the work." Stella walked to the window and looked out. "How do we fund this? Well, we have many fine benefactors; we get some money from the adoptions, the state gives us an annual grant, and we make our own maple syrup and sell it." She returned her attention to Penny. "And with volunteers like you we can provide many more services."

Sugar Moon was just as it seemed to Penny. She was thrilled to be part of such a wonderful organization. She thought about the maple syrup. "Could I see how the syrup is made? I've read a great deal about it, but I have never seen it."

Stella wiped her hands on her apron and then looked at Penny. "The basement is off limits to anyone other than the caretakers. It's unsafe and we fear a lawsuit. I'm sure you understand."

"Of course," Penny answered but wasn't quite sure how an unsafe area would be all that great for making syrup. "Now, why don't I get started with some of those anxious students we left in the great room?"

"Oh, I knew you were a go-getter from the moment I met you," Stella tittered as she led the way back down to the cheery room and the young women.

Stella handed Penny the literacy workbooks and then hurried to the kitchen to finish making dinner. Penny excitedly distributed the handouts. "Now," she said, "if you will be patient with me I'll do the same for you. Reading is great fun." She thought for a moment. "Do you like romantic stories?"

The women's faces lit. "Yes," they said in unison.

"After a few classes of the basics, I will begin reading a romance novel to you and you will have to learn to read well enough to read the ending."

The young women were excited and Penny knew her reward would be the students' growing self-confidence when they learned to read. After what seemed like minutes, Stella entered the room. "Ladies, it's time for dinner." She turned to Penny and asked, "Would you like to stay? It's one of the benefits of being a volunteer."

Penny glanced at her watch, "It's eight already and I do have things to do at home." The truth was she wanted to see if Mack had phoned. She hoped he had. Then he would know she wasn't sitting at home waiting for him.

"Of course, dear." Stella hugged her. "Don't forget I'll be by on Thursday to clean."

Penny smiled at the older woman as she was leaving. "I'll be back tomorrow night and I look forward to seeing you on Thursday." Penny bounced down the stone steps. At the bottom stood two men who looked like they'd been working in the dirt all day.

"Hi," she greeted them with a huge smile.

"You must be Penny, that new teacher Stella told us about," one of the men said.

"Yes, I am and who might you be?" Penny asked, still smiling brightly.

"I'm Fred and this here is Phil. We're the caretakers here."

"I'm pleased to meet you and I might add, you do a very nice job on the grounds," Penny said.

The men seemed surprised. "Thank you, ma'am," Phil said. "We try our best to keep Sugar Moon the nice place it is supposed to be." They tipped their fingers to their hats and walked away.

Penny heard from Mack once in two weeks. His message was so short it almost hurt. She ran the words over in her head many times. "Hi, just checking in; in accordance with one of our rules I am letting you know I'll be gone for a week, maybe two. I'll try to call again but Cavine and I are hot on a couple of leads and I'm not sure where I'll be." There was a long pause and then he said, "Penny, take care of yourself."

She sat in the dark rocking and thinking about their situation. She glanced at the clock. It was nine. Penny wondered if Mack would phone or even come back but as the days passed she was giving up on both. While he'd been gone she'd spent the time convincing herself what she felt for

Mack was lust, but whenever the phone rang, her heart raced to answer it. And every time she answered the phone and it wasn't he on the other end, she was both sad and angry. How could what they did mean so little to him?

The clock ticked loudly in the silent cabin. Unconsciously Penny was rocking in time with the ticks. The faster she rocked, the louder the squeak in the floor called out. The louder the noise grew, the angrier she was at Mack for leaving with that woman and just after they'd been so intimate. If he ever returns, she thought, he'll be out of here so fast he won't know what hit him. The squeaking board was almost deafening. Unwillingly she dragged herself from the chair and pulled it off the small braided rug it sat on.

"Ah-ha," she said to hear a human voice. The squeak she'd heard for years was a lose board in the floor. Stepping on it, she could see that one of the nails holding it down had worked its way to the top. She glanced at the clock; a half an hour had passed. "Give it up!" she yelled at herself. She wasn't going to sit and think of Mack. It was time to move on. It was time to get her life back to where she wanted it. Penny half laughed as the noise seemed to grow louder, "It's time to fix that noise."

She rummaged through all of the kitchen cabinets and drawers looking for tools and found none. She was determined to fix that noise. Placing her hand on the front doorknob, she hesitated. Penny didn't really think there was anyone around but since Mack had instilled in her the possibility, she'd been very careful not to journey out too late. "Oh, hell," she said, scolding herself. "You're going to live here alone for a long time." Pulling the door open she walked to her truck, looking in every direction.

The mid-May air was warm and filled with new-growth fragrances. She inhaled deeply. She loved the fresh, heady scent of the north woods. Penny noticed the full moon; the glowing beams covered the area with a soft diffused light. This was the cabin and the north that she loved. It was peaceful and out of harm's way. Before Mack had put her on guard, she would've slept out here under the stars without giving her safety a thought.

Releasing the lid of the large toolbox, she reached in to get her toolkit. Penny decided she was going to put all of the worrisome thoughts instilled in her by Mack and her wild imagination behind her. She wasn't going to fear her beloved cabin and the woods that surrounded it. Smiling to herself, she pulled the kit out and closed the lid on the large one.

Bravely she walked around the cabin and felt more confident in herself. As she rounded the side of the cabin, she heard a vehicle driving slowly down the road. Cautiously she moved behind a tree. Not that she was afraid, she told herself, but she was alone and had to be careful. She kept her stare fixed on the older car as it crept down the road, and then stopped a few hundred feet from the cabin.

She saw the outline of two men slide from the car and quietly close their doors. Her heart began to pound erratically as they moved toward the cabin. She edged her way back in the direction of the old dilapidated storage shed. Damn it, she thought. My gun is in the house.

As the men drew nearer, Penny was able to see their faces

in the moonlight. Recognizing them as the caretakers at Sugar Moon, she breathed a sigh of relief. She opened her mouth to call out to them and then closed it. If they were just looking for something they would've come to her place and asked. Why were they sneaking around? She fell back in the shadows, clutching her toolkit to her chest. Holding her breath she watched as the men walked toward her.

As they prowled toward the shed, she moved back toward the small creek that ran through the rear of her property. Her feet slipped into the shallow icy-cold water. The splash wasn't loud, she knew that. What if they'd heard the noise? She held her breath and stayed in place. Her feet had turned to icicles but she knew she dared not move. Her heart violently thumped against her rib cage. She quietly released the breath she was holding and took deep ones. Penny was trying to quiet the roar in her head and the drumming of her heart so she could hear the men's conversation.

The men opened the storage-shed door as if this was an everyday occurrence. "If you would've taken care of this, we wouldn't be here tonight," one of them groused to the other.

"Just get that damned box and let's get out of here before she sees us," the second man ordered.

"She's in bed. She won't hear us," the first man uttered and then added with a jeer. "Good thing the little ranger works hard and goes to bed early. Otherwise, we would be here in the middle of the night." The men chuckled wickedly. "Sure would like to see that little brown girl in bed."

"Don't get any stupid ideas. A romp with her would mean the end of our money supply." The second man spit out his criticism.

"Nah, she would disappear." The first one spoke as if this were a normal activity.

Penny had never felt so threatened in her life. Thank God, she wasn't in her bed but then again if she were, at least her gun would be with her. She stared at the shed. She hadn't been in it since her arrival. The old building had been sagging for years, and all those years her father had said it needed to come down. It would now.

Her fear was turning to anger. What right did these men have rummaging around in her family's things? Even if what they were looking at was rubbish? And what right did they have discussing her as if she were just a piece of meat?

Confronting them was in her mind but then she thought better of it. Nothing in that old shed was worth dying for…unless they'd put something there. What if they weren't stealing something but instead were taking something they'd stored there? If that were the case, she wanted to know what it was.

Daringly, she quietly slid her freezing feet down the small creek and positioned herself to see what they were carrying away. Somehow, she would find it at Sugar Moon and inspect it. She listened closely, waiting for them to leave.

She heard a loud thump and heard the second man curse. "Damn it! If you would've got this when you were here a week ago, we wouldn't be back tonight."

Startled they'd been there a week ago, Penny held her breath to keep from gasping and jerked as her toolkit splashed in the shallow creek. Icy-cold water penetrated her pants and trickled down her legs. Violently shivering she held the shriek rising at the back of her throat.

She froze in place, waiting for them to find her and wondering what she would do if they did. There was no doubt in her mind what they would do with her. One of them had made that plain in their conversation. After a few minutes she realized they were so busy with what they were doing they hadn't heard.

Carrying a wooden box between them, she watched as the men veered away from the cabin and into the woods. When she heard the car start, she crumpled into a pile on the ground. Pulling her numb feet from the creek and gasping for breath, she shivered from sheer cold and the aftermath of fear. She knew these crooks were causing the trouble for Sugar Moon and was relieved she'd been right about the people who ran the home.

Dipping her hands in the creek, she threw water on her face. As cold as she was, her face burned from the hot nerve endings that had pounded so wildly while the crude and terrifying men were in the shed. Penny sat listening and waiting; fear kept her in the dark with only the moon as a companion.

When she felt it was safe, she grabbed her wet tool kit and ran for the safety of her home. Once inside she took the loft stairs two at a time. In her room, she grabbed her gun, loaded it, and held it tightly in her hands. Surreptitiously Penny moved around the house making sure she was alone. After opening every door and closet and searching the nooks and crannies of the cabin, she fell into the rocking chair.

"Damn it!" The squeaking that had sent her outdoors was still there. She laughed at herself. The noise actually sounded welcoming now but she was wide awake and needed something to do. With her toolkit and gun beside her, she pulled the braided rug back and examined the boards.

Curiously, one board lifted about an inch above the others. The nail had worked out and was in need of her hammer. Penny took a long hard swing at the nail. She hit it so hard it should have ended in China, but instead it bounced out.

"Damn it!" she cursed again. The loose board squeaked and groaned as she tried to push it down with her weight. Once she got the board in place, she would drive that annoying nail back where it belonged. She stood on the opposite end of the loose board with plans to edge along it until it was flat. Instead, when her total weight was on the opposite end of the nail, the board flew up and smacked her full in the stomach. Jumping away, she rolled to the floor and held her aching tummy. "Good thing that wasn't a six footer," she told herself.

Her gaze fell to what looked like a notebook tucked in the floor opening left by the missing board. Penny looked around cautiously and then grabbed the book. Scooting into the corner where no one could see her, she opened the notebook and saw her father's neat script. "Oh, my God," she whispered. Inside the front cover, there was a note to her.

Penny, if you are reading this then something has happened to me. I know you are the only one who would attempt to fix the squeak. That's my girl. Hot tears flooded Penny's eyes and she could read no more. Long pent-up grief flowed.

Through all of her pain and grief, she heard the door-knob turning. Swiping at the tears, she grabbed her gun. Penny quickly rolled to a position where she could see the door but could not be seen. She lay prone on the floor with the gun pointed at the door. "Come on, you son of a bitch!" She screamed her fury at the intruder. She didn't care who it was…in a minute he would be dead.

She waited. The door didn't open. "Get your ass in here if that's what you want!" she commanded vehemently.

"Penny?"

Her breath caught in her throat. She was sure she was hearing things. "Identify yourself!" she knew she sounded like a commando. But she didn't care.

"Mack Holsey at your service, ma'am."

His voice wrapped around her like a blanket. She dropped the gun and ran to the door. Within a second, she was in his arms with her face buried in his chest. "God, I'm glad you're back."

"Now this is the kind of greeting a man likes." Mack chuckled.

"What are you doing here?" Penny pushed away from him. As much as she wanted to be held and protected, this man had left her to be with another woman.

"And that is exactly the question a man does not want to hear when he returns home." Mack looked over her shoulder. He could see the toolkit, the loose board in the floor, the rug and rocking chair out of place and… "What is your gun doing on the floor?" He studied the gun. "The thing is cocked!"

Penny shivered, drew her shoulders straight and pushed her determined chin out as she glared at him, "What difference does it make to you where my gun is?" she said as she grabbed it from the floor and released the hammer.

"Because you might kill yourself with it," Mack stated flatly, irritated at the way she was acting. One minute she was in his arms and the next, she was treating him like a stranger.

"I can take care of myself," Penny said as she walked to the couch and pulled her mother's afghan around her.

Mack couldn't help smiling. Her words and actions were totally in conflict. "Why are you angry with me?" he asked, completely baffled by her actions.

Penny's eyes widened as if that were the dumbest question she'd ever heard. "I'm not angry with you. I've had a bad evening."

Mack's survey took in the living room. "It looks like you've had more than a bad evening." He stared at her. The look of fear and terror was right behind the angry daggers she was shooting in his direction.

Mack sat on the edge of the couch where Penny curled in the corner all wrapped up. "Do you want to tell me what happened?"

Penny's body shook with emotions. At the moment she was so angry with Mack she could kill him, yet she knew he was the one person who would understand why she had the fear of the caretakers. She shrugged. "I don't know why you would want to know."

Mack stood and stomped to the kitchen where he poured

a cup of coffee. "Damn it, Penny, you know I care."

"If you cared so damned much..." She stopped, drew in a deep breath, and tried to stay calm. "I've been here alone for two weeks and you phoned once. That shows me how concerned you were."

"I was working, for Christ's sake." Mack threw his arms in the air and came to stand in front of her.

Penny hugged the pillow tightly to her chest. "I hope your job is going well." What she really meant was she was pissed that Cavine had such control over Mack that she could make him leave at the drop of a hat, but Penny wasn't going to give Mack the satisfaction of knowing she was jealous and hurt.

Mack gave her a look that seemed to bore right through her. "I'm here now. Do you want to tell me what this is all about?" his arm swept over the disheveled room.

Penny looked into his eyes. His sincerity overwhelmed her. Maybe he did want Cavine but he was sincerely trying to help her right now. "It's just that..." Her chin shivered and tears streamed down her cheeks.

He gathered her in his arms and comforted her. "It's okay now." He hushed her and gently brushed her hair. "I'm here now. It's okay." He spoke in gentle tones like those one would use for a terrified child. Something very bad would have to come down for this independent, strong woman to fall into a weeping pile.

After a few minutes, her shivers began to subside. "It was so horrible," she cried out and began shivering again.

Mack surveyed the room. In the corner was his partner's

notebook. He'd know that tattered old book any place. Cliff had carried it from the first day he'd become an agent. When it had been discontinued, his partner had bought all of the refills he could find so he'd never run out.

"Penny, you have to get hold of yourself and tell me what is going on." Damn it! Mack cursed to himself. He probably shouldn't have left her alone for so long, but she wanted to live alone here, he reasoned. And when Cavine called and told him she and Linc Cross had some leads as a result of their investigative work, he'd been anxious to follow those leads. But right now, he had to deal with the terror he saw in Penny's face and felt in her trembling body.

Penny looked up at him. Her face was tear-stained and teardrops sat on her lids. "I found Dad's notebook."

Mack nodded. "I noticed that." He glanced at the black book, anxious to know the contents. "Have you read it?"

"Only that he expected me to find it." She gulped hard; hot tears slipped down her cheeks.

Mack pulled her tightly to his chest and tenderly rubbed her back. "It's time for you to grieve your loss, hon." That was all he had to say. She yielded to the compulsive sobs that had built for years. Mack held her until she gently pushed back.

"Thank you." She dabbed at her eyes with her pajama top and smiled sheepishly at him. "I'm really not this weak. I don't know what came over me." She paused, thinking of the evening, and said, "Well, I do know."

For the next hour, Mack held her as she related the whole evening to him. "Oh, baby," he said as he dropped a kiss on the top of her head. "It's no wonder you were gun ready when I turned the doorknob. I'm glad you were." He paused as his face lit with a grin. "And I'm really glad you waited for me to identify myself."

Penny offered him a wan smile and a curious stare. "You know, I thought I was going to kill the person at the door."

Mack chuckled. "I had no doubt of that when I heard your longshoreman language."

Penny's copper cheeks stained a dark crimson. "Hey," he said as he tapped her chin, "you have no reason to be embarrassed. After what you've been through I think you were actually very nice."

Penny released a long sigh. "I've never been so scared in all of my life. I swear those men are pigs!"

"Tell me all about it." Mack encouraged her to let it all out.

"If it weren't so serious I would have to laugh at my reaction." She rose and walked to where the notebook lay. Lovingly she picked it up and brought it back to the couch. I think it's time we see what it was that Dad wanted me to know if he was gone. She pointed to the inscription and a lonely tear made a rivulet down her cheek and over her chin. She bit her lip. "Don't worry, I'm done crying now."

"You don't have to be." He sat close to her on the couch. "Now, let's see what our number one investigator had to say.

Mack couldn't understand Penny's anger at him. Just as she would do, he had gone where his job had taken him. But he knew this wasn't the time to discuss that. His heart filled with adoration for this brave woman. He'd longed to be back here with her but circumstances just didn't allow that. He was here now and maybe when she calmed down they could discuss the situation as two adults.

Chapter 11

Penny and Mack read late into the night. Mack kept the food coming as Penny read aloud. After reading, they sat and stared at the notebook. It was all there. Everything Mack suspected but not the proof.

One passage was especially interesting to them. They discovered there were many tunnels in the area. The tunnels had been used to hide enslaved ancestors on their journey to freedom. The passages were a few miles from the Canadian border, which was the last stop before their ancestors were free. Penny and Mack reveled in the history and were more determined to return to the tunnel they'd found. When Penny finished reading, she laid the book beside her. "I'd like to go back to that tunnel."

"I don't want you to go there by yourself. I have all of the equipment we'll need to do it safely this time." He smiled at her. "How long did it take you to recover from the last time we were there?"

Penny looked down at her hands. "Oh, not long. Within a couple of days I could move again." Penny knew Mack was talking about her pulling him out of the hole but she wanted to add that she still hadn't recovered from the hot chocolate or his sudden disappearance the next morning.

She drew in a deep breath. Penny knew she had to accept that Mack was more interested in Cavine. And who would blame him? Somehow, she had to put all of that behind her and concentrate on what her father had left for her. "Mack, I know there is something disturbing going on at Sugar Moon, but I don't think the people who run it are the ones committing the offense…whatever misdeed that is," she added.

"Yes, I agree in part and we'll look into it. But first, we have to go see Paige and Linc," Mack said as he placed the book back under the plank, flopped the rug over it and pulled the rocker back to where it belonged.

"I've been to see Aurora a couple of times while you were gone. She's fine." Penny studied his face as lines of consternation etched over his features.

He smiled softly. "I'm glad she's doing well." He paused for a moment and then continued. "There are a couple of things I have to tell you about the investigation. The night I met Linc, I was so taken with his honesty that I took him into my confidence and told him who I am and what I'm doing." His voice was soft and apologetic.

"I can see how that would happen. I feel the same way about Paige." Penny was going to tell him she'd taken Paige into her confidence, too, but as she stared at him, there was something else. "Why are you feeling bad about it now? What did Linc do?"

Mack shook his head. "It isn't what Linc did. It's what I did." He stood and paced the floor. "I asked Cavine to stay and help in the investigation—well, that's not completely true. She offered and I didn't turn her down."

"Oh, I see." Penny felt her heart drop. *Here's where he tells me what we had was a mistake. Well, while he was gone, I figured that out.* She pulled on her reserve strength. "Mack, I do understand. I know you and Cavine have something special and please believe me when I tell you I'm okay with it."

Mack opened his mouth to speak but Penny held up her hand. Smiling, she tapped him on the chin. "What we had was sex. Two people obviously needed release and sex was available. End of story." She said it emphatically and walked to the loft stairs. "Now if you don't mind, I'm whipped. I've worked two jobs these past two weeks and had a few other things to deal with." She faked a yawn and stretched. "In the morning," she glanced out the window and saw the sun peeking over the horizon, "or when we wake, we can discuss where we go from here...on the investigation, that is." She walked up the steps to show she was tired but she really wanted to run as fast as the wind.

Penny slept fitfully. She woke often thinking of Mack and changed her thinking to consider her father's notes. As hurtful as her father's notes were, the more she tried to ignore the truth, the more it persisted. On the calendar she and Mack had been together a short time, but emotionally she had lived a lifetime since she'd met him. She'd get through all of this and be a better person for it, she told herself, trying to give herself strength and an escape from her feelings.

Penny lay staring at the ceiling. It pained her that her father knew he was in danger and didn't ask for help. Yet she knew he hadn't had enough evidence to prove his theory of baby selling. She had a hard time believing that theory herself. Yet, when she thought of Aurora, she knew something strange was going on.

Her father had charted some of the comings and goings of people and babies at Sugar Moon. It had been his intent to follow up on the people to see who contacted them for the adoption. He'd penciled in a date to discuss this very subject with a willing set of parents but there were no entries after that. His gut kept leading him to the place and Penny did understand that feeling.

As much as Penny wanted her father and Mack to be wrong, she was sure they were right. But who at Sugar Moon would do such a thing? Of course, she suspected the caretakers but then again, they might have a completely different activity going on. And listening to them that evening, she knew they weren't smart enough to organize anything as intricate as selling babies.

Her mind whirled with all of the information she had . She pondered the evidence they needed to prove their theories. Penny gained a new respect for her father; she'd never thought about how difficult his job must be. And she had to admit to herself, this new revelation spilled over onto Mack. He was just as dedicated to his investigations as she was to keeping the forest safe.

She finally fell asleep only to wake with a startle. Mack was lifting weights. The barbells were clanging again. She rolled over and listened.

The cabin had grown silent except for the singing of

morning doves outside her window. She sat bolt upright. What had stopped him? She knew darned well he wasn't finished with his routine. After last night, she took no chances. Gun in hand she crept down the stairs and turned corners carefully. First the kitchen, she thought. As she jumped out and held the gun pointed at the kitchen, Mack crushed the eggs he'd been holding in his hands.

"Damn, sweetness! You're going to give me a heart attack doing that," he grumbled as he cleaned up the eggs.

"Why are you so quiet? I know you haven't finished your routine." She stood with one hand on her hip and the gun dangling from the other, glaring at him.

"I'm hungry and I thought you were sleeping so I was doing the socially acceptable thing, I was being quiet."

"Oh, well, don't do me any favors," she shot back as she realized he'd used her own words against her.

"No problem." He glanced at her and then away. "I'm having a late lunch with Linc and Paige today. Do you want to come along?"

"Why? Isn't Cavine available?" she said before she realized her mouth had opened. Damn it, I don't want to sound that way, she told herself.

"She's working," Mack answered bluntly.

Penny studied him as the muscle along his jaw line flexed ever tighter. So, he's angry she thought. Big deal! I've been angry a bit myself lately.

"They are your friends, too, and I have some news about Aurora to give them, so do you want to go or not?" Mack slammed the pan into the sink and started toward his bedroom.

"But right now I have to get my butt in gear or Linc and Paige will have lunch alone."

Penny wanted to see Paige. She needed to talk to another woman...one that she trusted, but she wasn't sure she wanted to go with Mack. And she wanted to hear the news about Aurora. If she didn't go with him then she'd be here alone again and after last night she didn't want that either. "Yeah, okay," she finally answered.

"Good." Mack looked at his watch. "You have fifteen minutes to get ready."

Penny opened her mouth to say she would drive herself, but then decided she didn't want to be any place by herself right now.

She shrugged and headed upstairs to the shower. Just as she leaned to turn on the water, she heard his shower running. Penny leaned against the shower wall and thought about his beautiful body dripping with water. If she were smart, she would fight for him. It might be an uphill battle but she couldn't win if she didn't try.

❦

"Hi!" Penny waved as she spotted Paige with Linc at the restaurant table. She was more relieved than she could say to see her new friend.

Paige looked at Penny. "I hope those dark circles are from spending the night with the man you love."

Penny felt the heat rising to her cheeks. She glanced at Mack and Linc who were still standing, shaking hands, and exchanging small talk. Penny leaned over to Paige and whispered, "It's a long story. Maybe we could talk later."

"Sure," Paige patted her arm. "We will excuse ourselves to use the rest room and then we can talk in the lounge."

Penny nodded at Paige as Mack sat down next to her. She was surprised he felt comfortable enough to be within twenty miles of her, let alone right next to her.

The server took their orders. Paige slid her chair back and held her hand on her shoulder. "Penny, I believe I've broken something. Would you mind coming and helping me?"

Penny stood on her cue and excused herself. In the women's lounge, the friends sat on the couch while Penny poured out her heart.

Paige patted Penny's knee. "Have you considered the possibility that he was working?"

"Yes, in fact I'm sure he was, but the fact is when Cavine says jump he asks how high." Penny's hands twisted in her lap. "I don't want to be like this, I don't want to sound like this, I just wish he would go away and leave me alone."

"If that is what you want then tell him that." Paige handed her a tissue. "But I don't think you want that."

"I don't know what I want." Penny stood and looked at her reflection in the mirror as she dabbed at her smeared mascara. "But I know I don't want to be part of a triangle where I have the weakest side."

"Then don't let anyone shut you out, not even yourself. If you want to be with Mack then you have to fight for that." Paige joined Penny and looked at her in the mirror. "You have all of the right equipment. He likes you, that's obvious, but if you keep on with this jealousy thing, he isn't going to like you."

Penny gave off a disgruntled laugh. "I would lie to you and say I don't care, but I know I do. I'm not sure just how far I am willing to go to win the fight."

"Pride goeth before a fall," Paige offered quietly.

"You sound like my mother." Penny stared at Paige in the mirror. "Have you been talking to her too?"

Paige shoved her makeup back in her purse, "If I sound like your mother then I would bet she sounds like the voice of reason."

"Okay, but I'm still pissed at him for leaving like he did," Penny pushed her makeup bag back in her purse and snapped it shut. "I don't think it is unreasonable to ask for an explanation."

Paige reached for the door, "Not unreasonable to ask but be careful that it's not a demand."

When they rejoined the men the food had been served. Linc asked. "Get it fixed, hon?"

Paige smiled broadly. "I'm sure it's temporary but with a few stitches it will be fine."

Penny knew Paige meant for her to take her time and make the necessary repairs to hers and Mack's relationship. She was a woman after all and she was the one in charge...even if Mack didn't know it.

✄✄*

Mack shifted uncomfortably in his chair; somehow, he

didn't think the women were discussing a broken strap. He decided there was no time like the present to give them all the news about Nikki. He'd worked hard the past couple of weeks to find her parents and he'd been successful but he wasn't sure how Paige and Linc were going to take it. That's all I need, he thought. When I deliver the message everyone at the table will be mad at me. He shrugged inwardly and said, "While I was in Chicago last week…"

With those words, he had everyone's attention. He could see Penny was shocked that he'd been out of town. I left a message for her, he thought defensively.

The other three sat waiting expectantly. Mack looked from one to the other and decided to give the background to the women before he dropped the bomb.

He reached for Penny's hand and then withdrew. Mack felt the cold wall that had been erected and he wasn't quite sure why. "While I was there I searched the missing persons files. Linc and Cavine were here working on a couple of leads and I'm sure we are moving closer to solving the reason the young woman was killed."

"Killed?" Penny asked, "It was an accident…wasn't it?" She was asking questions but her heart kept saying over and over he was in Chicago while Cavine was here.

Paige turned to Linc and questioned. "Honey?"

"Mack will explain. He and I discussed this yesterday while he was still in Chicago, and we knew we had to tell both of you today," Linc answered.

Mack nodded. "It's about Aurora." His facial features creased in sadness.

"What?" Penny asked as the shroud closed in around her.

"Aurora has a family," he answered and waited for their response.

"Oh," Paige uttered as the full meaning of his words sank in. "Are you sure you have the right family? Will they be coming for her soon?"

Mack nodded. "Yep, there's no doubt. We had the missing persons picture identification of Aurora's deceased mother but just to make sure, before we told her parents, we ran her dental records. The records came back as a positive match to the picture, and she actually was the daughter of school teachers from Chicago."

Now all three were staring at Mack in anticipation of the rest of the story. He heaved a long sigh. "While I was in Chicago, I had the unpleasant duty of telling the Masons of their daughter's death." He shook his head as if to remove the painful scene and then continued. "Our young mother, Nikki Mason was her name, was a runaway." Mack hunched forward and aimlessly shifted the silverware from one place to another. His face was bleak with sorrow.

"Go on," Penny urged.

"Nikki had left a note. She hadn't wanted to disgrace her family so she'd found a home for unwed mothers and planned to return when it was over." Mack drew in a deep breath. "Her parents reported her missing. They wanted her to know that no matter her mistake they would stand beside her, but the impulsiveness of youth led her down the wrong path."

"Oh, my God. That poor little girl and her parents, how

sad for all of them," Penny uttered through her finger-covered lips.

Linc whistled in astonishment.

Penny took Paige's hand as she saw the light leave her friend's eyes. "Are you going to be able to deal with this?"

Paige nodded. "I prayed for the authorities to find the baby's family but I also prayed that Linc and I might be able to adopt her." She glanced down at her hands and then back at the other three. "Aurora is a true gift, a wonderful child, and she deserves to be with her right family." She thought for a moment. "And for all of their sakes I hope the reunion happens soon."

"So this shows that Sugar Moon is legitimate," Penny offered tentatively.

Mack cleared his throat. "The FBI had been investigating Nikki's disappearance and when my report came through they connected their case with what we've been working on." He looked Penny in the eyes. "It's not just my case anymore. Cavine has been assigned as my partner."

✦

Penny bit down hard on her lower lip and dropped her gaze before she said something she knew wasn't true. Cavine probably was a good agent. Mack had said that. But she was not just his coworker and Penny knew that too. Not because of anything she'd learned, but her gut told her and that was good enough for her. Mack wasn't the only one who could listen to his gut.

She knew that Mack had to connect all the clues and

prove her father was actually murdered. But she wanted to be part of that. She wanted to do it for her father. Penny's stomach twisted in turmoil. She knew Mack didn't need her help but somehow she was going to do it whether he liked it or not.

When she lifted her gaze back to Mack's she was again confident or at least she portrayed self-assurance. "Whatever it takes to prove your theories and to stop the selling of babies, if that is what is happening," she paused. "You know I'm on the inside of Sugar Moon. If there is anything you want me to do or look for…just say it."

Mack was momentarily speechless in his surprise. Penny could see a glint of admiration return to his gaze as he spoke. "I'd like to keep you out of this, but I know that's impossible."

For the first time that evening, the small group laughed. Penny looked around at her friends. She let out the long breath she'd been holding. The others were relieved because the investigation was going well and she was glad of that, too, but she felt she and Mack were on different footing now and she wasn't going to slip if she could help it.

With Mack's help, Penny filled the other two in on the events of the previous evening and told them about the passages in her father's notebook. Paige and Linc stared at the two who seemed to be taking this all in stride.

"My God," Paige's hand went to her mouth, "Penny why didn't you phone us?"

Linc smiled lovingly at his wife. "I think she should have called the police."

"I never thought of either," Penny said as she wondered how she expected to live alone when she couldn't even dial 911. "I can't believe I didn't think of that." She fell back in her chair and glimpsed Mack's smiling face. "Don't even go there. I can take care of myself."

The other three roared with laughter and Mack added, "You can in fact, but the next time I come home I will be wearing a bulletproof vest."

"Good idea." Linc laughed, glancing at his watch. "I told Cavine we'd meet up with her at your cabin. She and my cousin Dan have been researching the tunnels. With their information and Penny's Dad's notes, I think we can explore undetected and see just what is happening to the women of Sugar Moon."

Mack shook his head. "I don't think it's a good idea for civilians to be putting themselves in harm's way."

Penny glanced at him and could see he was serious. "Okay, but you said that about me, too, and if I remember right..."

Mack laughed. "Yeah, okay." But if you find something, you leave and turn it over to experts. Agreed?" He looked from Penny to Linc.

Linc nodded in agreement.

Penny didn't answer. Her mind was already moving ahead to her own plans; plans that involved grabbing Mack's attention again and keeping it and plans to help find the people responsible for her father's death.

Mack looked at Penny expectantly. She knew he was waiting for an answer but she wasn't willing to give the answer he wanted; instead, she suggested, "If you are all coming to the cabin tonight, why don't I fix dinner for everyone?"

Mack's eyes widened in surprise and an open smile pushed up the worry lines on his face, "Did you install the vending machines while I was gone?"

They all laughed as Penny continued, "I can cook, but good cooking takes time and I don't usually have much of that. I promised Mack I would cook the smelt we caught." She looked at him and then continued. "He left kind of abruptly and missed the thrill of cleaning all of those little things, but he can learn that next time." She glimpsed Paige's face and knew her friend approved of her new tactics.

"You cleaned all of those fish." Mack's tone was skeptical.

Penny tapped him on the shoulder. "Yep, I sure did. You know my mom would say waste not want not. So I did it."

"But how?" Mack was still showing signs of not believing she did both of those huge buckets.

"I cut their heads off with scissors, slit the underside and popped the innards out with my thumb." She laughed at Mack's grimace.

"That would be how it's done," Linc agreed, "except some folks leave the heads on."

"I sure hope they taste better than they sound." Mack's gaze shifted around the table to see if they were pulling a joke at his expense. "Okay, then dinner at the cabin and we can discuss what we've all learned."

Linc looked at Paige. "You don't suppose you'd have

time to make some of your sweet potato pie, would you?"

Paige laughed. "Sure can." She looked at the other two, "I've been turning this Indian into a soul food lover."

"Nothing better," Mack agreed.

Penny spent the rest of the afternoon making a dinner that she knew would please Mack. Cavine had special talents but so did she. Penny knew that she and Mack had sexual chemistry and now she was going to work at having more than just that. Not, she thought, that she didn't want that too. Her face heated as she shredded cabbage to boil for fried cabbage.

"Penny?" Mack hollered as he entered the cabin.

"In here." She turned and looked at him. His face was as bright as sunshine.

"It smells great in here." He came over and lifted the lid on the frying bacon. "Fried cabbage too?"

"Yup, you aren't the only one with cooking skills." She turned and stirred the macaroni. "Besides, how can anyone think on an empty stomach?"

Mack leaned over her shoulder. "There are other ways to feed the body."

Penny's blood rushed through her arteries down to the pit of her stomach. Just the hint of making love with him turned her into a hot lava pit. "I know," she answered, her voice hoarse with growing passion.

"Baby?" He brushed a kiss over her soft lips as he spoke. "This stuff can cook without us." His last words smothered on her lips as she kissed him with a hunger that belied her outward calm.

He kissed the pulsing hollow at the base of her neck. Her body pressed into his, giving freely of her passion. Reclaiming her lips, he crushed her to him. Parting her lips, she raised herself to meet his all-consuming kiss. He was hers, for now.

Penny felt the heady sensation of his lips against her neck and as his lips traveled to her mouth, she felt a dreamy intimacy with him. They were a couple, even if she hadn't spoken the words. She knew it.

They mutually pulled back and stared into each other's eyes. They didn't need to speak. Their lips met and soothed them with the tune of a peaceful harmony. She felt the effortless lifting of her body to meet his. They drew together as if they were opposing magnetic fields; his fervor for her pressed against her tummy. Penny floated on the cloud of a renewed relationship as Mack carried her to his room and laid her gently on the unmade bed.

He leaned down and traced a series of slow, shivery kisses over her face. He dropped a kiss on her nose, and then her eyes and finally he satisfyingly kissed her mouth. "Mmmm," she murmured as her tired soul melted into the kiss. She trailed her fingers over the wide expanse of his chest and wanted so much to believe this was really her man.

Sliding her hands over his sides to his butt, she pulled him down to her. She wanted him close, she wanted him to be part of her body. Penny felt the need to be one with the man she knew she loved. His rock-hard shaft penetrated her and urged her to open the door to its new home. Penny locked her legs around Mack's hips and held him close until they became one. He moved slowly as her hot juices poured out to welcome him.

Penny's instinctive response to him was so powerful she innocently arched, yielding to meet the torrent of his heated excitement. Hot flesh on hot flesh met and shivered with the contact. Climbing to the peak, Penny's heart filled with joy. Clouds of doubt disappeared as they became one in their urgency. Penny's long-awaited climax burst as she felt Mack explode and thrust until the last of his liquid energy rushed to mix with hers.

Spent, they lay in each other's arms. Penny rolled toward him, curled into his body, and drifted into a peaceful slumber.

Mack gazed down at her for the longest time. Every minute with Penny was intense. It didn't matter what they'd been discussing eventually the turmoil of their growing relationship surfaced. He knew he cared greatly for her and wanted to explore that further but not until all of this was over. Cavine was a concern. While she was conducting an exemplary investigation, she kept the pressure on him to have a repeat performance of their one night. He brushed the hair from Penny's cheek. Somehow, this little nymph had a hold on him and he would feel guilty if he were with any other woman. But she had to learn, just like him, his job came first and if they were to have a relationship then she would have to accept that.

Mack heard the clock chime five times. The others

would be there in a couple of hours. He knew Penny needed time to finish making the dinner but he wanted her again
and they were there, he reasoned. He covered her mouth
with his and plunged his tongue into the depths of her
mouth. Penny wrapped herself around him in response.
Mack smiled inwardly. Their bodies had made the decision.

Chapter 12

Penny rushed through her shower with the lingering passion filling every nerve in her body. If she could just stay on an even keel with Cavine here tonight, she might win the war, one battle at a time. She'd conquered her inadequacies but Cavine was still in the picture. And Penny knew that even if Cavine hadn't wanted Mack before, now that she knew someone else was interested, she was going to make a play for him.

When she climbed down the loft stairs Mack was stirring the macaroni and cheese. She leaned over his shoulder and brushed a kiss over his cheek. "I'm going to set up a buffet because it's obvious we don't have room for everyone to sit at the counter."

"One more kiss like that and the buffet will be moved to the bedroom or...," he laughed, "we just won't make it out of the kitchen."

"I think it's hot enough in here right now," she laughed as she stacked the buffet items on the snack bar that separated the kitchen from the living room.

Mack slid over to where she stood and placed a hand on each of her butt cheeks. "You are such a nice handful."

Penny didn't move. The heat from his hands traveled up

her back and made her quiver. "Keep that up and we'll have to lock the doors and turn off the lights."

"Sounds like a good idea," Mack chuckled.

The front door flew open just as Mack was saying that. "What sounds like a good idea?" Cavine asked as she strutted into the cabin.

Penny drew in a huge breath. This was going to take all of the reserve strength she could muster. "Hello, Cavine," Penny said in her most welcoming voice. She looked to Mack to answer the intrusive question but he had turned back to the stove.

"Hi ya, sweetie," Cavine said in a condescending tone as she walked into the small kitchen and hugged Mack. "Welcome back, sugar," she slapped his butt. "Mmmm, that is such a nice ass." She turned to Penny. "I'd bet we could both attest to that."

Penny had to swallow hard when Cavine greeted Mack in such a familiar way. Mack had given Penny a reassuring wink over the other woman's shoulder, just before he winced at the slap on his backside. She thought about answering the snide comment with one of her own but she would wait. Eventually she would unexpectedly slide her own comment in on Cavine.

"Thanks," Mack said as he gently but firmly pushed Cavine from around his neck. "When the others arrive we can go over all of the evidence and see where we are." Mack's voice was quietly firm.

"Sure, baby." Cavine grabbed a carrot stick and munched on it. Her gaze roved over the buffet as she turned sideways to look at her image in the window. Cavine drew her hands up her hips and settled on her small waist. "How on earth do you expect a girl to keep her figure with this kind of a layout?"

"It doesn't hurt even the best of figures to eat this kind of food once in a while. You'll be fine," Penny answered condescendingly even though she knew Cavine had only asked to draw attention to her curvaceous body. Penny watched the door, willing it to open and bring in Linc and Paige. She glanced at Mack. His face was unreadable. He had dropped his investigator's mask in place and it seemed to cover those beautiful eyes she'd read so well until Cavine arrived.

Mack and Cavine opened their notebooks and sat discussing the case. Penny felt as if she were invisible. She thought of many things to say but kept her mouth shut. Her mother's proverbs were always running through her mind. Right now, she could hear her mother saying, it is better to remain silent and thought stupid, than to speak and remove all doubt. So, with great effort she kept her mouth shut. The last thing she wanted was to give Cavine more fodder.

Mack and Cavine had a long history. Penny didn't want to think about them as a couple-ever, but in her heart, she knew there had been something. Just as she felt she would explode, Linc and Paige arrived.

Penny greeted them with great fervor. Paige glanced in the living room and then back at Penny. "Oh," she whispered in Penny's ear, "she is a beauty."

"Thanks," Penny whispered back. "I needed that."

Paige handed Penny the sweet potato pie and then handed her another container. "What's this?" Penny lifted the lid to peek.

"One of my grandmother's favorites, Sprite pound cake." Paige gave Penny a reassuring smile.

"Did I hear pound cake?" Mack stood and came to the kitchen.

Penny opened the lid and showed him. Mack bent down to smell it but caught and held her confused gaze for a moment. She was sure he was reassuring her but then how could she know?

Cavine dragged herself from the couch as if the others had insisted. She moved to the kitchen and looked at the cake and pie. Shaking her head she said, "I can't believe what you people put in your body." Her British accent was very prominent, as if she meant it to be.

Mack laughed. "And I suppose you would prefer fish and chips?"

"Oh, sugar." She tapped Mack on the chin. "I like fish and chips best when you and I are in London eating them...remember?" Her sultry laugh rippled through the cabin.

Paige tapped Penny on the shoulder. "Let's get everyone eating so we can discuss the situation. Linc and I have to be home at an early hour tonight." She winked at Penny.

"Sure. Why don't you all grab a plate? Paige and I will set all of the food on the counter. I hope you like the smelt. I used cornmeal and special secret spices from my mother." She laughed but she didn't feel like laughing. Her insides were seething. Cavine was trying to goad her and it was working, but she wasn't going to let anyone see her sweat.

After dinner, everyone gathered in the living room with the information each had. Penny retrieved her dad's note-book and sat in the rocking chair thumbing through it. She watched as Cavine and Mack spread out the tunnel maps, and Mack placed a temporary evidence and findings board against the wall.

Linc showed Mack the ins and outs of the tunnels where he'd spent a great deal of his childhood. The whole scene was so unreal. A little more than a month ago, she had been a forest ranger making a career move and now she was in the middle of a living nightmare.

Her thoughts wandered over everything she'd done, seen, or heard since her arrival. Suddenly her heart thumped loud-ly as she realized what she'd seen at Sugar Moon and only given mild thought. She stopped rocking. "Mack!" she cried out in her excitement.

Mack and Cavine looked up as if she had interrupted something more important than what they were doing. "What?" His usually lively eyes flickered with weariness.

"There are three babies in the nursery right now. If someone at Sugar Moon is really selling babies, then would-n't they want to sell each to the highest bidder?"

They all stared at her blankly. Penny rushed on with her thoughts. "Couldn't we have someone go there and ask to be put on the list? And tell them money is no object? If it's really a selling ring, then they should offer to sell one that is already there." Penny glanced at Cavine who was glaring at her with a smirk on her face. Penny wanted to slap Cavine but held herself together.

Mack paced thoughtfully. "You know it might be the quickest way to a resolution." He moved to the makeshift board and began setting up the plan of action.

"Okay, Cavine. I'm sure no one at Sugar Moon has seen you." He smiled. "You are such a night owl, I doubt if anyone has seen you in the daylight."

"You only say that because you know it's true." Cavine stuck her lower lip out in a pout.

Penny couldn't believe how Mack could miss all of the obvious references Cavine made to their relationship. Or maybe he wasn't missing anything. Maybe he was just ignoring the quips until they were alone together. Paige walked past Penny on the way to the kitchen and pressed her hand into Penny's shoulder. It was a friendly reminder to stay calm but Penny was ready to scream. She rose and began cleaning the kitchen. She would do anything, even clean, to stay out of the reach of that woman's claws.

"As I was saying, no one at Sugar Moon has seen you, so you will have to do some undercover work."

Cavine moved next to Mack. "Okay, sweetie. Do you want to be my husband this time?" she asked and then added, "We wouldn't have to pretend much."

Mack shook his head, ignoring her implications. "I think you can do it solo. The right amount of money can get you what you want at Sugar Moon. And you know I'm not good at undercover." His mouth spread into a thin-lipped smile. "Call the department head and see how much you can spend."

Penny slammed the refrigerator door harder than she had wanted to, drawing all eyes in her direction. She shrugged. "Guess I'm stronger than I realized," was the only explanation she could offer. Penny turned back to the cleaning but inside she was fuming.

She was furious that Cavine kept bringing up her and Mack's relationship and Mack kept ignoring it. He never denied it…just ignored it. Paige moved beside Penny at the sink and spoke loudly. "That was a great suggestion you made. I bet it will give the FBI the information they need."

"It was good alright but honestly we would have gotten to it eventually. But of course, sweetie, we will listen to all ideas." Cavine's voice dripped in sarcastic syrup.

Penny wrung the dishrag she was holding so tightly that it was almost dry. Paige whispered, "If you let her get to you, then she has won."

"I know it, damn it," Penny said through gritted teeth. "I just wish everyone would leave." She immediately felt bad that she'd insulted Paige. "I don't mean you, please forgive me, I'm not really myself right at the moment."

Paige patted her wet hand. "I will try to clear the place out as soon as I can."

Mack continued giving assignments. "Linc, I need you to go through the tunnels near Sugar Moon if you can get that close, and report anything unusual to me."

Linc nodded and held his hand out to Paige. She took it and smiled at her husband. "There's no time like the present to begin. Besides I promised your mother we would be home early tonight."

Linc looked at her questioningly but Paige squeezed his hand. "Did you forget? Your mother has a council meeting tonight."

"Yeah, I guess I did." Linc looked from Paige to Penny but didn't ask what they were up to. Penny smiled inside. The one thing she had going for her over Cavine was her friendship with Paige.

Cavine settled in on the couch. "I'll set myself up at another hotel tomorrow and become a desperate mother wanna-be." She kicked off her shoes, and stretched out in one fluid motion. "I hope you don't mind." She looked at Penny, challenging her to say anything.

"She probably doesn't mind but I do," Mack said. "I want you to set up at another hotel tonight. You work better at night and it's night." He chuckled as he threw her shoes to her.

Cavine hesitated but then grudgingly pushed her feet into her shoes. "I guess duty calls."

Paige nodded and tugged at Linc. "We'd better go. Our duty is calling too." She smiled at Cavine. "It's hell to have to work for a living, isn't it?"

Cavine grunted and threw her jacket over her shoulder. "I'll see you all soon," and then she stopped in front of Mack. "As soon as I'm set up I'll phone you and let you know where to find me." She hugged him tightly and brushed a kiss over his lips. "That's for luck." Her laugh rang through the night air as she stepped outside.

"Okay, you have a good evening," Mack said as Cavine finished her wanton display and moved past him.

Linc turned to Mack and shook his hand. "Don't do anything without your back covered. I think the group we are dealing with isn't beyond doing serious harm to keep their little operation."

Mack nodded in agreement and turned to Penny. "Sweetness?"

Penny glanced at him; all of a sudden, she was sweetness again. She didn't know whether to laugh or cry. Awkwardly she cleared her throat. Pulling herself together, she realized Paige was staring at her. "I guess this is all more than I'm equipped to deal with," she said as she hugged Paige.

Paige hugged her and whispered in her ear, "Just go with the flow. When this is over it will be time enough to sort out your emotions."

Penny smiled as she released her friend. "Please call and let me know how the kids are."

Mack stepped beside Penny and put his arm around her as they watched the last of the collective group leave. When the door closed, he turned to Penny. "I know it's late but I think I'll go out to the old shed and try to discover what the caretakers might have had there and why."

"Okay," Penny answered tentatively. She wasn't sure she wanted to go back to that place but she knew she didn't want to be alone. "Let me get my jacket." Confused by his actions, Penny struggled with what to do. The minute everyone left, he wanted to work. That proved his job was number one with him, just as hers was to her. Yet, he acted as if Cavine had not been on the attack all night. And she knew if she brought it up, he might see her as a jealous, silly woman.

She drew in a deep, cleansing breath and decided to do as Paige had suggested, go with the flow. As she tugged on her jacket, she muttered aloud, "Only fear and common sense are holding me back."

Mack stared at her and then burst out laughing. "Ah, the wise words of Cliff Hart. I heard that many times."

His laugh was infectious. Penny smiled and then her sense of humor took over. She joined his laughter. "He was probably right but he took that from Mom." She pulled the door open. "Let's see whether fear or common sense should have ruled." Penny was so confused over the whole scene with Cavine that she really wasn't as worried as she probably should've been.

Mack smiled at her as they stood in the door. "See, that's just another reason why I love your mom. She is one wise woman and she gave birth to you."

"You are such a sweet talker. But I love it, and I know Mom does too." Just forget Cavine, she kept telling herself.

"Speaking of the woman who made it possible for us to be here together." Mack smiled broadly. "She says you finally phoned to let her know you arrived safely."

"Oh." Penny felt guilty that she hadn't phoned her mother more this past month. And more than pleased that her mother didn't speak to Mack about the rest of the conversation Penny had with her. She smiled to herself. Penny knew her mother had mentioned the phone call to Mack to see if he was aware of Penny's confused state of mind. She would love to know the rest of their conversation, but she wasn't going to ask. She gazed into his glittering golden-black eyes and smiled. "I'll phone her tomorrow."

Mack glanced down at her as he stepped outside and gave her a smile that set her pulses racing. "You do whatever works for you."

Penny almost pulled him back in and then thought she had to face her angst and help discover her father's fate. "You work for me," she answered and pulled the door shut behind them.

As they moved along the shadowed path toward the shed, Mack said quietly, "I noticed this old thing when I first came and thought it should be torn down."

"It's going to be," Penny agreed, determined to put anything remotely concerned with the fear she'd felt the night before behind her.

Mack cautiously opened the wobbly shed door and shined the flashlight at every corner before they entered. Sensing Penny's fear, he clasped her hand and held it tightly. He knew she was afraid and with good reason. He knew Penny was upset with Cavine's actions but that was Cavine; she didn't mean anything by all of her teasing. Understanding women took way too much of his concentration, and he knew he didn't have any to spare. The best he could do was offer Penny reassurance when he could.

"Wow, this stuff is really old junk." Penny surveyed the small area. "Oh, look." She moved a couple of boxes and tugged on a bike. "I wondered where this was." Mack watched as the prominent apprehension she had carried in her eyes for the past twenty-four hours shifted to pleasant childhood memories.

He spied to a large wooden crate in the corner. "Hmmm," he said thoughtfully as he tugged on it.

"What?" Penny turned and offered him a faint smile tinged with sadness. "Oh, that's all of Dad's fishing stuff. He tied his own flies for fishing, you know."

Mack shook his head. "No, I didn't know." He pulled the crate out of the corner and examined it. A lock held the top securely to the bottom. He glanced at Penny, whose stare was fixed on her dad's belongings. "Do you know where the key is?"

She shook her head. "After all this time I doubt there is one." Her voice cracked a little but she managed a small, tentative smile.

"Mind if I open it?" Mack asked softly, knowing that to her he would be opening the past.

Pensively she shook her head and answered, "No. Go ahead. I'd like to see too."

Mack grabbed a metal pipe that lay on the floor beside him and pried the lock until it popped off. He held the light inside the crate. He heard an intake of breath from Penny. He turned and stood quickly as he saw the tears on her cheeks. "Oh, sweetness. If this is too much for you..."

She shook her head. "I just haven't seen Dad's stuff in so long." Mack held her close, wondering why there was no dust on the crate. Penny gently pushed away and dropped to her knees in front of the large crate. Tenderly, she touched the items. Mack didn't want to disturb her memories so for a few minutes he stood quietly behind her.

He laid the flashlight on the items and dropped down

beside her. As he lowered himself, he noted the beam of light was shining through the crack between the lid and the bottom of the crate. He studied the corner where the crate had been, trying to make out what he thought he saw. It was a wooden lid with a handle. Like a door, he thought. No. He shook his head. Why would there be a trapdoor over there?

Penny looked at him and whispered, "What?" Apprehension glittered in her eyes.

His arm automatically went around her as he pointed to the corner.

The heavy lashes that shadowed her cheeks in the dim light flew up and she was instantly alert. "You don't think…?" she began and then shook her head.

"Yeah, I do think that." Mack shimmied his way between the crate and the other boxes stored in that corner and knelt beside the trapdoor. He held his ear against it for several minutes. When he heard no noise, he turned off the flashlight and slowly opened the lid to the tunnel below.

Staring down into the hole, he could see it had the same features as the tunnel at Sugar Moon. He heard Penny as she knelt beside him and was glad she didn't speak. Her eyes were as wide as he was sure his were.

He pointed that he was going down. She shook her head. Mack lowered the lid and asked, "Why?"

"We aren't going anywhere without our guns or our escape equipment." The fear he'd seen earlier had changed to sheer determination. He smiled broadly and hung his head in false shame.

Penny punched him in the shoulder. "Come on. Let's

get the stuff."

Mack's heart lightened as Penny's did. He'd hated the pain and fear left with her but had no idea how to help. Now he could see all she needed was a challenge and she responded like an old fire horse. He smiled to himself. *And I bet she would hate that description.*

Within minutes, Penny and Mack were in the tunnel exploring. Penny was amazed at the wooden structure that kept the dirt walls from caving.

Mack pointed to tracks and Penny looked at him and smiled. "The crooks are smarter than we are. We could've brought my bike down. They followed the bike tracks for at least a couple of miles until they came to a bend where they saw a sliver of light. Penny's heart began pounding hard and she patted her chest. Since she'd arrived in the Upper Peninsula, her heart had had a better workout than it had in years.

Leaning against the wall she watched as Mack pantomimed they should depart. For once, she couldn't agree with him more. Now they knew why the men had been in the shed; it was a passage out for them. This knowledge alone was more than she wanted to know but she knew there would be more. Her dad had been on to something bigger than she could have imagined.

The ringing phone popped Penny's eyes open. Mack

rolled over and plunked his arm over her as he answered. He rubbed his forehead. "Yeah, I can. What are you doing up so early?" Penny felt his gaze saturate her body as he held the phone close to his ear.

She smiled broadly, realizing he was talking with Cavine but making love to her with his eyes. The sweetly intoxicating musk of his body overwhelmed her. She curled into him and felt his immediate response.

"Yeah, I'll be there shortly," Mack spoke into the receiver and then dropped it back in its holder. His voice had taken on a rasping tone as his eyes drifted over Penny.

Words weren't necessary as Mack and Penny slid into their own world of heated passion and then returned satiated, lying in each other's arms. Each time they made love, Penny's eager response to him surprised her. She wanted him every minute she saw him. And she was glad that they'd made love before he went to Cavine. She pushed the sheet aside and poked him in the ribs. "You'd better go, duty calls." That was the hardest thing she'd ever said but she wanted to take the high road—well as high as a woman could go when she was fighting for her man.

Mack rolled over and searched her eyes thoughtfully. "You are one special woman."

Penny's lashes briefly shuttered her eyes so Mack couldn't read any of her fear. When she looked at him, she smiled broadly. "Thank you." Pulling herself from the bed, she walked to the door. "I'm going to shower. If you leave before I'm down, have a great day." She escaped his scrutiny and ran to the loft.

"You're welcome," she heard him holler as she stepped into her room, but she also heard the chuckle in his voice. She smiled. Keeping her mouth shut about him running when Cavine called was the hardest thing she'd ever done, but she wasn't going to let that woman break her. Not now. Not ever.

Chapter 13

The next day Penny dragged herself out of bed and went to work. She'd waited all day and night for Mack to return. At midnight when he hadn't, she curled up in the loft and lamented that Cavine and Mack were together.

All day at work, Penny prayed there wouldn't be a fire to fight, and thankfully, her prayers were answered. She loved her job but she'd been so tired coming to work she feared she would do something terribly wrong. Glancing at her watch, she frowned; in an hour she would be on her volunteer's job at Sugar Moon. Penny knew she didn't have to go, but she'd promised to help.

As she drove to the home for unwed mothers she mentally ran over all of the instructions Mack had given her the night they'd all been together. If Cavine were there, she couldn't know her and that was that was fine with her. Penny didn't want to know her anyway. She wished she'd never known Cavine in the first place. She was not to discuss that Aurora's family had been found with anyone. If Penny hadn't wanted her father's killer found so badly, she would just ignore his orders, just as he seemed to be ignoring her.

She sighed heavily as she walked up the steps of the home. Before she opened the door, she put on her best smile and reminded herself of everything she should or shouldn't do. The door thrust open just as she reached for the knob. Brilliant smiles spread over the faces of her students who greeted her.

"Hi," Penny said with a great deal more spirit then she felt. She glanced around the young women into the great room. Everyone was chattering in enthusiastic voices and clearly celebrating. "What's all the excitement about?"

"It's just the best news," one of the young women squealed.

Penny frowned when the squeal pierced her ears. "Whew." She rubbed her ears. "This had better be good news. I'm losing my hearing over it."

One of the young women leaned closer to Penny. "It looks like another one of the babies will have a great home," she whispered.

"Why are you whispering like that?" Penny asked.

They hushed her. "Because the woman is still here. She is gorgeous and dripping with money."

"Ohhhh." Penny glanced around. She knew Cavine must be there.

"We think she doesn't want to have a baby because it would mess up her perfect figure." They laughed as they filled Penny in.

"Give the woman a break. It's not her fault she's gorgeous and rich. She is a woman first. And what do most women want?" Penny thought, Now I'm acting because I agree with the students. If Cavine ever had children, this is how she would do it; she loves herself too much to have

232

babies normally.

"Babies, a great man, and lots of money," one of the young women answered with a huge smile.

Penny patted her on the shoulder. "That about sums it up; you go to the head of the class."

They laughed as they joined the buzzing room. All of the women were quietly cheering the new adoption. Penny stared into the fireplace. She let out a long breath. She knew Aurora uniting with her grandparents depended on closing this case. If the people who might be baby selling got wind of what was happening, they could hide whatever evidence there was. At least the case would soon be over, and Cavine would be out of her life. But would Cavine ever be out of Mack's life?

"Of course you'll have to wait for the proper papers," Mrs. Rowe was explaining to Cavine as she walked her to the door. "But I'm sure that won't take too long."

"Anything...and I mean anything I can do to speed this along you just let me know. Money is not a problem. You just call me at my hotel and let me know what I have to do to gain this wonderful baby as my own."

Penny smiled to herself as she watched Cavine squeeze the baby lovingly. Cavine certainly looked and acted the part of a woman aching to have a child. She should've been an actress, Penny thought and then grudgingly, but then, I guess, that's what makes her such a good undercover agent.

Penny deliberately didn't look Cavine in the eye. She wasn't an actress and wasn't about to be the one who messed with Mack's investigation. If she did that, he might turn to her, she thought.

"Penny?" Stella touched her arm. "Is there anything wrong?"

"Oh no." Penny tried to sound as excited as the rest were. "I was just thinking how wonderful this place is and all they do for the young mothers and their babies."

"I know," Stella answered thoughtfully. "Sometimes I..."

Penny eyed her closely. "Sometimes what?"

Stella shook her head and forced a smile. "Oh nothing, I'm just a silly old woman with a vivid imagination." She wiped her hands on her apron. "I just wish we could stop the cycle. I would love to work my way out of this job."

Penny could see her new friend really meant what she said and that something was bothering her. If we talk enough, Penny thought, I'll find out what is on her mind. Penny hugged the older woman. "Stella, I swear. You'll work your way out of a job before long." She bit her lip. She'd said enough.

"Oh, I hope you're right." She let out a long breath and glanced around at the young women who were waiting to deliver babies. "It's just that sometimes it can be so depressing. I really think many of them would like to keep their kids but they're trapped by circumstances. I remember when I had to make the decision." The older woman pushed back straying gray hairs from her cheek and gazed wistfully at the young women.

"I'm sure it was the most difficult decision you ever had to make." Penny spoke softly to Stella, as she noticed the vacant look in the older woman's eyes.

Penny had talked with the young women at the home and for the most part, they wished they didn't have to give up their babies. But she really felt that the people who ran Sugar Moon were trying very hard to do the right thing. If there was something despicable happening there, the people Penny had met were not doing it. She was sure of that. She was also sure the caretakers were up to no good, but she could not see how they could sell babies out from under Stella Rowe's nose. The older woman watched all of the young women like a mother hen with her chicks.

Penny arrived home to find Cavine and Mack in deep concentration. Mack looked up and greeted her. "Hi. How did your day go?"

How did my day go? There was a night in there too, Penny thought. "My day was long." Exhausted, she slumped into the rocking chair.

Cavine laughed. "Well, we sure the hell don't want to disturb you." Cavine walked to the door. "Maybe we should leave."

Penny shrugged but kept rocking, "Do what you have to do."

"We're almost done here," Mack said as he looked at Penny questioningly.

"Whatever," Penny said flatly. She was just too tired to argue and didn't really care what they did.

"Oh, by the way," Cavine said, "I had some concern that

you might show a sign of knowing me today but you did a good job."

"Thanks." Penny kept her eyes on the window across from the rocking chair. "I just want the investigation over so I can lead a normal life." As an afterthought she added, "And everyone was convinced you wanted a baby too." She didn't say they all thought the rich woman was afraid of losing her figure.

"See, Mack," Cavine said laughing, "it's Oscar time."

"Wait till tomorrow. After that's over we'll see if your cocky butt is still in the running for an Oscar."

"Tomorrow?" Penny asked. All of a sudden, she wasn't as tired as she'd been.

"After Cavine returned to her hotel room she had a phone call from Mr. Proctor. He is the man who manages Sugar Moon, right?"

Penny nodded, her curiosity growing rapidly.

"Mr. Proctor has set up a meeting with Cavine and the woman who does all of the adoptions. They are going to meet for lunch tomorrow and Cavine is going to be wired, so other agents can listen."

"Who is the woman who does the adoptions?" Penny asked, wondering who was at the bottom of this.

Cavine and Mack exchanged looks. "We don't know that yet."

Penny saw the exchange but decided whatever the two of them wanted to keep from her was fine. She just wasn't going to worry about it.

Mack stood and stretched. "I wish the vending machines

were installed." Penny forced a light smile as Cavine's forehead creased in question.

"He's crazy," Penny stated bluntly but she was glad this was something Cavine didn't know about.

"I guess so." Cavine stood and moved to the door. "I have to make an early evening of it if I'm going to perform tomorrow."

"Okay, partner. I'll see you in the morning."

"You bet, hon," Cavine said as she left.

Penny dragged herself from the rocking chair. "If you don't mind, I'm going to take a shower and go to bed."

Mack's brow furrowed as he looked at her. "Is there something wrong?"

"No," Penny answered. She knew that wasn't true but telling Mack what she really felt about Cavine would accomplish nothing. "I'm just tired. I can't keep going to work feeling like I should have brought my bed with me."

"Okay," he answered but she could hear the doubt in his voice.

"When all of this investigation is behind us..." She paused. "I think we'll have to discuss different living arrangements. Especially if you are going to complete your one-year leave of absence."

"I see," Mack answered slowly. "We'll just have to cross that bridge when we come to it." He smiled and put the matter away with his usual good humor.

Penny hesitated before she climbed the stairs to the loft. She didn't know whether to kiss him good night or shake his hand. This is stupid, she thought. We make love and I don't know whether to kiss him or not? "Mack," she said quietly.

He moved to where she stood. "Yes?"

"I...good night."

Mack came to her, pulled her into his arms, and kissed her tenderly. Penny could feel her body responding to his loving kiss and moaned inside. She was so tired.

Mack released her, tapped her on the nose, and turned her toward the loft. "Now before you cave in, get yourself to bed."

Penny climbed the stairs to the loft, wondering if she would ever admit to Mack what she knew herself, that she loved him. She sighed heavily. What she wouldn't give for a quiet, normal day.

As Mack wired Cavine for her meeting, he thought about Penny. He'd left the cabin before she was out of bed. He'd stood at the bottom of the loft stairs wondering if he should go tell her, but then she hadn't given him permission to break rule number one, yet. As soon as this was over, maybe Penny and he could get into some serious conversations and he didn't want one of them to involve different living arrangements as she'd mentioned.

Mack pressed the last piece of tape on Cavine's back. She yelped. "Hey, take it easy, bud. That's tender skin you're working with."

"I'm sorry," Mack muttered, still distracted by thoughts of the shining face he'd grown to care for, and the shadows behind her eyes that didn't belong there.

"Yo, lover boy." Cavine snapped her fingers. "I'd appreciate your mind staying on the job."

Mack jerked her blouse down over the wires and made sure it wasn't visible. "My mind is where it belongs."

"I hope it is." Cavine gave him a big smile as she tucked her silk blouse into her leather skirt and then pulled on the matching leather jacket. Twirling around she asked, "Do I look like a rich mama wanna' be?"

Mack laughed. "You look fine." He glanced out the window. "The surveillance team has been setting up all night. I talked with them this morning. There'll be a couple of agents in the restaurant at a table near you—just in case."

Cavine tested the sound with the team and then gave thumbs-up to Mack. "Guess, we'd better get this show on the road." She hesitated. "Where will you be?"

Mack looked at her as she tucked her purse under her arm. "Are you worried?"

"Just a little," she admitted. "These people aren't nice, ya know." She offered him a nervous smile.

"I'll be in the van with the surveillance team and we won't let anything happen to you." He gave her a reassuring hug and patted her on the back. "If you need an out, just do one of your fake sneezes."

Cavine gave Mack a playful shove, "My sneezes aren't fake." She checked the sound one more time and enthusiastically cracked, "Okay, let's do it."

The team sat outside the restaurant while Cavine took her place and waited. Mack slid on the earphones and watched the door, wondering who was going to show to sell the baby. When he saw Carol Young open the restaurant door and look around nervously, he whistled. "I never would've thought." He pointed her out to the others on the team. "I bet that's her."

Mack held his breath hoping he was wrong. She seemed so nice and so caring. But as his mind went over his brief encounter with her, the pieces began to fit. At the hospital that first night, she hadn't wanted Penny to push the placement issue. She'd allowed herself to be pushed until she made Penny happy. He'd thought she was being kind to them, but now he knew she was just protecting herself. He shook his head. "I should've seen it."

The others glanced up but said nothing. "Mrs. Eastman?" Mack heard in his earphones. It was the caseworker's voice. He listened.

"Yes," Cavine answered in her sweetest voice, making Mack smile. She was at her best when acting.

"I'm Carol Young. It's nice to meet you. I understand we have a common interest in seeing a sweet baby find a good home."

"He is the sweetest little thing. I had a hard time parting with him yesterday," Cavine answered sincerely.

"Well, I'm the baby's caseworker. If you'll fill out these papers, we can get the ball rolling. The state can be very slow acting on these things. And of course they'll have to do background checks on you and your husband."

She sounds on the up and up, Mack thought. If she is, then they would have to dig deeper for the perpetrator. There seemed to be a long pause. He gave the other agents a questioning look. They nodded everything was working and shrugged.

"The background checks wouldn't be a problem," Cavine finally answered, "but the time factor could be." Mack heard her let out a long, wistful sigh. "We've wanted a baby for so long…" She let her voice fall off as if she couldn't imagine another day without a child.

Another long pause followed. Mrs. Young cleared her throat. "I understand that, but you know how the government works. Red tape and more red tape."

Mack heard Cavine's spoon in her coffee. He could picture her stirring and waiting for the right moment. He'd seen and heard it before. He listened intently. There, he thought, the stirring had stopped.

As if on cue Cavine asked, "Oh, I know you have to do your job, and I know that can be stressful." Another long pause and then Mack heard her move in for the kill. "Is there anyway we can cut through the red tape?"

"I don't see how," the caseworker said thoughtfully.

"Well, if it would help I can hire a lawyer who is really great at cutting through the government's maze."

"No," the caseworker said quickly.

Mack was surprised at how fast Mrs. Young answered. Then he heard her explain. "What I mean is…if lawyers get involved then it takes even longer."

"Oh, I see," Cavine answered sweetly. "Well, then you just tell me what to do to speed this along."

In his mind, Mack could see the women sizing up each other and hoped Cavine was giving her usual great performance. The silence was almost deafening. He glanced at the other agents again, and again they gave him a nod.

"There might be a way to do this and make everyone involved happy," the caseworker said, as if she'd just thought of a plan.

"Whatever it takes," Cavine said eagerly. "I mean, my husband and I have tried for years and we would truly love to have a child." Mack could hear the tearful sob she choked back. She might get an Oscar for this, he thought.

"The baby needs a family and permanent home. Good ones are hard to come by," Mrs. Young said thoughtfully.

"Yes, the poor baby should be in a good home," Cavine said earnestly and then encouraged the older woman. "What would that way be?"

The cat-and-mouse game was afoot and Mack hated the waiting, but he knew it would all come together if played right.

"I hate to sound crass but I'm quite confident if you can...well, you know...give a donation to the home. I know the papers can be processed faster."

"Donation?" Cavine asked dumbly.

That's how it's gone undetected. Mack was always amazed at the ingenuity of criminals. He'd almost bet that half of their transactions were in donations and the rest in just plain cash dealings.

"Any other way and the authorities would say we were baby selling. And you and I know that is not the case," Mrs. Young said, as if the idea was the last thing on earth she would do.

"Of course not!" Cavine answered as if affronted by the idea. "How much of a donation would it take to get the ball rolling," Cavine asked in almost a whisper.

"Oh, my goodness. I hadn't thought of that. I've never had to deal with an adoption this quickly." Mrs. Young let out a long sigh.

"Oh, I understand that," Cavine said encouragingly.

"I'll have to have some cash, you know, to satisfy the ones who might see this as something it's not and go to the authorities." The caseworker spoke in a conspiratorial tone.

"Okay, then part should be in cash and the rest should be in a donation check to Sugar Moon?" Cavine asked.

"Yes, I think that would be best." The older woman sighed as if reticent to do business like this.

"I don't have cash right now but I could have it by tomorrow night." Cavine pushed for an amount. "How...I mean what would it take?"

Mack heard a pen scratching on paper. And then Cavine stated, "The fifty thousand in a donation check will be no problem. I can do that right now. The twenty thousand in cash, I fear, will have to wait until I can have my husband wire the money to a local bank."

All was quiet for what seemed forever. Mack thought Mrs. Young might not be happy with Cavine stating aloud what she'd written on paper. They waited, holding their combined breaths for the older woman to commit herself.

Finally she spoke. "I don't think having the cash go through a local bank is a good idea. I'm willing to wait until you can maybe have your husband bring it to you." She paused. "You know what I mean. This is such a small, close-knit area that a transaction of that size would surely raise eyebrows."

"Oh, I hadn't thought of that," Cavine answered and Mack could tell she was relieved. "My husband has a private plane. I'm confident when I tell him all you are doing for us that he will get the money and bring it to us by tomorrow night."

"That would be wonderful. Then we'll meet here tomorrow night and I'll have your baby with me."

"Thank you. You have no idea what you have done for us. We will be forever grateful. I would bet that my husband will make Sugar Moon one of his regular charities."

"Oh, Mrs. Eastman, that would be wonderful. The young women at Sugar Moon need benefactors such as yourself. It's been a pleasure meeting you. We'll wrap this up tomorrow night then?"

"We certainly will." Cavine grew quiet as Mack heard rattling paper noises and then nothing. After a few minutes she said, "Oscar nominee?"

Mack and the other agents laughed.

Mack had the surveillance team meet him back at the cabin where they finalized what they needed in the exchange of money for the baby. He was relieved when the last agent left. Penny wasn't working at Sugar Moon that evening and he wanted to be alone with her.

Chapter 14

Penny gazed at Mack across the intimate candlelit table he'd arranged in a private corner of the Ojibwa restaurant. "This is so sweet of you."

"I aim to please, ma'am." Mack's handsome face was once again relaxed and happy.

"You told me everything went okay today but you didn't tell me who Cavine met." Penny wondered if he could tell her. "But if that's information for the FBI only, I understand."

Mack shook his head and laughed. "I think you know more about this case than most of the agents that are here now." The smile quickly slid, leaving his features somber. "It's just that I missed the clues as to who it was and I'm uncomfortable about that."

"Who is it?" Penny's voice was filled with questions.

"Mrs. Young," he answered simply.

"Oh, my God," Penny gasped and began to fit the puzzle together as Mack had earlier. "It's no wonder she didn't fight our demands the night Aurora was born. She didn't want a big public display."

Mack moved his silverware from one side of his plate to the other and then back. "I don't know if I was so preoccupied with finding the people who were responsible for my partner's death or if I was just..." He stopped and smiled at Penny.

She felt heat rushing through her as the double meaning of his look became evident in his sparkling eyes. "Oh no, you can't blame this on me," she teased. "I'm not the one in control of your hormones."

"Sweetness, you have no idea how much in charge you are; not only of my hormones but more to the point, my heart." His large hand covered hers.

Penny looked down at their hands and thought how beautiful they were together. When she brought her eyes to Mack, she could see the loving tenderness shimmering there. They shared an intense physical awareness of each other but more important to her, they were gaining an emotional and mental understanding. There was a tangible and undeniable bond between them.

A passionate fluttering rose at the back of her neck. She glanced around as if others would see the effect he had on her. "I think it's time for us to leave," she said barely above a whisper.

Mack smiled broadly. "I knew it wouldn't take long." He opened the brown leather folder holding the restaurant check and placed money under the clip.

"Stop that." Penny barely stifled her laughter. "I think we have tied up the table long enough." She stood and waited for him to join her. Penny really didn't care if the restaurant ever had other customers but it sounded good.

Mack's smile grew broader. "And I don't think they'd let

us tie the table up for that."

"Oh." Penny laughed lightly as heat filled her cheeks. She stepped through the exit door he was holding. The very aroma of Mack turned the bottom of her stomach into a rolling, screaming pit of desire.

The late spring evening was warm and laden with the scent of new growth. Mack and Penny walked out of the restaurant and across to a park near the Soo Locks. The foghorns sounded as another ship entered the locks from Lake Huron. They watched as the ship rose slowly in the lock until the water level was high enough for it to transfer to Lake Superior on the other side.

Mack possessively took Penny's hand as they walked through the park. "Would you mind if I stayed at the cabin for a couple more weeks after we wrap this up?" He leaned down and asked her in her ear.

Penny shook her head but didn't speak. She didn't want him to leave—ever. But she knew that was not going to happen. His life, his job was in the Windy City, and she just couldn't see herself there. She sighed heavily.

Mack gripped her hand. "Let's worry about that later." As usual, he could read what she was thinking. She loved the feeling of having someone who knew all about her and loved her anyway. She smiled her answer to him, but she couldn't help thinking they would soon face a hopeless situation.

Mack was guiding her through the park to the waterfall with the streaming fountain in the center. She could hear the music and knew they weren't far. Her dad had brought her there many times as a child. She inhaled deeply. "I really do love it here. Everything is so fresh and so new."

The path ended and they stood in the enchantment of a silvery misty haze near the waterfall. Colored lights shimmered over the spraying water and swirled in the pool below. Soft music streamed from somewhere in the background. Mack wrapped his arms around her waist and she leaned back against him. As they stood admiring the water dancing in the lights, she heard Johnny Mathis crooning a love song.

Penny twisted in his arms and glanced up at him. "How'd you do that?" His look was so galvanizing it sent a shiver of wanting through her.

"Do what?" He smiled mischievously and then glided her over the grass slowly as he hummed the song to her.

"You are relentless," she murmured softly as she pressed a kiss into his neck.

"It's not for me to say," he whispered as he pressed his lips to hers, caressing her mouth more than kissing it. Penny snuggled closer, drinking in the intoxicating man who radiated a vitality that drew her like a magnet. His lips feather-touched hers with tantalizing persuasion.

Mack pulled her into his arms. As if she'd done it all her life, her legs wrapped around his waist. "Right here?" Her whispered words caught in the passion of her breath. Mack moved into the shadows of the waterfall where a gentle breeze, misty like a dream, washed over them.

Their hips swayed in perfect harmony. Penny locked her arms around his neck as Mack nuzzled her breast. Her tongue flicked his ear and she felt a heaving shudder run through him. Mack brought his hands under her skirt and moved her panties aside. Penny felt his erect manhood plunge into her. Her skirt fell over them but she knew if anyone came along, they would know what was happening. For an instant, she thought about stopping but the heady drug of passion had removed all reason.

Mack thrust into her as she fervently pressed down. Her breath came in short spurts; her need for relief was her single thought. Soon they were in a perfect rhythm. Together they moved through the realm of fervor, oblivious to the outside world. Mack jerked and thrust as he reached the zenith of passion. Penny threw her head back as she felt the hot fluid of his love heating her insides to the boiling point. Together their lovemaking brought them to a mutual pinnacle. Mack held her tightly as he shuddered repeatedly. Penny gripped his shoulders as she arched back with ultimate relief.

Gently Mack lowered them to the ground and held her tightly. When their breathing slowed, he murmured, "We are dangerous together."

Penny laughed nervously and glanced around. They were alone but she couldn't say if they'd been that way for the whole time. "Next time, I think we should get a room." She was teasing but knew it was true. Never in her life had she been so enthralled with anyone as she was with this man.

After dragging themselves from their love tryst, they laughed as they walked across the dew-covered grass of the park to his truck. "I think we'd better go home where things like this are accepted better." Penny couldn't help laughing. She'd never done anything so iniquitous. Now that she had time to think about it, she hoped she didn't let go like that again.

She glanced at Mack as he manipulated the truck through the traffic and off onto the lonely road they lived on. She admired everything about him, even his... Damn, she said to herself. You are sounding brazen...at least in your mind.

He caught her in her sidelong glance. "It's a good thing this console is between us. Huh?"

"Oh, aren't we the cocky one?" She laughed softly.

"I can be. Should we stop right here?" Mack chuckled.

"No. I think we should get home. I still have to work tomorrow, you know." She shifted in her seat at the thought of stopping and making wild passionate love again. He sure knew how to hold her attention. She laughed demurely.

"You want to stop, don't you?" He put on the brakes and the truck stopped with a jerk in the middle of the road.

"No. Now stop doing that." Penny couldn't believe how much fun they had with only the simple things. She sighed wistfully and laid her head against the seat.

Mack laughed, released the brake, and continued on. "Are you sure?"

"Yes." Penny folded her arms over her chest. Her mouth said yes but her body was beginning to scream stop.

The truck slowed. "What's that?" Mack asked, his voice still husky from lovemaking.

Penny sat up and looked at him. "Do you think we could just make it home?" She smiled.

"No, I'm serious. Look on the side of the road over there." He pointed to a man and woman hugging and rocking, standing outside of their car.

"Oh," she said. "I thought you were…"

"I know what you thought, and it's not a bad idea but now we have people around." They laughed and studied the couple.

"I think they need help," she said as she stared at the embracing couple.

"Oh, they look like they can do it all by themselves," he teased.

"Stop that. I mean they look like they're in distress."

"What makes you think that?" He turned the truck onto a two-track logging road where they could see the couple but were out of sight.

"That is not a passionate hug," she answered adamantly. "He is consoling her. And Mr. FBI, if you haven't noticed, their license plate is from Illinois, your home state. If they are in trouble, I would think you would want to help them. Andddddddd, I don't think they drove from another state to mess around on a back road."

Mack stared at the couple. "What if they did?"

"They didn't."

"Are you sure?" he asked doubtfully.

"Yes, I'm sure, now let's see if we can help them." She turned toward him and added, "If we don't help them we'll have to sit here and argue about it all night. I'd rather help and get home, wouldn't you?" she asked in a sugary voice.

Mack swallowed hard, pretending he had no choice. "Yup, I'd much rather do that." He backed the truck out of the side road. "Get your cell phone out. We'll call for help, and then get on our way."

Penny laughed. "Oh, you are so much the good Samaritan."

"I know." He laughed. "Just another thing you love about me."

"But it's not for you to say I love you," she teased, thinking of the wonderful song-and-dance in the park.

"Nope, I'm just hinting." Mack smiled broadly as they pulled alongside the other vehicle.

"You folks need help?" Mack asked earnestly.

The man released the woman. "No." He shook his head.

The woman's face turned scarlet. "We're fine." She shuffled her feet and stared at the ground.

"Oh," Penny said knowingly as she looked at Mack who was smiling broadly.

"Well, then we'll be on our way so you can be on yours." Mack's I-told-you-so smile lit his eyes until the gold sparkled radiantly. He drove away chuckling.

Once they were on their way Mack said, "Do you have anything to say?"

"No," she answered, muffling a giggle.

"You don't want to say, 'Mack, you were right, they were doing what you and I did and want to do again?'" Mack let out a loud roaring laugh.

"Well, if they are going to do that kind of thing, they should pull off the road," Penny said as if she would never consider such a thing.

"Or," Mack offered, "maybe they should head for the

water fountain in the park. It worked for us."

Penny reached over and tugged on his shirt. "You know what I mean."

"I sure do, sweetness."

When Penny and Mack arrived at the cabin, Linc and Paige greeted them. Mack liked the couple but he really wanted to spend the rest of the evening with Penny. As the four of them walked into the cabin, Mack asked, "Is there a purpose for this visit?"

"Mack!" Penny admonished.

Linc and Paige laughed. "We understand what you mean," Linc spoke softly, "but we have a favor to ask of you."

As they moved into the cabin and sat in the living room, Mack wondered what it was they wanted. Whatever it was, he hoped it wouldn't take long. He shot a sidelong glance at Penny who was making coffee. "Whoa," Mack exclaimed, "I can't believe you are making coffee and all without a vending machine."

Penny smiled at Mack and then asked the other couple, "What can we do for you?"

Paige looked at Linc and then back at them. "Cavine has told us that the Masons will be here in a few days to pick up Aurora."

Mack nodded. "They are anxious to have their grand-child and there is no reason for us to wait. Unless you have something we need to know?" he stated plainly, but his voice was filled with sadness for them.

"We know," Linc said. "If you could, we'd like for one of you to pick up Aurora and surrender her to the Masons. We want to say our good-byes to her at our home. We know the Masons have every right and deserve to have her. It's just that we've become attached to her and to see the finality would be a bit much."

Penny went to Paige and hugged her. "I'm sorry. I know how you love her but the Masons have nothing of their daughter and this could heal some real wounds. I bet they would let you keep in touch with them."

"We plan to send a letter with Aurora and ask permission to visit. I would bring her to them myself, but I'm sure I'd break down and that would not be good for anyone." Paige wiped at a tear rolling aimlessly down her cheek.

"Then we'll do as you ask," Mack said, "and if you change your mind we will understand that too." Mack plopped into the easy chair. "I've seen so much crime and every time the case is over there are victims. The victim circle spreads wide and reaches everywhere. And, I know when this case concludes, there will be many more victims. It's a shame how some disreputable people will think only of themselves and money and never give a thought to the innocent people they are hurting."

Penny sat on the side of Mack's chair and slid her arm around his neck. His chosen career brought many rewards but it also brought many painful times. She was beginning to understand his love for his job and why he moved so quickly when duty called, even if Cavine was the one delivering the duty message. No, she thought, I will not think of her tonight. Our night has been blissful and I won't let anything or anyone change the mood.

"We still have some of that wonderful Sprite pound cake you brought over." Penny smiled at them, "Would you like a piece?"

Mack smiled broadly. "I would like a piece." Penny pinched his neck as she stood and went to the kitchen. She knew what he meant, and her heart warmed thinking of how he desired her. But she wasn't sure his desire for her was nearly as strong as hers was for him.

Paige followed her and pulled four plates and cups from the cupboard. "We won't stay long," she whispered to Penny.

Penny felt heat rising from the back of her neck and spread over her face. "It's that obvious?"

Paige laughed. "Only a nun or a monk wouldn't recognize the signs."

"Paige, I'm sorry about everything. I wish it could be different but I really believe Aurora belongs with her natural family." Penny glanced at Paige as she cut the cake. "Is there anything I can do?"

"You are doing it." She smiled. "It's really great to have a friend so close. I know Aurora belongs with her real family, too, and I'm truly happy for them."

The women took the coffee and cake into the living room and served the men. Mack laughed. "Brother, I think this is the way it should be."

Linc held up his hand. "No comment. I want to live to see my old age."

Laughter rang in the cabin. The sadness of the occasion

was made whole by friendship.

With the arrangements for Aurora made, Penny and Mack were alone again.

Mack turned to her. "I don't suppose we could pick up where we left off, could we?"

Penny stared at him for a moment and said, "I wonder what you'll be like when you have gone completely crazy."

He shook his head. "I don't know but after the past few weeks I'm kind of looking forward to it."

"You know," she said, smiling, "I think you'll make the transition very nicely."

He grabbed her and pulled her to him. "Oh, you do, huh?" Penny fell into his arms laughing.

"Do you want to hear something even more incredibly crazy?" Mack whispered seductively in her ear.

"Not sure," she whispered back with mirth in her voice.

"I need to have Sugar Moon bugged for a few days to see how deep the illegal activities go." Mack hoped she'd volunteer without him having to ask.

"How are you going to do that?" she asked, missing his implication.

"Well, there is this certain woman who volunteers her time, who might offer," he said cautiously.

Penny stared at him. "You're right, that is incredibly crazy. I have no idea how to do that."

"It's simple and I'll teach you. It just has to be done without anyone, including Stella, knowing about it." He knew they had the evidence against Mrs. Young but they had none against others working there. And if others were involved, he wanted to nail them all.

Penny looked at him thoughtfully. "You know, I really don't think the others are involved. The girls are happy with their situation. Mrs. Rowe and Mr. Proctor seem totally committed to the young women and their plight."

"That's what we need to discover." He paused thoughtfully. "I know Mrs. Young isn't doing this by herself. There has to be someone in there who helps her."

Penny shrugged. "Well, we know the caretakers are kind of mixed up in the whole thing. They were here and I heard them."

Mack didn't want to bring it up, but his original interest in her father's death was still unsolved. "Penny." He turned her to him gazing into her shimmering copper eyes. "I'm sure someone there had something to do with Cliff's death. After reading his diary, we know he was onto them. I want to help the young women at the home and have Mrs. Young and whoever else is part of this scheme locked up. You know I need to prove what happened to your dad."

Penny nodded. "Okay. I know someone else was involved and I know we need to prove who." Her voice was unsteady but he could tell she was determined.

Hearing the resignation in her voice, he hugged her tightly. Remembering her dad and what might have happened to him was painful for her and he knew it. "Once this is over we can lay it to rest. Your dad deserves a commendation for dying while doing his job, and your mother needs to know she was right about her husband."

She nodded and a soft smile came to her lips. "Mom will be able to move forward with her life and I know Dad would have wanted that." She thought for a moment. "Okay, Mr. Agent, teach me." She laughed softly.

"You do it so well, I don't think I have much teaching to do."

Penny tapped his lips with her finger. "Stay on the subject. The bugs you want planted!" she scolded.

"You are something, sweetness." Mack hugged her tighter to his chest. "I think I know just the classroom."

Penny laughed as she realized he was taking her to his bedroom. "This is going to be a class I truly enjoy."

Chapter 15

Penny stared down at the intimate, silent world of the forest as she glided in the fire reconnaissance plane over the Hiawatha National Forest. She surveyed the area for fires but let her mind go to the events of the past week. Cavine had successfully bought the baby and temporarily secreted him away with the Crosses until he could be placed with real adoptive parents. And the Masons would soon have Aurora. That sweet baby would be in the arms of her grandparents that night.

She smiled as she thought of Mack showing her how to plant the bugs and how proud he was when she placed them successfully. He'd had a surveillance team listening and watching day and night for the past week. He reported to Penny that it seemed she'd been right; the main house seemed to be a completely normal operation.

She knew Mack was disappointed. Not that the home seemed legal but that with all of the FBI investigation he couldn't put a finger on the people who had to be helping Mrs. Young, and that he couldn't tie the whole thing to his partner's death. Mack was right, she thought. There had to be something.

The tunnels were being explored daily but the underground network of passages was so intricate that it would take months to cover it all. Well, Penny thought, that would keep Mack in town for months and that wasn't a bad thing. But she hoped he could do the rest without his partner. She mentally scolded herself for being selfish and tried to think of something she could do to put an end to the investigation. For Mack and her mother it would be closing a book on a painful time in their lives. For Penny, she'd finally be able to face the pain she'd put aside when her father died. She sighed heavily. And closing the case would mean she and Mack would have a chance to explore their relationship.

As the plane flew over the back of Sugar Moon, Penny sat up straight and came to full attention. In her reverie, she'd still been subconsciously viewing the terrain. She stared at what she thought she saw until it came into focus. On the farthest section of the Sugar Moon estate, she noticed a small building.

Penny turned to the pilot, whom she'd barely spoken to for the entire flight. "Would you fly over that area again?" He nodded. Then he turned the plane to make another pass.

Penny studied the building carefully and wondered what might be stored there. Then as the pilot flew closer she saw an old beat-up sedan that looked like it had been mud bogging. Her fingers covered her mouth to hold back the gasp. Visions of Nikki's body flying through the air fast-forwarded through her mind. And as if she had a pause button, the vision stopped for a second on the car she'd seen. That car hit Nikki!

After the plane landed, Penny quickly filled out her daily

report and literally ran to her truck. "I have to get to Mack," she said anxiously to herself. Her heart was pounding with the news that might uncover the evidence they needed to finally put her dad's memory in its proper place.

Barely stopping her truck, she jumped from it and ran into the cabin. "Mack!" she shouted with excitement as she pulled open the door. Mack turned from the coffeepot and looked at her. He raised an eyebrow and then nodded toward the living room. "Oh, I'm sorry, I didn't know anyone was here."

Mack smiled. "Mr. and Mrs. Mason, I would like you to meet the woman who owns this cabin." And as he walked past her he leaned closer and said, "and my heart."

Penny smiled anxiously at him and then walked to the couple with her hand extended. "I'm very pleased to meet you." She paused seeing the grief in their faces. "And I can't tell you how sorry I am about Nikki."

Mrs. Mason held her hand tightly. "You were the last one to talk with my daughter, I've heard."

Penny could see Nikki's mother was holding on to every ounce of strength she could muster. "Yes, Mack and I were," she answered softly and continued looking both of them in the eye. "I think Nikki was a very brave young woman, and I was proud she chose us to make sure Aurora got to where she belonged."

Penny looked at Mack. "Where is their Aurora?"

"Cavine is bringing her here in a few minutes," Mack answered.

"That's wonderful," Penny said to the Masons. "I know

nothing will take the place of your daughter but Aurora is one of those children who could fill the hole in the ozone."

Fresh tears flooded their cheeks. "Our granddaughter," Mrs. Mason said as if she hadn't had time to accept the reality of her yet. "Aurora?" the grandmother questioned through tears.

"Oh, I'm sorry, I named her that because she was born under the Northern Lights but I'm sure you will have a name for her."

The grandparents smiled and held each other. Mr. Mason said, "Aurora." He glanced at his wife. "I think that's a beautiful name. Should we keep it?" Mrs. Mason nodded and glanced at the door in anticipation as it opened. Cavine stood in the door with the baby wrapped in a bundle of blankets. She walked to them and held out the baby. Mrs. Mason accepted the tiny bundle and held her tightly to her chest. "Thank you, all of you."

Penny turned to Mack. "While they make up for lost time and bond, I would like to talk with you." She opened the door and indicated they should go outside.

Mack smiled. "That was sweet to leave them alone."

Penny scrunched her face and smiled back. "It probably was, but that's not why I did that. I made a discovery today while flying fire reconnaissance and I know you'll want to follow up on it."

"Really? What?" Mack asked quickly. "Wait." He held up his hand and called into the cabin for Cavine.

Penny's stomach sank. Why must that woman be part of everything they did or said? Cavine came out and stood next to Mack. Inwardly Penny wanted to punch her but she pulled herself together and said again, "While on fire reconnaissance today I saw something on Sugar Moon that I'm sure will interest both of you.

Mack and Cavine were at full attention.

"On the back of Sugar Moon and I mean way on the back of the estate, there is a small building."

"But when we took that canoe trip, Mack, we didn't see a shack back there." Cavine glanced a Penny and then back at Mack.

Frown lines creased Mack's brow. "I guess we didn't go far enough. That estate is larger than I thought."

Canoe trip? Penny thought. When the hell did they go on a trip down the river together?

"We can get a warrant," Cavine said quickly.

"Yeah, but if we do, then we might lose the chance to see them in action at that shed," Mack said.

Penny snapped out of her rumination and stared at them. She shrugged inwardly, just get this over with, and get on with your life, she told herself. "Wait," Penny ordered abruptly as they began making plans. They turned toward her expectantly. "You haven't heard the best part." She glanced toward the house and then moved farther away to protect the grieving parents from her painful disclosure. "The car that killed Nikki is parked behind it."

She watched their eyes grow wide and dart as if searching hers for the truth. "Are you sure?" they said in unison.

Penny answered with more sarcasm in her voice than she'd wanted to show. "I know I'm not an investigator, but

I'm trained to view and identify objects from the sky." She was extremely incensed that they would question her observations even if they'd had a cozy little canoe trip down there. She drew in a deep breath and made a concerted effort to sound normal, "If I hadn't witnessed the accident, I wouldn't be this positive. But I know what I saw, and that is the car."

Mack squeezed her shoulder. "I'm beginning to think you are an agent."

Penny's brow creased in frown lines. She couldn't tell if he was placating her or if he really meant it.

"Damn yes!" Cavine laughed. "You go, sister."

Penny glanced at Cavine. Sister? She actually sounds like she means it. The compliment wasn't much but it was the nicest thing Cavine had said to her since they'd met. She could see that Cavine and Mack worked well together. But Cavine's constant references to their past and her innuendoes that there might still be something, made it impossible to like her. Penny knew Cavine was a capable agent but she wished Mack's partner was a capable man who wasn't interested in him. She forced herself to smile and answered, "I think I'll leave the investigation to you."

As the two agents began planning how to get closer to the area that held the car and when to get the search warrant Penny went inside. She just couldn't stand Mack and Cavine's closeness.

The new grandparents were smiling brilliantly at Aurora. As she walked through to the loft stairs, Penny said, "We will all be leaving soon. Please stay as long as you like. When you leave, turn the lock on the door. Then as an afterthought she added, "Feel free to grab snacks or whatever from the kitchen. The bathroom is right down the hall." She pointed in the direction of Mack's bathroom and for a moment thought of how she and Mack had shared a snack there. She ran up the stairs after they nodded. The last thing Penny wanted was for anyone to see the effect just the thought of Mack's bathroom had on her.

Penny showered and dressed quickly. She was sure Mack would want to do something later and she wanted to be ready. The thought brought heat from her toes to her nose. "Not that," she scolded herself. Now she was beginning to think like him.

When she alighted from the loft, Mack and Cavine were waiting for her. "Come on, we have to run to the courthouse and pick up the warrant."

"You're going to search it right now?" she asked, wondering why they weren't waiting and watching as Mack had wanted.

Mack shook his head. "Nope, we just want to be ready, just in case they decide to destroy the evidence. Cavine is going after the warrants."

"Oh," Penny said as she let him lead her to his truck. "Where are we going?"

"We have a surveillance set up near Sugar Moon. You and I are going there. Cavine will join us when she has the warrants," Mack said as if she should have known.

"Oh," Penny answered quietly. She'd hoped Mack had wanted to be alone with her for a while but she should have known they were going to wait for Cavine.

They drove in silence. Penny's emotions were on a roller coaster. At times, it seemed Mack didn't want to be without her. And other times it was as if she was not in the same room with him. But, she had to admit, those times Cavine was present. Penny looked at Mack. She was sure his mind was totally on the job and he wouldn't want to discuss her emotions.

Suddenly Mack pulled the truck onto a two-track and turned the engine off. Penny looked around but didn't see a surveillance vehicle. In fact, this was a very secluded area in the Hiawatha National Forest. She turned in her seat to face him. "What are we doing here?"

For an instant, wistfulness stole into his expression. He opened his door, came around the truck, and opened hers. His expression stilled and grew seriously determined. "I am going to say some things to you. And damn it, you are going to listen." His extraordinary eyes blazed and glowed.

Penny slid out of the truck and stood in front of him. They stared at each other for a long, charged moment. "Go for it," she challenged him with a look of scorn. Penny just knew this was where he told her that he and Cavine had something going and he was trying to decide between the two of them.

Mack bridled at the order, "Never mind. I guess you aren't interested in what I have to say." He grabbed her hand and led her back to the truck. "When you are ready, I'll be here."

Penny nodded. It was almost a relief not to hear what he

was going to tell her. She fought back tears. She wasn't going to let Mack or Cavine turn her into a pile of rubble.

The trip to the site was short. They joined Cavine and the other agents in the surveillance vehicle, which had taken up a camouflaged residence in the woods near Sugar Moon.

Penny noticed Cavine and a couple of other agents were dressed in black as she and Mack had the night they found the tunnel at Sugar Moon. She turned to Mack. "I would've thought you would want to be there to see that car."

"I do. I mean I did…" He stopped what he was saying, and looked at her.

"What?" Penny asked, completely baffled by his reluctance to go.

Mack looked down at his shoes and then back at her. "I didn't want to leave you here alone and…"

"You don't have to worry about your partner's daughter getting hurt. She can take care of herself." Penny slapped her hands on her hips and glared at him. "Mack Holsey," she said through her gritted teeth. "I wouldn't want you to interfere with my job and I don't want to get in the way of yours. If you are uncomfortable with me here, I'll go back to the cabin and wait."

"No," he said emphatically.

"If you don't go, I'm going home," she warned quietly.

"Okay, okay. I'm going, but I think you'll be safer here. Wait for me."

Orders, Penny thought, all I get from him are orders.

"Sure," Penny said offhandedly. She glanced around the surveillance vehicle and noted the other agents who would be there with her. The agents were so involved in their listening that they hadn't heard her and Mack. She gazed at Mack. "I'll find something to entertain myself." She forced a smile to her lips. Her heart was still stinging from his abrupt anger when they'd been talking on the two-track.

He nodded and then looked at her. "Just remember, when you are ready I have some things I want to say to you." He gave her a meaningful look as he dressed for his job.

"Sure, I'll remember that." She answered in neutral tones as if she could forget. As she watched him leave, she knew she'd wait forever; all he had to do was ask.

The agents who were in the surveillance vehicle equipped her with listening devices and taught her how to switch from the house to the team in the woods. Mack was in the woods and she sat listening as he saw the car. "By God," he said quietly. "Penny, you are right, that is the car." She grimaced. He knew she was listening. He seemed to know her better than she knew herself.

"And," she heard Mack say, "I'll bet we have that wooden crate you described." Penny thought, He's talking as if I'm the only one listening.

She heard the men as they whispered that they had the files they needed. Happiness filled her as she realized she'd helped in a big way to solve her father's murder and help the young women at that place. She looked at the house with disgust for the people who were selling babies and then thought she saw a flickering in the woods.

She stared at it, trying to decide if it was a line of fire and then heard Mack shout. "Son of a bitch, the place is on fire.

Grab as much as you can and let's get our asses out of here."
Penny's heart throbbed and tightened in her chest. The man
she loved was in danger and she could do nothing.

Her pager began flashing. She stared at it as if it were a
foreign object. Penny had seen the fire and had forgotten she
was on call. She took off the headgear reluctantly and wrote
a quick note to Mack. "Duty calls. I couldn't wait. Oh, and
sorry, I had to take your truck." She hesitated before signing
it, she wanted to sign love but after the scene in the woods,
she worried he had something to tell her that she wouldn't
like. She thought for a minute and then remembered a message he had left for her when he was off with Cavine, then
signed, *Take care of yourself. Penny.* She folded it and asked
one of the agents to give it to Mack.

She grabbed Mack's cell phone and reported in.
"Yep, I'm close and will be right there," she told her supervisor as she flew down the road. She loved her job, but part of
her was back in those woods with Mack. She prayed he'd be
all right and that the fire wouldn't get way out of hand.

Penny joined the others running to the station.
Everyone dressed rapidly as excited voices were hollering out
information that they knew. She turned to her supervisor. "I
saw it start and I swear it looked like a deliberate line of fire."

"How did you happen to be there?" he asked as he
shoved his helmet on.

"It's a long story." Penny had to yell to make him
hear over all of the others.

"Ride with me and tell me on the way," he shouted as he
did a last check of his equipment and barked out orders to the

others.

Penny and Dan sped through the dark woods. He glanced at her. "Tell me what you know about the fire." Every nerve in her body jolted with the additional adrenaline that pumped through her. She tried to decide how much to tell Dan. Then she determined after tonight it would be all over anyway.

"My roommate is an FBI agent. They have suspicions about the goings on at Sugar Moon. The agents were investigating that small shack on the back of the estate when I saw the line of fire and heard them holler that there was a fire." She watched his face as it grew solemn.

"Is Cavine there?" He sped up and the fire truck rumbled from side to side on the old trail.

"You know Cavine," she half stated and half asked wondering how and when.

"Yes. Quite well." He glanced at her, "I thought you knew."

"How would I know a thing like that?" she asked. "And yes, Cavine is with Mack in the woods where the fire is."

Worry lines formed over Dan's brow. "Guess we'd better do a damned good job of stopping this fire then." He offered her a drawn smile. "It's hellish close to the jack pine and if we lose it, we'll be here for days."

She nodded. "I'd swear it was started with some kind of incendiary. The line was straight and moved fast."

"Damn it!" He cursed as the fire came into full view.

The firefighters jumped from the vehicles and took up their post. Dan shouted orders the minute his feet hit the ground. He turned to Penny and barked, "Backfire the area along the northern line."

Penny looked around to see where her fellow firefighters were. She called out as she lit her torch and began to run the backfire line. The fire roared in her head along with the vision of Mack trying to escape from the flames. She prayed he would get back and read the note. What a fool I've been, she thought. What would it have hurt if I'd said I love you or even signed the note with love?

After finishing her backfire line, she stood staring into the distance and realized she hadn't heard another voice for some time. She called out and waited. No answer! Her heart began to pump rapidly.

Penny called to Dan and waited. She heard no answer. "Damn it!" she spit out. "Where is he? Where is anyone?" She called out to anyone and again no answer. Penny turned around and realized her mind had been somewhere else and in its absence, she'd become surrounded by fire.

She pulled her bandana over her mouth and nose and tried to think over the drumming of her heart and the howling of the fire. In the darkness, she couldn't see where there might be a short jump through the fire. She listened. All she could hear was the thunderous fire; no firefighters, no equipment, nothing but the deafening roar of the fire.

"For God's sake, don't panic," she yelled at herself. "You've been in this spot before. Do what you were trained to do." Giving orders to herself calmed her enough to push her into action. Quickly she emptied the bladder bag in a wide circle around her and began to dig. Frantically she used her Pulaski to throw dirt beyond the water circle trying to buy more time.

The fire was rushing toward her. She dug frantically until she had no time to dig. She had a shallow burrow dug. Just as she lay down in the hole, she thought how much it looked like a grave. Shaking off that thought, she pulled her fire shelter out of her backpack and covered herself with it. She thought of the firefighters out West who'd died under similar shelter but knew this was her only chance.

Lying in the shallow pocket of earth she hysterically dug with her hands. No, she kept telling herself, she couldn't go like this. Her death would mean double pain for her mother. Penny moaned aloud as she thought of Mack. God, if she'd only told him.

"Dear heavenly father," she prayed frantically. "Let those I'm leaving behind know what was in my heart. Let them know I loved them and believed Dad's death wasn't an accident." Her hands dug rapidly while she prayed.

Suddenly her right hand slipped through the ground and dangled in a hole. Shocked, she dug faster. Dirt filled her eyes and mouth. Her vision blurred and she spit to clear her throat. Penny stopped for a second and listened. The fire roared so close she held her breath and pressed her body tightly to the dirt bed under her. Her right arm fell down in the hole. She drew it back and continued to dig next to the hole, hoping and praying it would be some kind of natural phenomena like a sinkhole.

Tears pushed dirt from her eyes as she felt the heat of the fire that was moving over her. She punched her fist into the ground beneath her and cursed through sobs. "Damn it!"

The earth below her gave way and Penny plummeted to the bottom of a pit. She lay in shock for some time. Shock that she was still alive and shock that she had somehow dropped into the earth.

Her hot skin met the cold air of the hole, causing her to shiver violently. She stood trying to shake it off. Darkness surrounded her. She had no idea where she was or how she'd get out. The fire burned out of control above her and she didn't know which way to turn now. But she had another chance at life. "Thank you, Father," she whispered.

Penny tried to orient herself. Before she'd gone into her thinking fog while fighting the fire, she'd noted she was at the edge of the woods by Sugar Moon. My God, she thought. I'm in the tunnels!

She rummaged through her pack for her compass and pulled it out. She pushed the button and the glow light came on. Wiping her eyes with her bandana, she stared at the compass. Penny studied the instrument through blurry eyes. If she walked straight, she would be moving toward Sugar Moon. If she turned around, she should be moving in the direction of her cabin.

But the cabin was ten miles away. She slid down, wondering what she was going to do. "And I can't see a damned thing," she said, trying to keep the fear from creeping in.

Penny pulled her canteen and flashlight from her pack. She would have to conserve both but right now, she needed a light. Before she switched it on, she noticed a flicker to her right. Was the fire falling in? She stared in the direction of the faint light. If the fire fell in, she was going to run in the opposite direction.

Penny held her breath and watched. The light grew brighter and she edged back, preparing to run. What was that? She held her breath and listened closely. Someone is running and panting hard, she told herself.

Other firefighters must have fallen in. She stepped into the oncoming light. A blood-curdling scream came at her as she stepped out. Penny shivered and stared

"Stella?" My God, what are you doing in here?" Penny couldn't help, noticing the terror in the older woman's eyes.

Stella ran to her and hugged her. "It was all so awful. I can't believe what I found."

Penny rubbed the housekeeper's back to calm her. "Tell me slowly but only when you have your breath."

After a few minutes of deep breathing, Stella regained some of her composure. "Do you remember the other day when I said sometimes I just don't know?"

Penny nodded.

"Well, for a few days I had been snooping around in the basement." Her cheeks stained crimson. "I would never have done that if I hadn't suspected something strange was happening."

"Of course not," Penny reassured her.

"Each day when Phil and Fred left I went down. I found things that made me wonder, like stacks of blank adoption papers with the state seal already on them. I know that isn't possible because they have to come right from the state after they are completed."

Penny knew this would be helpful but they already knew baby selling was taking place. What they didn't know was who was involved and how her dad's death fit into it. "Yes, go on," she urged.

"I also found blank death certificates with the state seal on them. And a couple of the certificates were completed with baby's names that I know did not die. I thought they were adopted out with the mother's permission but if the mother thought they were dead..." The older woman began to sob. "How could they do this to those innocent mothers and babies?"

Stella was dragging a bag of things that she pulled beside her. She gave Penny a grieved look as she reached into the bag and pulled out something. "I found this in the caretaker's room. I remember your father. I used to clean for him on occasion too." Stella held out the object to Penny.

Penny accepted it and opened the small leather-looking holder. Her father's FBI identification lay in her hand. His picture was on one side and his shield on the other. Tears rolled down her cheeks as she saw her father's smiling face looking back up at her. "Thank you, Stella."

"Oh, Penny that's not all. Fred caught me snooping. He was going to kill me. He told me he was. And because he thought I'd be dead soon he told me how he and Phil threw the cop off the Cut River Bridge." She shook her head. "Fred said your father contacted a couple who'd adopted a child. That couple got worried that they would lose their baby, so they called whoever does the adoptions and asked what was happening. That couple unwittingly let the criminals know, and they killed your father to keep him quiet."

"Oh, my God," Penny drew in a deep breath. Her father's journal had said he was meeting with someone who had adopted a baby and Penny was sure it wouldn't take much to discover who that couple was. She stared at the older woman who was obviously physically and emotionally drained. "How did you get away from them?" Penny asked incredulously.

"Phil was starting the fire and it got out of hand. Fred locked the door and left me in the basement so he could go help Phil get files or something. She caught her breath, "Anyway that idiot didn't realize that the locks in an old house all have the same master key and I carry one." I really thought those men were nice. I am such a fool."

Penny held the woman tightly. "Shh. Everything is going to be okay. How could you have known what was going on?"

"I shouldn't have stuck my head in the sand," the old woman said sobbing. "I had inklings a long time ago but I cast it off as an overactive imagination."

"Sometimes our imaginations can get us into more trouble than we want so you were probably right to wait." Penny wasn't thinking of the older woman's imagination as much as she was thinking of her own. Her worry over how Mack felt about Cavine had kept them on a roller coaster and now here they were both in danger and she had not told him she loved him. She had to get out, help with the fire, and find Mack, if it wasn't too late.

"Stella, are you able to walk?"

Stella nodded. "Yes, but I'm slow. You go ahead without me."

Penny considered it, then thought of the fire. She had no idea if it would stay above ground now that she had left the hole there. She knew she could move faster alone but part of her job was to save people too.

"I'm not going anywhere without you." She held her hand down to Stella and pulled her up. "We will walk and rest until we find our way out."

"I knew you were a dear sweet thing the moment I met you," Stella acclaimed as they began their long trek.

After the FBI team had gathered and escaped with as much as they could, Mack returned to the surveillance vehicle. He read the note from Penny and smiled broadly. Take care of myself, he thought. When this is over, I'll show her how I want to take care of myself and her.

He helped as the items were loaded onto other vehicles and stood watching the fire.

Cavine stood beside him. "You did one hell of a great job of driving that damned car out of that fire."

"Thanks, I didn't want to lose one drop of evidence. Penny would have shot me for that." He laughed and thought of Penny standing with a gun pointed at him. His stare moved over the fire, and he wondered how the efforts to squelch the inferno were coming.

"I know Dan is in there, too, but that's their job and they are good at it," Cavine said as she stared at the blazing forest.

"Dan?" Mack asked. "Do you mean Dan, Penny's supervisor?"

"Sure do." She laughed. "Did you think I was going to wait for you to come back from little-miss-country?"

Mack shrugged. "I never gave a thought to what you were doing when we weren't on the job."

"I hope to hell I've left more of a lasting impression on Dan," Cavine laughed.

"I know you," Mack said grinning. "You have impressed him."

Cavine checked her gun and nudged him. "We have an arrest to make."

"I passed it off to Agents Nash and Carnes." He shrugged under her scrutiny. "They can pick up those bastards as easily as we can. With their boss in jail they won't know how to turn off the lights."

Cavine laughed. "Mrs. Young sure was surprised when I paid for the baby with handcuffs."

"She had better get used to them. She's going to be spending her life in shackles," Mack said as he spit, trying to expel some of the smoke and dirt from his mouth. With one last look at the fire, he turned to where he'd left his truck. "I'm going to the ranger station to see what I can do to help." He gave a sheepish grin to Cavine. "But it seems I'm without wheels. Would you mind taking me there?"

"Mind?" She laughed. "I wasn't going to let you go without me. I'm not finished with Danny boy yet."

Mack stared at her. "Hmmm," he said thoughtfully. "I think a hunter has captured more than just the surface of

Agent Eastman."

"Get out of here." She poked him. "Dan and I have become great friends and that's all." She stalked off to her red sports car and Mack followed her, laughing.

At the ranger station, Mack and Cavine found themselves in a hive of activity. As a fresh crew of rangers reported for duty, the weary, smoke-covered firefighters came dragging into the station. Volunteers served refreshments and took messages for the families of the rangers who were returning to the firestorm.

Mack searched the faces of exhausted rangers as they came in the back door of the station. Dan came through and Cavine perked up. Mack saw a man who'd been fighting fires all night but also a man with a cloud of grief in the shadows of his eyes. He shoved his way through the crowd to Dan, and Cavine followed close in the path Mack had opened through the jungle of people.

Dan didn't look in their direction. He slid into a side office. Mack followed him. "Dan?"

Dan's empty eyes looked up at him. He stared at Mack for a moment and then shook his head. "I don't know."

Mack's heart rolled over and thumped heavily in his chest. "You don't know what?" He asked the question but was afraid to hear the answer.

Dan rested his elbows on his knees and dropped his head into his hands. "Penny was with me and then she wasn't." He kept his stare firmly fixed on his charcoaled boots.

Mack's mind whirled. "But you don't know that she is...I mean she is probably out there someplace." He felt

Cavine's hand on his back as his voice broke in panic.

Dan didn't look up. "I don't know how she could have lived through it." His weary voice cracked but he continued. "We've searched all of the safe areas. It'll be days before we have this under control and…"

"Take me out there," Mack demanded.

Dan looked up as the sharp order shot at him. "Mack," he stated firmly but his eyes were pleading. "All I can tell you is that Penny is a damned good ranger. She has fought worse fires than this. If there was a way out, she found it." He leaned back against the wall and stared at the ceiling. "The only thing anyone can do is pray."

"Does that mean you are not going to look for her?" A flash of wild grief tore through him. "How could this happen?" Mack swiped at his eyes where uncontrollable tears rolled off his lids and streamed down his face.

Cavine, who'd gone to Dan, reached out to take Mack's hand. "Mack, I'm positive she is being looked for; just like we would look for another agent who was missing."

Mack looked at Dan for confirmation.

Dan nodded. "More rangers arrived from Montana this morning, not only to contain the fire but to search for Penny."

Mack wanted to protest that they forget the damned fire and concentrate on the love of his life, but he knew Penny wouldn't want that. Mack's shoulders sagged as he dropped his arms to his side. He glanced at the desolate couple in front of him and felt more alone then he'd ever felt in his life.

Walking as fast as he could, he exited the station and

looked around the parking lot. His truck was parked crooked as if Penny had flown in and jumped out. He smiled sadly and prayed that wasn't the last time she would park his truck. He was going to leave it for her to use when she came out but then decided he would be there to take her home.

Mack didn't want to think of the inevitable that was looming before him. As he drove home, he called Penny's mother and told her that her daughter was missing. He heard the heart-wrenching scream on the other end of the phone and shrank inside.

Chapter 16

Three tortuous days had passed since Penny had disappeared while fighting the fire. Penny's mother had arrived and taken over as hostess to the group of friends gathered in the cabin. Mack felt as if they were all at a wake but no one wanted to admit it.

Mack answered the phone and listened as the ranger on duty gave him the latest report. They'd found Penny's scorched fire shield but no remains. He placed the phone in its holder and quietly told the small group in the living room the news. The cabin buzzed as Diane Hart took the news as hopeful and shared with the others how positive it was that her daughter's remains weren't found. Mack couldn't see anything hopeful about the latest news but he knew voicing that feeling would only add to Mrs. Hart's agony.

Mack stood aimlessly in the kitchen thinking about Penny and the wonderful life they could have had. The life they could have already started if they both weren't so involved in their careers.

He listened as Diane Hart made small talk with Paige and Cavine. Linc and Dan had joined the women but Mack couldn't bring himself to just sit and wait. He had to do something. But what?

In his mind he could hear Penny laughing as she looked for quarters for the vending machines. His heart hurt. He'd found that one special woman. The one who'd put up with his bad jokes and sloppy ways and now she was gone.

He squeezed the towel he was holding to avoid screaming. He was supposed to be a man, and men didn't scream or cry. This man was going to have a break down soon if he didn't get out of his and Penny's love nest.

"I'm going for a walk," he announced to the group in the living room. "Could I get you anything before I go?" Looking at Diane Hart's face broke his heart all over again. How could he have let this happen? He knew Penny had been tired this past week and he'd known she was on call. She'd needed her rest. Yet he let her keep late hours working with him on the case and he'd insisted she stay at the surveillance site when she could've been home resting. He sighed heavily.

"No, I'm fine," Mrs. Hart answered, and the others shook their heads.

"If you need me, call. I'll be close." He wasn't taking any chances with losing a third Hart.

"Mack?" Mrs. Hart's voice had the same ring as Penny's. Just that sweet sound made his heart tighten in anguish over his loss.

"Yes," he answered, anxious to do anything he could for the mother of his beloved Penny.

"We will find her, and she will be alive. I want you to stop blaming yourself for what has happened. You couldn't control Penny anymore than I could. She is irresistibly independent." Her smile lit her face when she spoke of her daughter but the smile didn't reach her eyes. The sadness he saw there almost overwhelmed him.

"Sure." Mack nodded and tried to smile in return, but he had to be realistic. Penny's fellow firefighters were looking for a body now, and he knew it. He slipped out the door before anyone could say more to him. He just wanted to be alone with his thoughts.

Mack walked without direction over the grounds around the cabin. Morning dew glistened on the ground and the morning doves sang. A lonely tear slipped down his cheek as he thought of how Penny loved the freshness of a new day. "Oh, God." Mack looked to the sky as his grief besieged him. "Why her? Why now?"

His fist clenched and he whirled around. He had to do something. A few feet in front of him stood the old shed. With little thought he picked up a crow bar and began its demise.

He told himself that once the authorities confirmed Penny's death, he would be gone and he wouldn't return. Tearing down this old building was the least he could do for her. Mack tore into the shed with a vengeance.

That tunnel entrance would be something they'd shared and one of his fondest memories. He wasn't going to share it with anyone. She was so cute standing there that night. *I miss her so much*, he thought. *She's gone and for what?* Mack tormented himself with questions with each blow of the crow bar.

After all they'd been through, he hadn't been able to

come up with conclusive evidence that his partner's death had been murder. He thought of the carpet samples and the notebook. He knew there were many common threads but nothing to make a whole shirt. He sighed heavily and fought back sobs.

Mack tightened his grip on the crow bar and fiercely pried against the old planks. The screeching of the nails as they gave way sounded almost human. He stopped and stared at the wood. He heard the screeches again and this time the crow bar hung by his side. His heart pounded heavily in his chest. Cautiously, he opened the wobbling door of the shed. Stella Rowe fell into his arms. "What the hell?" he hollered as he caught her.

"Oh, Mack," Stella spoke in an exhausted voice. "It's so good to see you."

Mack set the older woman on a crate and stared into the shed. "Where did you come from?" he commanded in astonished tones.

"Get Penny out," she urged breathlessly as if he knew what she was talking about.

"Penny?" Mack was surprised to hear his own shaky voice. "Penny's in there?" His heart thudded in his chest, he was sure he was hearing things. Penny? He had to be hearing things or losing his mind. Penny was dead. But still. Quickly, Mack pushed his way to the corner and shoved his arm down the hole. "Penny?" he repeated, hoping against hope that she would answer.

"Mack, where have you been?" He heard the sweetest sound he'd ever heard. He laughed as tears ran down his cheeks.

"Right here, sweetness." His voice choked with tears and laughter. Mack sucked in a deep breath and added. "For three days I've been waiting for you to emerge." He was sure he was hallucinating but if that was the case, he didn't want to be brought back to reality.

"I thought you would search in here for me." She tried to sound surly but he could hear the joy in her voice.

"I thought you were dead," he said as he yanked once and had her in his arms. He held her so close neither could breathe. "I can't believe you're here." His voice choked as he murmured against her cheek. His senses filled with the aura of her. He could feel her, touch her, smell her, and hear her, but he couldn't believe she was in his arms.

"I thought I was too." Penny gazed into his shimmering eyes; the gold had almost disappeared into the black. The pain of the last three days lay in the storm just behind the mist. Tenderly, she kissed him. "I can't believe it's over." She felt hot tears rolling down her cheeks and shivered.

"I can't believe you're here." Mack's voice grew quiet in disbelief. Mack held her close as the shivers subsided.

Penny leaned back and laughed through her tears. "Me either!" She turned back to Mack and hugged him tighter.

Stella rose from the crate. "I'll leave you two alone. I'm going to the cabin. I need food and I really need to wash up." The older woman stared down at her filthy clothes and then smiled at them. "Is this any way for your housekeeper to look?"

Penny and Mack laughed as they watched her walk slowly to the cabin. "We'll be right there," Penny hollered out to her. She saw Stella wave her hand in acknowledgement and continue her trip to safety, food, and something clean.

Three days with Stella, wondering if she would ever escape, had given Penny an entirely new outlook on life. They'd never given up. Their faith that Providence would bring them out was all they'd had to cling to.

Penny said as she grabbed Mack's hand, "Stella and I have some things to tell you that will amaze you."

"I'm already amazed," Mack said as he squeezed her hand tightly. "I'm ready to listen when you are ready to talk," he answered, trying to understand how this all happened. "Oh, my God." Mack stopped and pulled her back. "Your mother is here. She will be shocked into an early grave when Stella appears and tells them all you are safe. We'd better hurry. I'm sure no matter what she says she thinks you are gone."

"Mom doesn't shock easily." She smiled at him and couldn't say how relieved she was that Mack and her mother had held to each other during the ordeal. He held her hand so tightly, she could feel her hand going numb. But after the last three days, even that numbness felt good.

She smiled as he gazed at her; his eyes were still saying he didn't believe she was there. Determined features set over his face. "You're not going to be out of my sight," Mack stated firmly as he opened the cabin door and bowed gallantly.

Penny held him back and gazed into his eyes. "Thank you for being here for Mom and for me."

Mack swooped her in his arms and laughed whole-heartedly. "I wouldn't be anywhere else, you nut."

He sat her down just inside the door. Mrs. Hart jumped up, her face filled with a myriad of emotions and then she raised her hands. "Oh, thank You, Jesus! Thank You, Lord!" She gave thanks repeatedly as she ran to her daughter and held her tightly.

When her mother released her, the others took over. Penny laughed. "I see you're glad to have Mack's keeper back." They all laughed and cried.

"He is a handful," Cavine joked and smiled at Dan.

Penny hugged Dan. She knew what he'd been through and knew the sheer horror of searching for a missing firefighter. "Is everyone else okay?" she asked.

Dan nodded and returned the hug. "Yes, and the fire is almost contained." He stared at her as if he didn't believe what he was seeing. "When this is all over I want a report from you."

All baffled faces turned toward him.

Dan shrugged. "I want to know how the hell she got out of there. I think her next assignment will be writing a training manual on surviving a firestorm." He laughed and picked up the phone. "I think I know a whole bunch of rangers who want to hear this."

"I bet you do," Mack said.

Mack fell against the wall in exhaustion. As their eyes met and held, Penny's heart turned over in response. Without looking away from him, she smiled and said, "Yes, he is a handful, but I can handle him."

The other women exchanged knowing looks and went immediately to the kitchen. "You take yourself out of here and give my daughter a proper welcome," Mrs. Hart said while shooing Mack away.

"Gladly." The heartrending tenderness of Mack's gaze wrapped around Penny and sent her own heart into a flight of fantasy. For a moment she felt as if they were alone, no one existed but them. She heard the other women as they laughed and then she thumped to reality. "I-I need a shower," she stammered and then moved quickly to the loft stairs. "I'll be right back." She shouted over the laughter and then to Mack she whispered, "We'll take care of this later."

"Yes, we will." His eyes glittered. "Don't be long or I'll be up there."

"Rule number one." She laughed softly as she ran up the steps.

Penny wanted to stand in the warm shower forever but she wanted to be with Mack more; there was so much she wanted to tell him. She dressed in a hurry and ran back downstairs. The cabin was an outbreak of action. She heard Paige tell her mother she would go get the rest of the groceries needed for dinner. Penny sighed. It was such a relief to have them there and taking over.

Mack was standing at the bottom of the stairs, waiting. Penny stared down into his eyes. The gold was glittering in the black again. Her heart swelled with love for him; she couldn't wait to tell him. "Let's go for a walk," she whispered.

"I think that's a good idea," her mother shouted as she

worked in the kitchen preparing the celebration dinner.

Penny took Mack's hand and smiled at her mother. "Thanks, Mom, for everything..."

"That's what mothers do." The older woman smiled at her daughter. "Now go for that walk."

Their hands clasped tightly as they walked toward the creek. "I learned a lot from Stella and about myself." Penny looked at the shed as they passed.

"I'm sure you did." Mack let go of her hand only to wrap his arm around her waist and pull her closer as they walked.

"Never give up was our mantra." Spending three days in a dark tunnel gives a person time to reflect and really teaches what the important things in life are." She gazed into his eyes. "And I learned the lesson."

"Oh, sweetness..." Mack's voice choked and he couldn't finish.

"I know." She smiled at him. "Me too."

"Penny, I want to tell you what I tried to tell you in the forest, that day we were going to the surveillance post. This time I won't be stopped." He paused for a moment and then added, "For us to begin a relationship we have to get all of our differences out and discuss them. I don't want to wait for a couple of days or months and let them hit us again."

"I agree with that." Penny smiled at his determination but she was willing to listen this time anyway. "Okay, I won't say a word until you're finished.

Mack smiled. "Good. Now, first, I have tried to tell you that Cavine and I are coworkers and yes, friends. Once, we dated. Just once, and we knew we were not right for each other. Next, I've tried to show you how much I care for you in every way I can, but you've refused to see. Next, half the time you were pissed at me for investigating your dad's death and the other half, I don't know what you were pissed about." His voice grew calmer but stayed steady. "Next, what we had was not and I quote, 'just sex.' You and I both know it was more than that. Now if you want to ignore those feelings, that's your right. But damn it, don't tell me how I feel! I do know the difference between making love and having sex."

Penny didn't know whether to laugh or cry. He had held all of this in for a long time. She wavered, trying to comprehend all he was saying and struggling to keep her old weaknesses at bay. This was what she'd wanted to hear. Was he saying he loved her? She turned and stared out into the woods. "Okay, I won't tell you how you feel because I really have no idea." She shrugged to hide her confusion.

Mack grabbed her by the shoulders and turned her to face him. "Okay, I will say it then. I think you are the most wonderful, beautiful, independent, confident yet vulnerable woman I've ever met. I don't know what causes the vulnerability I see in you, but I'm willing to stick around and find out because my feelings for you are much more than a casual relationship." He stared at her, confident in what he was saying.

Penny studied him. For the first time he'd completed a paragraph without adding a quip or a big smile. All her loneliness and confusion welded together in one upsurge of yearning. She wanted to believe what he was saying but her mind was spinning with emotions. Penny was sick with the struggle within her. She couldn't speak. She merely stared, tongue-tied, into his eyes.

Mack dropped his hands. "Am I wrong? I thought if I said it, you would know we were more than just a blip on the sexual radar screen." He shrugged. "Maybe I've read more into our feelings...at least yours."

Her heart was singing and aching at the same time. He'd almost said he loved her but he'd stopped short of that. What was she to do? Should she share her innermost feelings of inadequacies or would that leave her heart wide open for hurt?

She shuddered inwardly at the thought of letting her guard down. But she'd learned from her brush with death that it was now or never. "Mack," she finally spoke, keeping her voice deceptively calm, "first, I accept your explanation of the relationship between you and Cavine. She seems like a sharp woman but I hate the way she is always bringing up your past together and insinuating that there is a present." She heaved a deep sigh as his features relaxed.

"Next, I wasn't and I quote, 'pissed' about your investigations of Dad's death. I was concerned for Mom. But when I began to realize there were some real facts behind your investigation, I had to face the horrible truth that Dad's death wasn't an accident. I was pained to think that someone disliked him enough to kill him, and I just didn't want to believe that." She looked at him and saw nothing but understanding in his eyes.

"Next, the other half of the time you thought I'm pissed, I was hurt. We make love, you get a phone call from Cavine, and you are gone without an explanation." Penny almost stopped but then she thought he might as well know everything she'd been thinking. "When Cavine is in the same room with us, you ignore me as if I wasn't there."

"Next," she paused for a few moments. This next point was her most vulnerable point and the most difficult to address. She took a deep, fortifying breath. "I…" She stood staring down at her shoes.

"Oh, baby." Mack pulled her into his arms.

She shook her head against his chest and gently pushed back. Shrugging, she said, "It's only fair to say it. I just don't know where to begin."

"At the beginning?" His bright smile had returned but his eyes were filled with loving concern for her.

"Okay." She took a deep breath. "I wanted to believe against hope that when we…well, you know." She felt heat start at her toes and climb to her hair roots thinking of their lovemaking. "We'd known each other such a short time, I thought it couldn't be real." She clasped her hands to stop the trembling of her fingers.

Mack waited expectantly but didn't say a word.

"Here's the truth. All of my life I've been overweight and unsure of myself. I'm still not a thin beauty like Cavine, and I never will be. But I like me the way I am. If you like what you see now, that pleases me. But could you love me if I gained weight?" Mack moved toward her but again she held up her hand. "Please let me finish. My other thought has been, Is the guilt you carry over Dad's death making you feel responsible for me? I don't want to be anyone's charity case. If and when I have a relationship, I have to know the man who says he loves me, loves me for who I am." Her rigid shoulders relaxed as she finally verbalized what her heart felt. Penny sighed. A load the size of the world lifted from her body, and she felt no worse for having shared her emotions with him.

Mack could hardly believe all he'd heard. He didn't know how a woman who seemed so independent in every other way could carry the societal burden of something as unimportant as body size. Or how she could possibly think Cavine was better looking then she was.

He chose his next words carefully. "I met the girl who was heavy. When I saw her at her father's funeral, I thought how sad, strong, and beautiful she was. I remember how you stood by your mom, holding her together." He drew in a deep breath. "I know when I'm on a case I become single-minded and that is the only reason I might talk with Cavine over you." He shuffled his feet. Now that she had bared her heart and soul, he knew more than ever that he loved this woman. But was this the time to tell her? He'd missed the chance before and almost missed it altogether. There is no time like the present, he decided.

She stood in front of him with her hands folded but he could see her fingers twisting. She looked so sweet, his heart swelled with undeniable love. Taking her in his arms, he held her close without speaking for several minutes. He loved everything about her.

"Penny," his voice came in a hoarse whisper, "I'm in love

with you." He felt a small jerk from her as his words settled over her. "I'm in love with the woman who is so fiercely independent, yet vulnerable. Of course, I've noticed how beautiful you are." His finger traced the freckles on her cheeks. "But that outside beauty is not what I fell in love with." His voice grew so soft it surprised even him. "I do feel guilt over Cliff's death but that guilt is separate from us."

Silence fell over the couple by the creek. Mack lifted Penny's chin and looked into her eyes. The only emotion he saw was relief. He'd waited for her to confess her love for him, but she hadn't. It would come in time. He was sure of that.

"Baby?" His heart warmed as she gazed lovingly into his eyes. He brushed a kiss over her soft lips as he spoke.

Penny wanted to shout her love for Mack and if she'd learned anything from this whole ordeal, it was to say it now while she had the chance. "I love you, Mack. I love you more than life itself." She paused for a moment. "When I almost died, my heart was pained because I had not told you. I shouldn't have worried about rejection. I know that now, and I promise I'll never let anything as silly as jealousy or vulnerabilities come between us."

They mutually pulled back and gazed into each other's eyes. They had no need to speak. They held each other and swayed to the soft, warm, gentle May breeze.

When they reached the creek, they sat in silence and watched as the water rushed over the rocks. Penny's stomach growled, breaking the silence. They laughed and Penny said, "After the last three days of not eating I could probably eat that half cow like you did our first night together."

"You mean on our first date," Mack chuckled, and then added, "I knew you would come around to my way of eating." He turned her toward him and held her by the shoulders. "Never in your life will you worry about your weight again. If you want to keep the extra pounds off for your health that's fine but if you gain weight, my love for you will not change. I'm in love with what is inside of here." He tapped on her head and then her chest.

A tear escaped Penny's eyes. "Thank you." She touched his face. "I've learned what is important in life and that problem isn't on the top of my list anymore."

Mack feathered kisses over her forehead. "When do we call the vending machine company?"

Penny looked at him and then crumpled in laughter. "Soon."

Mack lay down beside her and wrapped his arms around her. The laughter enveloped them as they rested by the creek. Penny had never felt the peace and love she had at this moment. Her mother and friends were scurrying around taking care of everything for her, and lying beside her was the man of her dreams. It doesn't get any better than this, she thought as the warmth of his body lulled her into a sweet, welcome sleep.

"Hey, you guys!" Cavine's loud voice shook them awake.

Penny and Mack had fallen asleep wrapped in each other's arms.

Penny jumped up and looked around. She was almost afraid she'd been dreaming. "Oh, I, no, I mean, we must have fallen asleep." She gazed warmly at Mack.

Mack rolled over lazily and whispered in her ear, "I know, sweetness, but we'll get to it later." His smile was as intimate as a kiss.

Penny looked down at him. "Better late then never." Then she looked at Cavine who was motioning them to come to the house. "Okay," they hollered.

"Come on." She held her hand down to Mack.

He grasped it and pulled her into his arms. "They can wait."

Penny brushed a long, slow kiss over his lips and murmured, "The sooner we get this over with, the sooner later will come."

His laughter floated up from his throat as he drank of her with smoldering eyes. "I'm a great supporter of later...as long as it comes sooner." Together they made their way back to the cabin.

"Oh, my God!" Penny exclaimed, amazed at the transformation in Stella. She was almost the normal Stella, a little thinner but normal.

"Yes, I would say God is where all of this goodness comes from." Her mother smiled at her.

Penny hugged her mother. "I know, Mom." She released her mom but held her hand. Smiling at Stella she asked, "Are you ready to tell the agents your story?"

Stella nodded and spent the next hour telling them everything she had discovered. When she'd finished she looked at all of their faces. "I can't believe baby selling went on right under my nose and I didn't see it.

Stella suddenly turned to Mrs. Hart. "Penny told me about your husband, her father. I did meet Cliff. In fact there were times he had me clean the house because he knew you would not like what he did to it."

Diane Hart dabbed a tear with her apron and then she smiled. "That was so like Cliff to hire someone to clean for him and then not tell me. I knew though."

Stella reached in the huge bag of evidence she had drug from the basement of Sugar Moon and pulled out Cliff"s FBI identification. "I know your husband would want you to have this."

"Thank you." Diane hugged Stella.

Mack stood and whistled. He paced in thought for a moment and then turned to Cavine. "That's why the carpet samples from Cliff and Nikki were the same. They'd both been in that basement. Those samples we grabbed the other night should prove that true."

Cavine nodded. "And now with Stella's information, we'll find that couple Cliff had made an appointment with and," she added the rest with enthusiasm, "we should be able to wrap this one up quickly, and I can get back to the city."

"Had enough of the country life?" Mack laughed as he handed Cavine the phone. "Why don't you call the office and get the search of Cliff's phone records under way."

Cavine accepted the phone. "With pleasure, sir." She

smirked as she dialed the number.

Penny watched the interaction between the two of them. It was true. When they discussed a case, they did lose track of everyone around them. Penny smiled at them, turned to her mother, and said, "I'll help you. When they are working everyone else is invisible."

Penny pushed the phone into its cradle. She couldn't believe after all they'd been through in the last few weeks, Mack had to leave for Chicago without coming back to the cabin first. She'd asked for how long he'd be gone and he had no idea. Tonight would've been their first night alone since she'd crawled from the tunnel with Stella.

At the airport that morning, she'd said her good-byes to her mother and hurried back to wait for Mack. "Damn it," she cursed and whirled around. "Now what am I supposed to do?"

She plunked in the rocker and set it going fast. The past few weeks had been filled with happy reunions and painful revelations. Many of the young women who'd elected to keep their babies had been told they were dead, and now it was proved the babies were alive and adopted by unsuspecting couples. Untangling this web would take a considerable amount of time. The FBI had set up a temporary office to sort through all of the evidence and somehow Penny had thought Mack would be able to stay for at least a while.

She thought about the agents and all of their work. They'd taken the files they'd salvaged from the fire along with Stella's story, and discovered where the babies belonged. Penny had been so proud of Mack and the other agents when they'd started the process of placing the children back with their mothers. She was also proud of the young women who chose to keep an aunt-like relationship with their children to keep from destroying their children's homes.

She leaned back in the rocking chair and closed her eyes. Penny felt great joy and pride at being the one who'd found and brought forth the evidence that put her dad's death to rest. The caretakers from Sugar Moon would be in prison for a long time.

She felt sorry for Stella Rowe and Mr. Proctor; they'd been innocent of everything reprehensible that was happening at Sugar Moon. They truly believed in the cause of helping unwed mothers and their children, and now they were working together to restore the home's reputation and bring it back to its real purpose.

Penny had made new friends and put away old vulnerabilities. Overall, her time at the cabin had been very healing. Her greatest joy had been seeing Aurora's grandparents when they first held their grandchild. Well, not quite. She smiled to herself. Her love for Mack had put her in a state of bliss she hadn't believed possible.

She pouted to herself. *And now I have to wait for who knows how long.*

But, she thought, *I don't have it that bad.* Her heart went out to the unsuspecting parents who'd been part of the nightmarish scheme. The investigation proved that most of them had actually thought the adoptions were legal.

With all of that out of the way, she couldn't imagine what Mack was doing. She sighed heavily; yes she could. Mack had told her the process of finding the Sugar Moon adopted babies and making them legal would take years. And he was probably working on that.

Penny rose quickly from the rocking chair. "I'm not going to sit here and wait. It's Saturday and I have shopping to do." She and Mack had agreed their relationship would be a long-distance one and she guessed she'd have to get used to it.

She pulled the door closed behind her and walked toward the truck. Just as she reached it, she heard the phone ring. Penny hesitated. If it was Mack, she didn't want him to think she was just sitting and waiting for him. No, she told herself. I want him to know I'm fine all on my own.

In the grocery store, she stood in front of the m&ms and almost wept. She so wanted Mack with her, but she wanted her career too and she knew he wanted his also. She took a deep breath and shrugged. "I don't like making choices."

"No shit, girl!"

Penny whirled around. "Cavine?"

"Damn, girl, you are hard to track down. I tried phoning you but you'd left already." Cavine stood with a hand on one hip and the other hip cocked.

"How did you find me and what do you need me for?" Penny didn't want to sound unpleasant, but she wanted to be alone with her feelings right now.

"Paige told me you shop here and I have to tell you something." Her eyes glittered mischievously.

Penny couldn't help smiling. This woman was full of surprises. "Okay. If it's serious we can go someplace else."

"No, girl!" Cavine stretched out that last word.

Penny frowned. "So tell me."

"Your smart-ass boyfriend is not going to Chicago." Cavine gave a disgusted grunt.

Penny's heart sank. Was he lying to her now? Suddenly she felt sick. Everything they'd been to each other and he was lying to her.

Cavine playfully tapped Penny's shoulder. "No, stop thinking like that. Mack wants you to think he is going away but instead he is being left in charge here to close this case."

"Then why did he tell me that?" Penny's mind raced for an answer.

"You know how he is. He likes to play jokes. He thought it would be funny to show up tonight and surprise you. And there is nothing a woman hates worse than a surprise like that."

Penny released a long breath and smiled. "No kidding!" She glanced at the m&ms. "I think I'll have a surprise for him. Two can play this game."

She hugged Cavine. "Thank you. Mack has no idea just how much a friend you are."

Cavine laughed. "Yep, I just saved his butt from a fate worse than death." Cavine glanced at the m&ms. "You do it!" She laughed said as she strutted away through the store.

Mack stepped into the dark cabin. He stopped and listened. Silence. He turned quietly and looked out the window, reassuring himself that Penny's truck was in the drive. That's what I get for trying to surprise her.

He walked toward the kitchen and put the bouquet of roses in the refrigerator. "I'll just wait," he said to himself and then stopped. As he walked, he heard crunching. Flipping on the light, he saw he'd smashed m&ms into the floor. "What the hell?" he asked to the night air. Then he smiled. "With the two of us, housekeeping is going to cost a fortune." It's a good thing Stella wasn't part of the Sugar Moon gang. We really need her.

He knelt down to clean up the mess and saw that there was a trail of candies leading to the loft. "The bag must've had a hole in it." He grumbled as he picked them up one at a time. Mack paused at the bottom of the steps and looked up. The trail of candy led all the way to the top. He shrugged and thought, It's better if I pick them up tonight than have her smash all the way down in the morning.

As he climbed the steps picking up the candy, he noticed that they were in a straight trail. That was odd for candy that was falling from the bag. On the landing, the candy trail continued to her room. Mack hesitated. If she were asleep, she wouldn't appreciate being awakened like this.

While he stood on the landing, he heard crunching and clicking noises from her room. He stopped. Then he heard giggling. What if she wasn't alone? He'd never thought of that. Mack's shoulders slumped and he turned to leave. Shaking his head, he said. "Like hell I will."

He tromped to her room, crunching candy on his way,

and threw open the door. There in her bed, bathed in the shadowy golden moonlight was a naked goddess. His smiling goddess lay covered in m&ms. Mack stared for a long minute and then he threw his head back and laughed. "I don't believe this."

Penny smiled up at him. "I just thought I would make your one fantasy come true. You can eat your way out of this one." She laughed impishly.

Mack stepped forward and then put his hands on his hips. "How did you know I'd be here tonight?"

Penny shoved her hand into a large pile of candies and held them up to him. "Women know things like this." She let a few trickle from her hand and fall back to the pile. "Are you going to start eating or would you like another snack?" She smiled radiantly at him. "Hot chocolate perhaps..."

Mack popped an m&m into his mouth and tenderly pulled his candy goddess into his embrace. "Oh, sweetness, you are all the snack a man could ever want."

<u>INDIGO</u>

Winter & Spring 2002

❧ February

Indigo After Dark, Vol. IV		$14.95
Dance of Desire	*Cassandra Colt*	
Skylight Rendezvous	*Diana Richeaux*	

❧ March

No Apologies	*Seressia Glass*	$8.95
An Unfinished Love Affair	*Barbara Keaton*	$8.95

❧ April

Jolie's Surrender	*Edwina Martin-Arnold*	$8.95
Promises to Keep	*Alicia Wiggins*	$8.95

❧ May

Magnolia Sunset	*Giselle Carmichael*	$8.95
Once in a Blue Moon	*Dorianne Cole*	$9.95

❧ June

Still Waters Run Deep	*Leslie Esdaile*	$9.95
Everything but Love	*Natalie Dunbar*	$8.95
Indigo After Dark Vol. V		$14.95
Brown Sugar Diaries Part II	*Dolores Bundy*	

OTHER GENESIS TITLES

You may order on-line at www.genesis-press.com, by phone at
1-888-463-4461, or mail the order-form in the back of this book.

Love Spectrum Romance

Romance across the culture lines

Forbidden Quest	Dar Tomlinson	$10.95
Designer Passion	Dar Tomlinson	$8.95
Fate	Pamela Leigh Starr	$8.95
Against the Wind	Gwynne Forster	$8.95
From The Ashes	Kathleen Suzanne Jeanne Summerix	$8.95
Heartbeat	Stephanie Bedwell-Grime	$8.95
My Buffalo Soldier	Barbara B. K. Reeves	$8.95
Meant to Be	Jeanne Sumerix	$8.95
A Risk of Rain	Dar Tomlinson	$8.95

Indigo After Dark

erotica beyond sensuous

Indigo After Dark Vol. 1		$10.95
In Between the Night	Angelique	
Midnight Erotic Fantasies	Nia Dixon	
Indigo After Dark Vol. II		$10.95
The Forbidden Art of Desire	Cole Riley	
Erotic Short Stories	Dolores Bundy	
Indigo After Dark Vol. III		$10.95
Impulse	Montana Blue	
Pant	Coco Morena	

Other Titles
by
Jeanne Sumerix

Meant To Be

Amy and Cord have been talking to each other about business matters by telephone and email for two years. When the prospect of meeting in person at an upcoming business seminar presents itself, they are both excited especially Amy, who has fallen in love with the voice at the other end of the line. When they finally do meet, Amy is shocked to find that Cord is African-American. But the attraction between them is stronger in person than it ever was on the phone and they plunge headlong into a love affair. In short order, however, the problems of an interracial relationship assert themselves and threaten to destroy more than just their love.

"A beautifully told story-you can't help but love the characters and share in their dilemma. The mix provides intrigue, humor, anger, and most of all, love."

-Rendezvous Magazine

Rendezvous with Fate

Leela and Jack's impassioned love affair of eighteen years ago draws them to revisit old feelings. They share a son that Jack knows nothing about, and Leela won't tell. They agree to be friends, but the embers are still burning and they are thrust back in time where history repeats itself.

"Jeanne Sumerix tells the story of an impossible love that just would not die...the strong writing, the steady moving story with its twists and turns keeps the reader turning the pages."

-Romantic Times Magazine

From The Ashes

by
Kathleen Suzanne and
Jeanne Sumerix

Paige Turner, a successful model in New York, returns to her childhood home in Michigan for a well-earned rest. She no more than arrives than her house burns, she meets two very different men, and she is suspected by the authorities of setting the fire that destroyed her home.

"...A story that will have readers quickly turning pages."
-*Bell, Book & Candle*

ORDER FORM

Mail to: Genesis Press, Inc.
315 3rd Avenue North
Columbus, MS 39701

Name _____

Address _____

City/State _____ Zip _____

Telephone _____

Ship to (if different from above)

Name _____

Address _____

City/State _____ Zip _____

Telephone _____

Qty	Author	Title	Price	Total

Use this order form, or call
1-888-INDIGO-1

Total for books _____
Shipping and handling:
 $3 first book, $1 each additional book
Total S & H _____
Total amount enclosed _____
 MS residents add 7% sales tax

ORDER FORM

Mail to: Genesis Press, Inc.
315 3rd Avenue North
Columbus, MS 39701

Name _____

Address _____

City/State _____ Zip _____

Telephone _____

Ship to (if different from above)

Name _____

Address _____

City/State _____ Zip _____

Telephone _____

Qty	Author	Title	Price	Total

Use this order form, or
call
1-888-INDIGO-1

Total for books _____
Shipping and handling:
 $3 first book, $1 each
 additional book _____
Total S & H _____
Total amount enclosed _____
 MS residents add 7% sales tax

ORDER FORM

Mail to: Genesis Press, Inc.
315 3rd Avenue North
Columbus, MS 39701

Name _____

Address _____

City/State _____ Zip _____

Telephone _____

Ship to (if different from above)

Name _____

Address _____

City/State _____ Zip _____

Telephone _____

Qty	Author	Title	Price	Total

Use this order form, or
call
1-888-INDIGO-1

Total for books _____

Shipping and handling:
    $3 first book, $1 each
    additional book _____
Total S & H _____
Total amount enclosed _____
    MS residents add 7% sales tax

ORDER FORM

Mail to: Genesis Press, Inc.
315 3rd Avenue North
Columbus, MS 39701

Name _____

Address _____

City/State _____ Zip _____

Telephone _____

Ship to (if different from above)

Name _____

Address _____

City/State _____ Zip _____

Telephone _____

Qty	Author	Title	Price	Total

Use this order form, or
call
1-888-INDIGO-1

Total for books _____
Shipping and handling:
  $3 first book, $1 each
  additional book _____
Total S & H _____
Total amount enclosed _____
MS residents add 7% sales tax